SHATTERED DREAMS

Rohan Sharma Thrillers Book Two

C. V. Chauhan

SAPERE
BOOKS

SHATTERED DREAMS

Published by Sapere Books.

24 Trafalgar Road, Ilkley, LS29 8HH

saperebooks.com

ISBN: 978-1-80055-799-4

Dedicated to Linda Cook.
For her love and friendship through the ages.

ACKNOWLEDGEMENTS

I am deeply indebted to a number of individuals who read early drafts of this novel. Helen Dhillon, Mike Fowler, Margaret Jones and Susan Kent gave freely of their time and helped me to shape early drafts of the book. As ever, my profound gratitude goes to Amy Durant and Matilda Richards at Sapere Books for their considerable editorial skills, and the tact and wisdom with which changes were suggested. My heartfelt thanks to all of them, although I take full responsibility for the final product.

PROLOGUE

When astronauts first orbited the earth in the 1960s, they confirmed the Great Rift Valley was, indeed, visible from outer space. A living crack, thousands of miles long and many miles wide, stretching from Jordan in the Middle East to Mozambique in southern Africa. A fissure on whose vast open grasslands, high mountains and arid deserts, the terrible game of life and death, of narrow escapes and unexpected annihilation, is played out by hunters and their prey every minute of every day.

On this enormous canvas, the astronauts would be forgiven for not spotting a pinprick of a town nestling near one edge of the Rift Valley escarpment, more than two thousand metres above sea level. The town of Naivasha in Kenya was named after the Maasai word for the local lake, 'troubled waters'. More than thirty years ago, it was nondescript, with a main tarmac road coming in from Nairobi, the capital city, and carrying on further west to Kisumu on the shores of the largest freshwater lake in Africa, Lake Victoria.

One day in late December, the weather sunny but cool at this altitude, Anil, the third generation of the Sharma family to be born in the town and now in his late-twenties, left his two inherited shops at lunchtime and told his low-paid Indian manager to look after them for the rest of the day. The larger of the two shops sold textiles and furniture, while the adjacent smaller one sold ready-made shoes imported from India,

Bangladesh, Cambodia and Vietnam. He drove to the local bar and hotel. A handful of locals, with a few wildlife tourists, drank and ate inside. Together with the loud, piped African music, their presence meant the atmosphere was smoky and raucous. Anil Sharma downed a couple of neat Scotch whiskies, bought a six-pack of beer and some sandwiches, clutched his briefcase tightly under his arm, and retired to one of the cheap, rented rooms at the back. There he spent a couple of pleasant hours in the naked embrace of his young lover, Mary, a woman from the Luo tribe. They had been meeting discreetly for about a year; she said she loved him, but he suspected her love for him became more intense with every shilling he gave her.

Going their separate ways in the late afternoon, Anil drove his Subaru estate to the local bank and withdrew a considerable sum of money. He would need to pay the wholesalers for his goods the next day. The year was soon coming to an end and his suppliers always increased their prices after New Year's Day. He would try to cut his losses and pay them in untraceable cash, ensuring the price hikes would not be too high. He drove out of the town along the dirt road, the red and brown dust seeping through the partly open window and the long-dead air filters. He stared at the bulging, cracked brown leather briefcase on the passenger seat. Crossing the railway tracks, which cut through the country for six hundred miles — the line built by thousands of indentured Indian labourers about a century ago — he tried not to think of Mary as a sex worker. But then why was he paying her? To make her life a bit better. Yes, that was it. Wasn't it? There wasn't any chance of a permanent future with her. He knew that. She knew that. But then why carry on? Well, why not?

As Anil headed home, the glistening waters of Lake Naivasha in the distance shivered as a cold, northerly wind blew across the valley from the snow-capped Mount Kenya and the Aberdare Mountain range. In front of him the black, undulating and foreboding Mau Hills were silhouetted against the darkening African horizon, the low sun a gloomy orange and yellow, ready to set within the hour. The dense forest of yellow-barked acacia trees stretched for several miles and was home to a colony of vervet monkeys, a ready source of food for the numerous pythons living in the tall reed grasses. Impala and Thomson's gazelle took the opportunity to graze one last time before darkness fell, hoping to avoid the lithe leopards that hunted in the area at night. Fish eagles nested in the tall trees, soared high under the equatorial sky and skimmed the surface of the lake, fierce, long talons ready to clutch and kill. At night, hippos ventured from the lake and grazed on the luscious grass fed by the rich, volcanic soil.

Although the long rains were over, the gathering storm clouds and the occasional clap of distant thunder meant it would rain again. Anil turned into the lonely track leading to the sprawling, stone bungalow built by a British settler just before the First World War. It was rumoured that Theodore Roosevelt, the American president, stayed in this very house when he came to Kenya on safari in 1908, killing hundreds of wild animals. Anil's grandfather had purchased the house in a dilapidated condition after the most recent British owners had left suddenly during the Mau Mau uprising in the early 1950s. It had been empty for several years and had fallen into a state of disrepair, but the Sharmas had improved it over the years. The house had high boundary walls and a main iron gate, both topped with barbed wire and broken glass. The two rottweilers stared at him as he drove past. The long driveway, edged by vibrant, colourful flowerbeds, led to the stone steps to the main house. The flowerbeds contained red roses, yellow roses, pink roses, carnations, marigolds, trumpet lilies, white lilies and a bird of paradise plant. Lata Sharma, Anil's wife, adored growing flowers as much as she adored her two children, Rohan, aged five, and Maya, three.

The Sharmas enjoyed an evening meal of curried tilapia caught from the local lake, with pilau rice and salad, finished off by a dollop of vanilla ice cream, a favourite of the children. The maid cleared up, washed the dishes, turned down the bed covers and, after asking whether her services were still required, said goodnight and retired to her quarters. The cicadas started their incessant screeching, with the occasional growl of a wild animal in the distance. The children played with the recently acquired baby African grey parrot, which Anil had accepted in part-exchange for a pair of shoes from a native Black customer. The children were trying to teach him words like *Kemcho* in Gujarati and *Jambo* in Swahili, but the big round eyes of the baby parrot looked sad as he perched in his cage. The family then watched a Bollywood film on *Zee TV*, and when Anil saw Rohan's eyelids drooping, and Maya asleep in her mother's arms, sucking her thumb and trembling occasionally through her dreams, he suggested they all go to bed.

The trees rustled in the strengthening wind and an African grass owl screeched nearby as Anil tossed and turned in bed after midnight, willing himself to sleep. His body was pleasantly tired and his thigh muscles ached. He lay on his back and stared at the ceiling, the bright moonlight peeping through the gap in the curtains, dimmed now and again by the passing, heavy clouds. He gazed at Lata, her low snoring intermittent and strangely comforting. He turned his back towards her and thought of Mary. Her glistening face as she arched her back, the guttural, moaning sounds, the pale pink tongue protruding through luminescent lips that hid ivory-white teeth, the big, moist eyes with their dilated pupils. He just couldn't say no, he thought, as he started drifting in and out of sleep, while the steady patter of raindrops on the roof helped him relax. The ground rumbled far away and the forked lightning grew brighter, ghostly images dancing on the walls and ceiling. As the drumming of the rain became insistent and the thunder louder, the family were in different states of sleepiness.

Anil tossed and turned, the clawing humidity of the low clouds making him clammy. He threw the duvet off his body as he drifted in and out of consciousness, sometimes muttering, sometimes woken up by his own snoring. The white lightning was fierce and bright; a deafening clap of thunder vibrated through the wooden bedposts. The rain was torrential.

Anil felt a hard shove in his back.

'Wake up, wake up.'

'Just a bit longer Mar—'

'Anil, Anil!' Lata was calling out his name.

There was a loud banging on the door.

He rubbed his eyes, blinked, and looked at the silhouette of his wife's face. A frantic voice on the other side of the door grew louder and louder.

'*Effendi! Mama! Amsha sasa!*' Sir! Madam! Wake up! The maid. Panic was rising in her voice.

They let her in.

'*Iko mwivi thatu. Na kuja hapa,*' she whispered. Three burglars. Coming towards the house. She had been on her way to the outside toilet, had noticed a torch beam, and had seen them scaling the perimeter walls with a rope ladder, all armed with guns. She couldn't understand why the dogs hadn't barked.

Perhaps they had been fed poisoned meat thrown over the wall.

Anil told her to go and hide, to escape in the night. He and Lata rushed into the children's bedroom through the dividing door. Lata lifted Maya from her bed, and Anil grabbed Rohan by the hand. Both children were startled, not knowing what was happening. Lata stifled Maya's sob while Rohan asked if it was morning already.

'Shh,' Anil said, as he led the family quickly into the lounge through the connecting doors. *Must be after the money*, he thought. But how the hell did they know? Did somebody at the bank tip them off? Or, God forbid, had he inadvertently said something to Mary about going to the bank afterwards? Surely not her?

Must get us to safety, must get there before it's too late. He and Lata bent down as they ran, Maya in her mother's arms, Rohan dragged along. They rushed into the lounge and Anil locked the door. He ran towards the heavy bookcase standing against the far wall. Grabbing one side, he pulled hard. Finally, it grated towards him, helped by the invisible castors at the bottom. Behind it, a secret chamber with wooden steps led down. This hiding place, no bigger than a small bedroom, had been built by the British family in the 1950s to hide from any Mau Mau fighters who lurked in the area. It had a phone connection to the local police station, and a hidden air vent led into the back garden. The family rushed down the steps. Anil's breathing was heavy and laboured. Lata was wide-eyed, with beads of perspiration on her brow. The children were half asleep and frightened as their parents whispered to them to be quiet. Maya let out a nervous giggle, her soft, chubby cheeks punctuated by two deep dimples. Her mother cupped her hand against Maya's lips, her other palm brushing the small, round birthmark at the back of her neck. Rohan was quiet, sensing something was terribly wrong.

Anil ran to the telephone on the low stand in the corner and lifted the receiver. Shit, it was dead. The thieves must have cut the outside wire, because he had tested it not long ago. He heard his own loud breathing. He lit the small, thin candle with matches that he kept next to the telephone. The smoke wafted towards the air vent.

And then they heard the loud, ricocheting bullets as they ripped open the lock on the lounge door upstairs. A heavy kick. The door crashed to the ground. Heavy booted footsteps wandered around.

'*Wapi mahindi? Wapi pesa?*' Where're the Indians? Where's the money?

Other doors opened and thudded. The sound of the thunder was deafening. Through it, there was a piercing scream.

Anil stared at his children and put a finger to his lips. Lata and Rohan were silent and terrified. Maya let out a sob, quickly stifled again by her mother.

Outside, the wind howled. Wooden shutters banged against their frames. The dust in the underground dungeon swirled. The air was dank, the ground hard.

The lingering scream came again.

Lata's breathing grew louder, her heart thumping against her ribcage. Oh, God, the poor maid. What were they doing to her?

Rohan tried not to breathe. The dust was tickling his sinuses. He pinched his nose. His father smiled at him through the dim candlelight.

The screaming stopped.

The silence was deafening.

They stared at the top of the wooden staircase.

Rohan sneezed loudly.

Seconds later, bullets tore through the bookcase and through the trap door. The family were discovered and dragged upstairs. Anil's arm was broken by a rifle butt after he handed over the stuffed briefcase. Lata was slapped and punched, her cheekbone broken in several places. Both Rohan and Maya sobbed, rubbing their eyes.

The young maid, wide-eyed, clothes ripped off, screaming, was frog-marched to the next room. Each burglar took turns to rape her again. Then there was the crack of a gunshot. The screaming stopped.

The Sharma family was lined up against one of the walls. One of the burglars pointed the rifle at Anil and fired. Lata and Rohan screamed. The bullet thudded into the concrete above Anil's head, showering him with pieces of mortar. The burglars laughed, looked at each other and turned around. One was clutching the briefcase under his arm.

Just as the last one was leaving, he turned, smiled at Maya, came back, picked her up and ran through the door. Lata screamed and chased after him, calling out Maya's name under the storm-bruised African sky. A bullet zinged against the front wall, just missing her forehead. Lata continued running, calling out her daughter's name, while the whining engine of an old pick-up truck faded into the distance.

CHAPTER 1

Location: Leicester, England
Time: the present

The slow, steady rumbling sound outside my bedroom window must have woken me up. I rubbed my eyes, squinted, and then looked sideways. The bedside clock told me it was almost five in the morning. The vibration from the freestanding wooden wardrobe died slowly as I heard the crunching gears and loud airbrakes of a lorry travelling slowly along my residential street of two-up, two-down late-Victorian terraces. The driver was obviously trying to take a shortcut to the dual carriageway, which would eventually take him to the motorway. Watery mid-July sunlight, fighting its way through the gaps in the fraying curtains, danced on the Artex ceiling. I knew I should find myself another place, something more modern, more permanent, something that belonged to me. But this area was home, and I didn't want to move to the suburbs. Not yet.

Half asleep, I stumbled downstairs and over to the front window in my boxer shorts. I stared at the lorry crawling away into the distance, undoubtedly waking up others on its travels, and heard early morning traffic noise coming from the main road, the Golden Mile in Leicester. Behind me, I could hear a restless Fernando in his cage, wanting his breakfast. My dear Fernando — my African grey parrot that my parents had brought along from Kenya with us, my constant companion — was the only one who understood me, or so I thought. Perhaps I ought to have spoken to a psychiatrist about my relationship with him. I got on better with him than with other human beings.

As I pulled off the square cloth covering his cage in one swoop, like a bullfighter swishing his red cape, Fernando shouted out, '*Olé!*'

'*Olé!* to you too, Fernando.'

He scratched his head with one of his claws, blinked at my tall, slim body with his big, round eyes and said, 'You're fit, Rohan.'

'Thanks Fernando. But the only fit I'm interested in is my Fitbit. Need to make sure I'm getting enough exercise. Not getting any younger.'

As I showered, I reflected on my recent holiday in Cyprus. People had noticed the effect of the sun on my dark skin. I felt healthy and properly relaxed after a gruelling schedule as a detective inspector investigating major crimes in the city of Leicester and the East Midlands. Life was taking on a predictable path with Faye, my ex-wife, who continued to tolerate me while I tried to maintain some sort of meaningful relationship with my daughter Yasmin, aged thirteen, and my son, Karan, nine. The people in both my personal and professional life treated me with some degree of respect after my team and I had managed to solve the murders perpetrated by a local serial killer with the moniker 'Shiva the Destroyer'. But the price I paid was not easy to forget. Pain and fame in equal measure.

Still, the world had moved on and I was hoping my life would too. I was still living on my own, with Fernando for company, although he was still out of sorts since my return from holiday. I had left him with a young Indian couple I had become friendly with and who lived a few doors down. Their six-year-old son would be delighted to have an unusual pet to play with and talk to for a fortnight, they said. I had tried to explain to them that Fernando wasn't a pet, he was older than all of us, that African grey parrots often lived longer than human beings, that they were highly intelligent and could mimic every sound they heard. This seemed to delight the couple even more. *Well*, I thought, *I can't leave him with anyone else*. Not even with my own kids, since I didn't think Faye would have agreed to it. After giving them detailed instructions on how to feed him, clean his cage and how often to change his water, I felt comfortable about his future welfare. Fernando, however, knew something unusual was happening because he became quiet, turned his head away from me, and wouldn't even say goodbye. As I left, he turned his back on me and pooped onto the newspaper lining his cage. The others had laughed.

While skimming the morning papers on my electronic tablet and munching my cornflakes mixed with apricot wheats, I glanced at Fernando.

'Rohan's been a bad boy,' he said.

'I'm sorry, Fernando, but I couldn't leave you at the cattery. They'd have made mincemeat of you.' I laughed. 'Perhaps not. You look a bit scrawny under your feathers.'

He stared at me with his big, grey eyes. A doleful look.

It was the middle of the week and I was taking my time off *in lieu* for all the extra hours I had put in recently. I planned to go for a walk in the local park since it was going to be a beautiful, sunny day, and then I was off to the National Space Centre. People visited the museum from all over the world and I had never been there, despite it being on my doorstep. When it cooled down in the evening, I thought, I might go for a jog.

As I tidied up the kitchen, the sun streaming in through the window, my mobile rang.

Looking at the number, I sighed. *Now what?*

'Sorry to bother you, Sir, but we have a problem.'

Like Apollo 13, I reflected, as the member of the admin team from HQ continued.

'We know it's your day off, and it's still early morning. Superintendent Breedon asked me to ring you. All the other homicide detectives are on holiday, or they're tied up with other cases —'

I sighed. This was one of the times I regretted being a detective inspector with the Major Crimes division. Your time was never your own.

'— but the body of a middle-aged man has been found in Charnwood Forest. Ben Carter and his team of forensic officers are already there. Mr Carter says there's something very odd about the body. Wouldn't say any more. The super would be grateful if you went to the scene...'

I knew I couldn't refuse, because it would be held against me at some point in the future. But in all honesty, I was also intrigued. What could be so odd about the body that Ben had held back? I quickly changed into some formal clothes, apologised to Fernando and left him some more pumpkin seeds, pieces of apple and black grapes, and hurried out of the front door onto the pavement.

I then bumped into one of the most attractive young women I had seen in a long time. I stared at her. She blushed.

'Are you the police? The shopkeeper on the main road, he told me you live here.'

She looked to be in her mid-twenties, with thick, glossy, shoulder-length black hair and soft olive skin. Her eyes were large and frightened.

I nodded.

'My friend and me. We need your help.'

Her eyes darted towards the main road, urgency in her voice. She wore heavy make-up — pale blue eyeshadow that glittered in the sun, black mascara on her eyelashes, and a black painted beauty spot on her chin. Her pale pink *shalwar kameez* was delicately embroidered with gold thread, a dainty dark blue waistcoat covering the top. A thin, gold chain with a small rose in the middle rested on her right ankle. She looked as if she had stepped out from the pages of *The Arabian Nights* or from the cinema screen as one of the stars in *Sinbad*.

'I'm really sorry, Miss. If you need the police, you must ring the correct number. Somebody'll help you.'

'Please, Sir, please help me. And my friend Amina. We are prisoners. We arrived in this country from Afghanistan. Paid a lot of money. If they know we've run away, they'll kill us. They'll send *Biju* after us.' She quickly glanced up and down the road. 'Please, Sir. Help us. My name is Hasina. Here, this is valuable. My friend Amina, she gave it to me. Please keep it. I don't want to lose it.' She thrust something hard into my hand. I looked at it. I looked at her. Her name meant happy and joyful. She was far from that. I wanted to help her with whatever predicament she and her friend were in. But I also had to get to Charnwood Forest.

I retrieved a business card from my pocket and asked her to ring the number of the main office there. It also had my number on it.

She snatched the card from me. 'They are already here,' she cried, and ran. I looked up and down the street. I could see a steady stream of traffic on the main road. One or two cars were coming towards us. And then I noticed two riders on a powerful motorbike, both wearing dark helmets with visors and black leathers. Before long, Hasina had turned a corner and was out of sight.

21

As I drove off, I felt bad about leaving her, but I had no choice. Why was she so heavily made up in the morning? She looked as if she was going to a party. The *shalwar kameez* was made from the finest quality silk. And who or what was *Biju*? In Gujarati and Hindi, the word meant 'other'. Who would send this 'other' after them? People traffickers? She couldn't have meant *bichchoo*, which referred to a scorpion? I hoped she would ring HQ, and then she would be put in touch with the appropriate officers who would help her. I comforted myself with the thought that there was nothing more I could have done in that instant.

As I turned right along the main road, the shops were getting ready for business. Boxes of fresh tropical fruit and vegetables appeared on wooden stalls on the pavements, fluorescent lights inside saree shops were switched on, and the gold jewellers pulled up their electronic metal shutters and deactivated state-of-the-art burglar alarm systems. Bright sunlight bounced off steel pots and pans hanging from metal hooks in other windows. New life was slowly being breathed into an awakening city.

CHAPTER 2

The sixty-seven square miles of Charnwood Forest covered a large part of north-west Leicestershire. The forest had extensive tracts of woodlands, but parts of it were also barren and craggy. Many quarries, some still used for stone aggregate, were dotted for miles, while others were filled with water and provided a haven for rare flora and fauna, and a variety of bird life. A couple of reservoirs complemented the natural beauty of the environment. The area was popular for hill walking and rock climbing for the hundreds of visitors who regularly used it for recreational purposes.

I drove my white Mercedes Coupé into the now-restricted public carpark and parked next to the forensic vans. I left my jacket on the passenger seat, nodded to the officer in charge who appeared to be expecting me, and climbed the steep incline towards the thick woods. The morning sun was getting hotter, the uneven country path rutted and cracked, the brown dust rising with my every step. As my breathing became laboured, sweat ran down my temples and down my spine, making it tingle. I loosened my tie. Two large birds of prey circled against the deep blue sky. Buzzards, I thought. As I struggled towards the woodland, the sound of sweet birdsong filled my ears, lifting my spirits.

Behind me, the ruins of Bradgate House, a magnificent Tudor mansion in its heyday, made an impressive backdrop, a herd of red and fallow deer grazing in the foreground. Old John Tower, a stone folly in the shape of a beer tankard, stood high on the hill to my left, brooding. The tinder-dry, brown grasslands and the sad sight of acres of charred woodland burnt in the recent forest fires stretched into the distance. The fires had raged for days, destroying not only the trees, shrubs and grass, but many wild animals too. Crews had tried to tackle the fire with water pumped from underground streams, and a helicopter with a large metal bucket had dumped thousands of litres of water dredged from local rivers and from further afield. The event had been severe enough to be reported on the national news.

As I approached the ancient woodland, some of which had escaped the catastrophe, the familiar blue and white crime scene tape was already in place across large areas. Further to the right, about fifty yards from the edge of the woodland, was a series of metal poles like shortened shepherds' crooks, pegged into the ground in a rectangular shape and tagged with more crime scene tape. Officers dressed in white full-body forensic suits scoured the area with equipment that looked like metal detectors, while others, with pincers and forks, picked up leaves, blades of grass, twigs and items of potential interest with tweezers, dropping them carefully into transparent evidence bags.

As I approached, Ben Carter emerged from behind some trees and held out his hand. I shook it vigorously, pleased to see the senior forensic investigator again. He smiled back at me, accentuating the crow's feet around his eyes in his deeply tanned face.

'Nice tan, Ben. Where've you been? Round the Med? Further afield?'

'Back garden during evenings and weekends, Inspector. Not had a break yet. But the wife and I are looking forward to a fortnight in Croatia before too long.'

'What have we got here, Ben? I was told it's odd, to put it mildly.'

'Please put on one of the suits and I'll show you. Not seen anything like it in my thirty years in the business,' replied Ben.

Well-gorged crows with glossy aubergine-coloured feathers jumped and danced nearby, ready to carry the souls of the dead to their afterlives. Hovering kestrels and kites looked down, ready to pounce. I took off my Fitbit and put it in Ben's van in case it got caught on the forensic glove. As I zipped up the white forensic suit, a figure approached.

'Hello, Sir. You must be Inspector Sharma,' she said. 'I'm DS Nicholson. Grace Nicholson. Been assigned to work with you on this case.' She was already in a forensic suit.

I shook her hand and smiled. She was tall and slim, with even, white teeth. Her brown eyes glistened in the sunlight. I had not heard of her before and assumed she was either new to the force or had transferred into the Major Crimes division from elsewhere in the service.

'Have already taken a statement from the lady who found the body,' she said, nodding towards the car park. 'I asked her to wait in case you wanted to speak to her. She's in her car over there, with her husband. The pathologist, Dr Malik, will be here shortly.'

I thanked her, impressed with her efficiency. It was the sort of thing my previous detective sergeant, Jack Shepherd, would have done, but he had been rightly promoted to detective inspector and was now working in a neighbouring police force.

We walked into the woodland and came across a large tract of grassland. Not far away was a grassy mound, with a dark shape sprawled near it. The birds stopped singing as we approached. A swarm of blow flies, like a dark woollen blanket, lifted a few feet into the air. As the insects flew away, the unmistakable, rotting smell of death clawed its way deep into my lungs, making me want to retch.

The body of a tall man lay on its side, almost in a foetal position. He was dressed in a full-length black wetsuit, a snorkel and gloves, a rubber fin on his left foot. The right foot was hidden by the left. An oxygen tank was strapped to his back, but the air pipe leading to his mouthpiece had been ripped away. What looked like a large watch was strapped to his wrist. The diving suit was shredded around the midriff, the neck and the legs. Grey, dry, decaying flesh protruded through, a landing ground for the blow flies.

'Probably animals, trying to get to the body,' said Ben, indicating the torn rubber. 'And that looks like a dive computer on his wrist. Would have told him how long he'd been underwater, how deep, how long he could stay at that depth. My wife and I go diving in the Red Sea in Egypt when we can.'

'But Mr Carter,' said Grace, 'we're in the middle of England.'

'Ben, please,' the head of forensics said with a smile. 'Yup. The closest beach is about seventy miles away.' He hunched near the body and turned the head towards him.

DS Nicholson gasped, put her hand to her mouth and looked away. The man's right cheek was missing, the putrid flesh crawling with thousands of maggots, some coming through the eye socket and nostril. Beetles and centipedes crawled underneath.

'Oh, good,' said Ben, pleased. 'Should help us narrow down the time of death. It's all down to the life cycle of the maggots. Might also get some pollen from trees and flowers that have now stopped pollinating. That will tell us a lot.'

None of us said anything.

I eventually broke the silence by saying, 'So, we've got a man in full diving gear, miles from the sea, in a forest in Leicestershire. What the hell's going on?' Then it occurred to me. 'He couldn't be from that dive centre in the south-west of the county, could he? The one that's used for training scuba divers?'

'I thought of that too, Sir,' said Ben. 'But he couldn't have walked here dressed like this. And there're no tyre tracks anywhere leading to this site. How did he get here? These white specks on the diving suit look like dried sea salt. The quarry is filled with freshwater, so no salt.'

'Could've been killed by the sea and dumped here?' suggested Grace.

'Always possible,' I replied. 'Are there any obvious signs of murder, Ben? Knife wounds? Bullet holes?'

'Can't tell yet — we'll get a definitive answer when we get him back to the path lab. Could have been strangled, of course.'

'What, with a snorkel around his face?' said Grace.

'Not discounting anything,' said Ben. 'The airpipe itself could've been used for strangulation — who knows? We'll find out when we perform the post-mortem.'

I was beginning to warm to DS Nicholson, but I could sense Ben was a bit miffed at her comments.

'How long d'you think he's been here, Ben? Any ideas?' I asked.

'Can't say, yet. Could be a few days or a couple of weeks. The hot weather means the body will have decomposed rapidly. We'll know more once the suit's been removed and the pathologist gets to work.'

'What's this round his middle?' I asked, indicating what looked like nylon string tied round his stomach, another metre or so trailing behind his back.

'No idea what that's doing there. Will get my team to look into it some more.'

'What about the lady who found him? What was she doing here?' I asked Grace.

'Walking the dog, Sir. Doesn't normally come to this part of the forest. Had taken the lead off and the dog was roaming freely. Came into the woods. Said he'd been gone for a long time. She shouted to him, whistled, but nothing. Eventually the dog came running with something in his mouth. It was only when she took it out of the dog's mouth that she realised what it was — the right foot, torn away from the rest of the leg. She screamed, dropped it, and ran. She rang her husband, who rang us. He's with her now. The scene of crime officers cordoned off the area. It's where the rectangular crime scene tape is.'

So, the right foot wasn't hidden after all. As I stared at the corpse, my mobile rang.

'Sorry, got to take this,' I said, walking away and unzipping the suit to retrieve my phone.

It was my mother. 'What time will you get here, *Beta*?' she asked. 'I'm preparing our lunch. Chicken samosas, just as you like them, tangy with a thin pastry, and your favourite dish of pigeon peas and potatoes. All with hot chapatis, straight from the *tawa*.'

'Oh, Mum, I'm really sorry but I'm at work.' I couldn't face the thought of food after seeing the victim's face anyway.

'But you said this was your day off.'

'It is — it was. I'm sorry, Mum, but something urgent came up. I've been called into work.'

The long silence twisted my heart. How could I have forgotten to tell her? I knew she would have spent hours preparing all the spices and herbs, and would have minced the chicken breasts herself, with any slivers of fat carefully removed first.

'Please freeze my portion, Mum. Perhaps we can have it some other time.'

'But it won't taste the same… Ah, never mind. Goodbye.' With that the line went dead.

I so wanted to rush to her, to hug her and say I was sorry, and to have lunch with both my parents, but I knew that wasn't possible.

I turned towards Ben and Grace. As I did so, we noticed a forensics officer coming towards us with, I assumed, the pathologist, Dr Malik. Ben also informed me that an entomologist, an insect specialist, would assist Dr Malik *in situ* to help estimate a possible time of death given the state of the body. After the introductions, I left with Grace Nicholson. The others would work on the scene, gathering all relevant evidence.

'Are you okay, Sir? You look a bit upset,' said Grace, as we walked towards the car park.

'Oh, it's nothing. Just a family matter.'

She didn't ask any further and I didn't offer any more. I spoke briefly to the woman with the dog and said we'd be in touch if we needed any further information. I also encouraged her to contact us again if she remembered anything else, however insignificant. Her husband put his arm around her shoulder as I gave them my card.

I hadn't expected to be in charge of this case. My paperwork from the last major case on gangs and knife crime wasn't yet complete, and I was planning to do that back at HQ. Turning to Grace, I directed her to organise teams of officers to conduct interviews with visitors, to visit nearby dwellings and to set up roadblocks, if necessary. They could try and catch passing traffic, to ask if they had seen anything unusual over the last week or two. Since people came here for recreational purposes or to walk their dogs, chances were there must be plenty of regulars. I also asked Grace to prepare social media posts appealing for any relevant information. I reminded her not to divulge anything about the state of the body until we had the full results from forensics and from the pathologist.

'Oh, and can you ask around if a young woman called Hasina has rung the domestic violence unit? Or the other departments which deal with vulnerable people, especially refugees and asylum seekers?'

'Why? Who is she?'

'Could be something or nothing, Grace. Just ask around. Please.'

She smiled and her brown eyes twinkled.

I knew it would all be done efficiently.

CHAPTER 3

It was the early evening — rush hour. I inched my Mercedes home along the busy Golden Mile. The tarmac was rutted in parts because of the recent extreme heat. A slight breeze came in through the open windows, but I was still sweating and looking forward to a cool shower. Crowds strolled along the pavement, occasionally stepping onto the road, not paying any attention to the traffic coming up behind them. I had to brake unexpectedly a couple of times. Since it was the school holidays, there were plenty of teenagers wandering about.

The people and the clothes they wore reflected the world on a pavement. An elderly Indian woman, her white cotton saree informing others she was widowed, shouted and laughed with another across the road. A middle-aged Sikh man in an immaculate white turban hurried along, black leather briefcase in hand. Young Hindu women in short skirts, bright silk sarees, or wearing a *shalwar kameez*, laughed with their friends, their sisters, their mothers as they ambled along, casting sly, interested glances at young men walking towards them. Young brides-to-be entered jewellery shops with their mothers and sisters, ready to choose the gold set that would adorn their bodies on the memorable day, and which would cost thousands of pounds. There were Somali men, Somali women, a few Middle Eastern people, and a handful of white faces. The sound of popular Bollywood songs drifted through the open doors of cafes. The shops selling Indian sweetmeats were especially busy. Trays of yellow and white *penda*, pink and cream *barfi* with a milk chocolate base, and reddish-orange *jalebi* were weighed in small cardboard boxes, and then paid for.

A saloon pulled out sharply from a road to my left. I slammed on the brakes and let the car through. I received no gratitude from the driver, who joined the traffic and inched along in front of me. A dark hatchback pulled up next to me. Four youths in their twenties were playing loud rap music, shouting over each other to make themselves heard. A Hindu priest, dressed in traditional white cotton trousers and a short coat, with a pointed white Nehru cap and a red mark on his forehead, rushed past a Muslim man in a *kurta*, both fingering prayer beads. Both men were praying to the same God but coming at it from radically different directions. The gap between the two sets of prayer beads had led to the massacre of more than half a million people when India had been partitioned in 1947.

Many shop windows displayed brightly coloured *rakhis*, a string bracelet interwoven with red and gold threads, which a sister would tie to the wrist of her brother on *Rakhi* day every year. In return, the brother would promise to look after her through any misfortune that may befall her in life. I loved the sentiment but hated the day, which would be celebrated soon. While millions of brothers and sisters celebrated the occasion all over the world, it reminded me of what had happened to my own sister, how my sneeze had betrayed our hiding place all those years ago in Kenya, and how I had not protected her. The guilt cut through me every day. My poor Maya. I hoped she was all right. Was she even alive? Who knew?

As I was about to turn left into my road, a middle-aged Indian couple pulled up in their car beside me. A famous song by Lata Mangeshkar floated from the stereo. A song about how life can be sometimes joyous, sometimes painful. For human beings, it was important to increase one and reduce the other. For many, however, the balance was never right. The couple looked as if they were engaged in their own struggle for equilibrium.

I parked the car, discovering a rare space not far from my house.

Fernando was chirpy and shouted out, 'Hello Rohan, hello Rohan,' as I walked into the front room.

'Hello, Fernando. I see you're glad to see me. I'm glad to see you, too. Hope you're not too hot.'

He jiggled on his perch and stared at himself in his small, round mirror. He then blew a wolf whistle.

'I see we have a high opinion of ourselves, Fernando.'

'*Make India great again! Down with Pakistan!*'

'Fernando! Where on earth did you learn that?'

'*Down with beef-eaters!*'

'Don't say that anymore.' I had to admit the thought of Beefeaters from the Tower of London being harangued while walking through the streets of Delhi put a smile on my face. But really Fernando's outburst referred to the fact that Muslims could eat beef while Hindus did not.

I thought hard about where he could have picked this up. The only answer could be the Indian family who'd looked after him while I'd been on holiday. He must have been watching some right-wing, Indian propaganda on YouTube or one of the Indian satellite channels. I could think of no other explanation.

Fernando went quiet at my raised voice.

I removed the dirty newspaper from the bottom of his cage, replenished his water tray, chopped pieces of apple and pear and pineapple for him, then went upstairs for a long, cool shower. Afterward, I poured myself a glass of cold lager, put my feet up on the coffee table, watched the news on television and wondered what to cook.

My mobile rang.

'Hello, Dad. How're you?' asked Yasmin.

My two kids were on FaceTime. They were on holiday with Faye and the man she left me for, Pierre Thiébault, in the Marmaris region of Turkey.

'Oh, I'm fine, thanks. Hope you're both having a good time?'

'We miss you, Dad. Wish you were here,' said Karan, who didn't normally express his emotions so readily.

I missed my children, and sometimes Faye, despite everything she had done to tear us apart. I hated the thought of Yasmin and Karan being with another man. Still, there was nothing I could do.

'Mum and Pierre keep dragging us to see ancient sites. Old, decaying temples, forts, piles of old stones. Older than you.'

'Very funny.'

'Today we spent ages inside a museum on a really hot day. We wanted to go swimming.'

'Well, your Mum's trying to broaden your education.'

'It'd be much more fun if you were here, Dad,' echoed Yasmin.

It broke my heart to hear that. I tried to find my own balance between joy and pain and couldn't always get it right. *Must get past it*, I kept thinking to myself.

We carried on with a few more pleasantries, said we would speak again before too long and ended the conversation.

I wandered into the kitchen and had started rummaging through the fridge when there was a persistent knocking on the front door.

'Sir! Sir!'

I couldn't quite make out the voice, but it had to be Hasina. I didn't encourage uninvited visitors. Well, at least I could return what she had thrust into my hand this morning and, hopefully, she would contact the appropriate people to help her.

I opened the door.

'Grace?'

She stared at me.

'What are you doing here?' I asked.

'She's a fit bit, Rohan. Fit bit,' Fernando interrupted.

Grace laughed. I blushed.

'I'm really sorry, Grace. That's Fernando you can hear, my African grey parrot.'

He must have remembered some of the words I had spoken to him that morning.

'Actually, he's right. You forgot your Fitbit in Ben's van,' she said. 'We weren't sure if you needed it back today. Ben told me where you lived. I said I'd drop it by since I pass this way on my way home. Hope you don't mind.'

This was the second time today a young woman had wanted to give me something.

I said I didn't mind and thanked her. She looked up and down the road and then up at the house. An aroma of fenugreek, mustard seeds and coriander from a nearby kitchen wafted through the air.

'I thought,' she continued, 'you might live in the suburbs. Not here.'

'Might do. Eventually. Just renting this place for the time being. Been here since my divorce. This is…' I paused. 'This is home. In more ways than one.'

'Oh, I'm sorry. I didn't mean to pry.'

I looked at this woman I hardly knew. Then I said something on the spur of the moment that I hoped I wouldn't regret.

'I was just about to cook, but have gone off the idea. If you don't have to rush off, do you fancy having a bite —'

'Bite me, Rohan. Bite me,' said Fernando.

Grace laughed and tried to hide her blushing neck.

'— to eat. I know a really good Persian restaurant not far from here. But if you need to rush back, it doesn't matter. Please don't misunderstand; I'm not asking you on a date. Just seems like a good chance to get to know each other. You can also bring me up to date on what you found today.'

She smiled and nodded. I told her the address of the restaurant and said I would meet her there after I had sorted out a few things in the house.

'Oh, Fernando, you do drop me in it sometimes,' I muttered, back in the front room.

Since I was going out, I left the television switched on so he wouldn't feel lonely and he'd have a bit of mental and visual stimulation. I decided to select one of the nature channels. It was running back-to-back episodes of *Life on Earth*. I thought this better than him picking up any coarse language from *EastEnders* or one of the other early evening soaps.

The West African tropical forest on the screen was lush, with large drops of rainwater sliding down large, rubbery green leaves. The howling of colobus monkeys and the screams of the vervet monkeys as they jumped across the high jungle canopies filled the room. From the forest floor, bands of chimpanzees looked up longingly at them. Wild pigs snorted as they trotted across the carpet of dead leaves, while a rainbow of vibrant, colourful birds flew from branch to branch, calling out to each other, warning of any approaching threats.

In the background, David Attenborough, a Leicester celebrity, narrated slowly and solemnly, 'Some people may describe this as a cacophony. To me it's a moving, musical rhapsody of Mother Nature, made even better by this flapping, noisy and happy flock of African grey parrots as they go searching for nuts and berries.'

'Home sweet home, Fernando.'

I looked at him as I closed the front door.

His moist, round grey eyes stared back at me.

CHAPTER 4

'So, how did you feel when you caught STD?' asked Grace.

'Pardon?'

'You know. Shiva the Destroyer.'

'Oh,' I said, and laughed, realising she was referring to the case I had been assigned to some time ago. 'Glad you didn't mean anything else.'

She looked at me, puzzled. Then a crimson blush floated up her neck. She giggled nervously.

We were sitting cross-legged on thick cushions on the floor at The Omar Khayyam, facing each other across a low, rectangular mahogany table. Plates and serving dishes made from fine brown clay from the mountains of northern Iran were placed on the table. We shared the starters: tahini with walnuts, hummus, and aubergine puree with yoghurt. Vine leaves stuffed with long grain basmati rice and delicately flavoured mince lamb were on another plate. A fine spray of saliva escaped Grace's lips as she chewed the vine leaves, an embarrassed look on her face. I smiled; she returned it.

I kept my response brief. Much of the hunt and capture of the psychopathic killer was in the public domain, and I was sure she would know about it.

Since it was early evening, the restaurant was deserted. We could not be overheard. I asked her about her day, whether she had discovered anything useful, but she shook her head. 'Got the uniforms out, visited nearby farmhouses, set up roadblocks to interview passing motorists, spoke to the ramblers and amblers. Nothing. Nobody remembered anything unusual. I've no idea where our land swimmer came from.'

'Well, we don't have much to go on, Grace. It will take several days for the various forensic tests to be undertaken — including trying to work out the time of death from the flies and maggots. In addition to the post-mortem, that is.'

The scent of frankincense and sandalwood from the burning rings placed around the restaurant floated into my lungs. I breathed in deeply.

'How do you know about this place? The food's to die for. If we don't think about flies and maggots on dead bodies, that is.'

I tried not to.

I explained that the restaurateur, Mr Rahimi, had escaped from Iran after the Shah was toppled in 1979. He was persuaded to move to Leicester by a friend. Seeing the burgeoning city and the various nationalities, he decided an authentic Persian restaurant might be worth trying, especially since he had a wife and three daughters to help him. It had proved to be a highly successful alternative to the local Indian restaurants. The cuisine appealed to all nationalities. The Indians liked the food because it was similar to, but not quite like, theirs. It was also popular with the whites and others who preferred their food with a range of flavours, not necessarily hot.

It was a place for lovers, who would eat soft Mejdool dates together; a place for friends and family — or for a singleton. It was a place where you could picture Sindbad the Sailor laughing, eating and dancing with his friends, the cream and blue silk drapes hanging down from the ceiling a wonderful backdrop. It was a place that promised the heavenly Arabian Nights with your lover.

Grace Nicholson's eyes twinkled in the light of the jasmine-scented candle placed in the middle of the table. She picked up an etched brass wine goblet and sipped some red wine. A cool draught from the air conditioning blew across the room, while soft music played on the zither, the flute and the lute, not loud enough to interrupt softly spoken conversations but pleasant enough to listen to.

'Anyway, tell me a bit about yourself,' I said.

She said there wasn't much to tell, really. Born and raised in a small village in Somerset, she'd gone to Bath University and studied English, and had one younger sister in her mid-twenties who was a nurse. She also had a stepbrother who was much older than her and had been an officer in the army but had recently left. He was now running some sort of import-export business, based mainly in London. Her mother and father had divorced some time ago. Her father had remarried, but that hadn't lasted long either. She also wasn't in a relationship at the moment, she volunteered.

She continued, 'I worked in insurance for three years after graduating — one of these big multinationals in Swindon — but I became bored with the endless computer work and the tedious office gossip. I wanted to make a difference and do something exciting, so I joined the fast-track course to become a detective with the Devon and Cornwall Police. I did a few years, became a sergeant, and then saw an advert recently saying they were recruiting in Leicester. I thought it'd be more exciting to be in a big, diverse city. And here I am!

'Also, I love all sorts of music — mainly pop, rock, rap, garage, grunge. But I have a passion for old Hollywood films of all different genres. I like the Western, *High Noon*, *Mogambo*, which is an African adventure, the Hitchcock thriller *Rear Window*, and *High Society*, the musical.'

'*Mogambo*? Really? With Clark Gable? I love that film, too. A lot of it was filmed around the town of Naivasha, Kenya, where I was born. My grandfather claimed to have met him.

I'm not so sure. You like modern music and old films. Me, I like all sorts of films, but mostly music from the sixties and seventies. And opera, especially Verdi.'

A slim, dark waiter, dressed in a pale tunic with a red cummerbund tied around the middle to match the colour of the fez on his head, came to our table. We had ordered three dishes to share: pieces of chicken cooked in a pomegranate sauce, spiced lamb meatballs and yellow saffron rice cooked with chickpeas. The scent of the food was intoxicating and made my mouth water.

'Mmmm,' said Grace. 'This looks fantastic. I didn't know I was so hungry.'

As we finished, Mr Rahimi walked through the door. 'Ah, Mr Rohan. How good to see you. And your pretty friend. I hope you're both enjoying the food.'

'As ever, Mr Rahimi, your food is excellent. This is a colleague, Grace Nicholson.' They exchanged pleasantries.

Later, he arrived with the bill, which I duly paid, even though Grace objected. We agreed she could leave the tip. She left a generous amount.

Mr Rahimi stood by the heavy wooden doors as we were leaving. I said, 'And how's Jalil? Not seen him for a while.'

'Oh, these Afghans. Let you down. Especially the young ones. He was desperate to get a job with me because we spoke the same language. I felt sorry for him being an asylum seeker, so I hired him as a waiter. He did well for a few months. But now he's disappeared. Nobody knows where. Doesn't answer his phone.'

Perhaps the authorities were after Jalil for working. I had no idea about his asylum status and, quite frankly, it was none of my business. I wished Mr Rahimi and his family well.

Grace and I parted company at the door.

CHAPTER 5

Several days later, there still had not been much progress in the case of the dead diver. The post-mortem had been delayed because of the need to prepare the body. The pathologist had also been called to undertake more autopsies due to the recent rise in unexpected deaths, most likely due to the heatwave, but each one had to be properly investigated. We had not been able to identify the victim through the missing persons database and nobody had reported him missing. As a result, there was no pressure from family or friends to determine the cause of death or to pursue any suspects, if he had been the victim of a homicide. While I waited to hear from the pathologist and the entomologist, who had been drafted in to determine the possible time of death, I was working on other cases. I was still winding down some complex matters relating to gangs and knife crime and was also called in to lead some training sessions with recent recruits on policing in a modern, multiracial community.

It was rush hour as I headed home from HQ. As I approached the Golden Mile in the late evening sun, the traffic had come to a standstill in both directions. Horns blared intermittently; car windows were wound down, but there was no cool breeze for the occupants. On the pavements, young women in summer dresses drew unwelcome attention from the young men, some athletic, bare-chested and good-looking, with perspiring brown bodies. Music blared from shop doorways and cars. Rap, bhangra, classical Hindi, pop, rock — something for every taste and most ages. There was also laughter and shouting in Punjabi, Gujarati, English.

In the distance, I saw the cause of the delay: a broken-down old hatchback was being pushed along the road by two men, one steering through the open window. They were trying to heave it into a nearby side road. Across the other side, an ambulance, blue lights flashing, blocked the inside lane, where an old woman in a saree was sprawled on the pavement. A crowd had gathered; others walked by.

The car's air-conditioning blew only warm air onto my face, so I turned it off and wound down my window. I puffed my cheeks and breathed out.

A few moments later, the passenger in the car next to me, a middle-aged woman, shouted, '*Hai bhaia*, what's that music you're listening to? The singers sound really happy.'

I was listening to Classic FM on the radio and 'Brindisi' from *La Traviata* spread its joyous message through the air.

'*Maasi*,' I said. 'It's Italian. From an opera. They're singing about the joys of friendship, of drinking fine wine, and of love. It's just one song — there are others which are sad, though.'

'Tell me some more.'

La Traviata was one of my favourite operas and I related the story of passionate love, jealousy, family honour, abandonment and then the untimely death of the young courtesan.

'Sounds like an Indian film. Probably just as long. At least she wasn't a widow bringing up two young sons on her own, then forced to shoot dead her grown-up son, like in the film *Mother India*. I would love to watch your opera. But I won't understand the language. You're so lucky.'

'Oh, *Maasi*, I don't speak the language. I just know this opera inside-out because I love it so much. They should make an Indian film about it. We Indians would all love it.'

'Yes,' she replied. 'The scales are balanced more towards sadness than happiness. Just like we Indians like it.'

She smiled as her car pulled away.

The road cleared quickly. I didn't fancy cooking tonight so I picked up some *aloo chat*, aubergine *bhajis* and spiced chicken drumsticks from a nearby restaurant for my evening meal. I would wash it down with some *mango lassi*. It was all perfect to eat on a hot summer's evening like this.

'Fernando, so many feathers! Are you moulting?' I said as I walked into my living room and changed the newspaper at the bottom of the parrot's cage. Normally, he perched on the edge of the settee while I did this. Today, though, he flew out of the cage and straight into the window, falling heavily on the carpet.

I rushed to pick him up, stroked him, and had a good look to make sure he had not hurt himself.

'Oh, Fernando. Why did you do that?'

He stared at me with his big, round grey eyes, as if in a trance. Then he blinked once.

My phone rang.

'Hello, Sir,' said Grace Nicholson. 'Just thought I'd touch base since it's been a while since we last spoke.' Like me, Grace was also working on other cases. 'The roadblocks and interviews with motorists didn't throw up any new leads on our victim. I asked around about Hasina, but nobody's heard of her. I looked at missing persons too. Nothing. Then I looked at the national police database and messages from other police forces about her. Again, absolutely nothing. Who is she, Sir? And why the interest?'

I explained the strange circumstances of my meeting her, how she knew where I lived, how frightened she was, what I'd advised her to do and how quickly she'd disappeared.

'Very odd,' said Grace.

'Odd, indeed.'

I didn't know why, but I decided not to mention what Hasina had thrust into my hand.

'Grace, I'm hoping the PM on our victim will be carried out soon. Then we can proceed. Hopefully, with better results.'

'Thank you, Sir. And see you soon.'

CHAPTER 6

The quiet chatter stopped as I entered the incident room early one afternoon. It had taken many days for the body to be cleaned up, for the post-mortem to be performed and other tests to be done. Ben Carter sat at one end of the conference table, with Grace alongside. Facing Grace was Dr Azim Malik, the pathologist. As I walked towards the table, Ben stood up, looked behind me and said, 'Hello, Sir, this is Dr Marie Easterlake, the entomologist from the university. She's been working with us on the case.'

I turned round, offered my clammy palm to Dr Easterlake, and she gripped it firmly.

'Pleased to meet you, Inspector Sharma,' she said, one side of her shoulder-length, straight, dark hair almost covering her eye. Whitney Houston at her most glamorous came to mind. 'Your reputation goes before you.'

'The pleasure's all mine,' I replied, smiling.

I nodded to Grace and Dr Malik as I sat down at the far end of the table, near the large digital smartboard on the wall.

'I'll go through the findings of the post-mortem,' said Dr Malik, 'such as they are. Things are not clear cut given the state of the body and the time it's been exposed to the hot, humid weather. Dr Easterlake will say more on that later.'

Dr Malik then loaded video images of the body as we'd found it, with some of the footage taken by a drone above the site. He explained that the victim had suffered multiple bone fractures, especially to the right side of the body. The right shoulder and ribs, pelvis and both legs had been shattered. The skull had fractures. The teeth, especially those at the front, were broken, smashed against the air mouthpiece he'd been using. There was no evidence of any gun shots or knife wounds. The flesh that remained around the neck, which had not been eaten by the maggots, showed no signs of strangulation.

'But that could still be debated, and it's not a conclusive finding,' he added. 'There was no evidence of water in the lungs, so he didn't drown. But as we know, he was definitely in the sea because the wetsuit is covered in salt crystals left from water that had dried by the time we found him.'

'Could he have had a heart attack while diving?' I asked.

'Difficult to tell, as the heart has decomposed a fair bit. But his body is muscular. Strong calf muscles, strong biceps. The guy appears to have worked out regularly. The blood vessels didn't show any signs of furring. A heart attack is possible, but unlikely.'

'So, am I right in thinking the cause of death was the injuries he sustained?'

'In the absence of any other firm evidence, we have to say it is highly likely, yes.'

'How could those injuries have occurred, Dr Malik?' asked Grace.

'Could he have been run over by a vehicle?' asked Ben.

'It's possible he was run over. That could explain some of the injuries, such as the broken shoulder and legs. But the shattered pelvis and the damage done internally to the hip joints could indicate falling from a height. Landing on his feet could then explain some of the fractures.'

'Could he have fallen or been thrown from an aeroplane?' I asked.

'Possible, but all speculation,' said Dr Malik.

'Sir,' said Grace, turning to me, 'I made some enquires with East Midlands Airport and other smaller airfields to see whether a pilot had filed in a flight plan for this area over the last few weeks. There were flights nearby, but nothing that matches the body deposition site.'

The whirring and clacking of the air conditioning disturbed the silence. I coughed as the cold and dust from the vents tickled my windpipe.

'And the elephant in the room, so to speak, is the scuba diving suit. We know he didn't walk to Charnwood Forest. He didn't drive there himself —'

'No, he would have had difficulty pressing the pedals with those great big flippers,' said Dr Malik.

Ignoring this comment, Ben continued, 'And he wasn't at the local diving centre, because that's a freshwater quarry. The nearest coastline is in Lincolnshire and Norfolk, about seventy miles away. So, how the hell did he get here?'

'And more importantly, who is he?' I said. 'Any thoughts on the length of nylon string tied round his stomach, Ben?'

'Tests under the microscope,' said Ben, 'show it has jagged edges where it was severed. Not a clean cut with a knife or another sharp blade.'

'Could a rusty edge have done that, Ben?' asked Grace.

'Possible, but why use a rusty blade? Did the victim cut the string himself? Or did somebody else do it? What was it for?'

'Certainly not for pulling a sledge through the snow, like Scott of the Antarctic,' said Dr Malik. 'We could do with some snow now. This heat is killing me.' The pathologist flapped a slim manila folder in front of his face.

We glared at him.

'Going back to the idea about being thrown from a plane,' said Grace. 'Even if it was done without a flight plan, why would somebody wait for him to walk out of the sea, then bop him on the head, take him to an airfield and then throw him out of a light aircraft?'

I turned to Marie Easterlake. 'What are your thoughts and observations, Dr Easterlake?'

'Oh, please, call me Marie. The science of entomology, as you know, is the study of insects and how they interact with their environment, other species and humans. And before you ask, no, *A Bug's Life* isn't one of my favourite films,' she added with a smile, probably to counteract anything the resident comedian might have said. 'Dr Malik and I worked closely to determine the time of death. But, given the state of the body and other factors, it's not been easy. Ben, can we have the video of the body and the deposition site please?'

I turned my chair back toward the screen. We stared at the corpse again, covered in thousands of flies, many of which flew away as the camera operative approached. They were quick to land back on the body. The footage was taken from all angles and showed the face covered in wriggling maggots. Grace looked away.

'I won't bore you with too much science,' Marie continued, 'but it's important to know some of the basics to understand what's going on. Four types of insects and other bugs start infesting a body once it dies. They arrive one after the other. Blow flies have an acute sense of smell. They can pinpoint a tiny drop of blood or signs of decomposition from about a hundred metres away. They're the first ones to arrive. We know a lot about their life cycle. There are many different regional varieties in the UK so we can tell where the death occurred, even if it was miles away. So, in answer to the earlier question that was raised, our victim died where he was found.

He didn't die near the sea or anywhere else.' She paused to let this information sink in.

She then explained that eggs laid on a corpse take about two weeks to become a fly. After about a day, the maggot is hatched and starts gorging on the body. In about four days it has grown ten times the size, from about two millimetres to two centimetres. Once fully grown, the maggot tries to hide near or under the body, so it doesn't become a food source for others, such as birds or small animals.

'So, Marie,' Ben said, 'we can assume that the victim has been dead for about four days because of the maggots feasting on his face.'

'Unfortunately, it's not as straightforward as that. Please bear with me. The maggot then changes into a pupa and fights its way out of the hardening outer layer after about ten days. Once free, it starts mating straightaway. After two days, the female lays her eggs, often on the same body that gave her life.'

'The circle of life,' said Dr Malik.

'What complicates matters,' Marie continued, 'is that other insects and bugs are not going to sit idly by and watch the blow flies have all the fun. Beetles start arriving once the body starts drying up. The parasites and predators of blow flies have a golden opportunity to gorge themselves and they arrive in droves. These include ants, bees and wasps, and they lay their eggs on the maggot or their pupa. Other insects come to the body, but their presence is benign. They just land on it by chance, because it's breezy or they have fallen onto it from nearby trees and bushes. So, it's obviously important to take into account the activities of some of the insects. But not others.'

Marie Easterlake explained that she had collected some live maggots and the shells of the pupae from the site so that she could analyse them and come to a provisional conclusion of when the first flies arrived. She had also boiled some maggots in water and preserved them in ethanol and kept others alive. Maggots grow fastest in heat, and she had measured the temperature every hour for ten days to check their size. She also compared these results with the results of the nearest weather station to where the body had been found. This enabled her to understand how hot the maggots were as they developed. She analysed the ones kept in the ethanol as well to determine their stages of growth and compared it with the live maggots until they became fully-grown flies. She then plotted the temperature data backwards to when the female blow fly first laid her eggs.

'And having done all of that,' she continued, 'it's difficult to reach any definitive conclusion about time of death. You see, the wetsuit our victim was wearing complicates matters. Perhaps Dr Malik can explain a bit more.'

'Yes,' Dr Malik said. 'The wetsuit stopped some of the bugs from eating the flesh, especially on the torso and the limbs. It also prevented heat penetration. But as you can see, they got to the side of the face and other exposed parts of the body. When we removed the wetsuit, the stomach was already bloated. This means bacteria in the digestive system had started attacking nearby tissue, producing gases which inflate the body. Fluid was also seeping from the body orifices and the wounds. So, the body was already showing some early signs of decay.'

'And that means,' added Marie Easterlake, 'that the evidence from the blow flies and the maggots has to be treated with great caution. It appears to indicate the victim could have died within the last two weeks, but it could be slightly longer than that. The summer heat and humidity would have increased the rate of decomposition, but the diving suit might have slowed this rate. Nobody can say for certain. The post-mortem interval could be about ten days to two weeks, or it could be longer than that.'

I took a moment, impressed with her knowledge and professionalism, and then thanked her. The other three in the room nodded, all having learned something new. I wasn't sure where this left the investigation, but we had to move forward. Now that we had a possible cause of death, identifying the victim was our next step.

I turned to Ben and asked whether it was possible to reconstruct an image of the face, either through computer-generated imagery or some other means. Since we had half a face, and parts of the nose and mouth, he confirmed it could be done using CGI without too much difficulty. I told Grace that once we had an image we needed to circulate it to other police forces and put it on social media and the traditional outlets, asking our colleagues and the public for any information about the identity of the victim. However, she was to liaise with me first before taking any action.

I thanked all of them and closed the meeting. Grace, Ben and Dr Malik filed out the door promptly. As Marie Easterlake started to leave, I thanked her and said how much I valued her contribution.

'You're welcome, Inspector. By the way, how are your children? Yasmin and Karan?'

I did a double take. How did a woman I had only met an hour ago know the names of my children, and why was she asking about them?

'Why the hell didn't you tell me about Marie Easterlake?' I blurted to Faye on the phone. It was evening and I was back at home after the briefing session. 'Why didn't you mention that she was your boyfriend's sister?'

'Don't raise your voice at me, Rohan. Easterlake's obviously her married name. What do you want me to say? Do you want me to go through everybody that Pierre knows? That *I* know? Well, let's see. He and I work with at least seventy other teachers, not to mention another hundred support staff. Oh, and there's the small matter of over a thousand students and their families. Okay, where shall we start?'

I paused. 'I'm sorry, Faye. And I didn't mean to raise my voice. It's just that she took me by surprise, asking about Yasmin and Karan. I didn't know she'd met them.'

'Pretty, isn't she?' said Faye. 'Just separated from her husband. He found out she'd been playing away.'

'I know how he feels.'

'Don't be bitter, Rohan. And get over it. Life's moved on.'

I reflected on what I had said to Grace the other evening. It seemed my life and my taste in music were both stuck in the past.

'You and she could hit it off,' Faye continued. 'She would be good for you. Time for you to be with somebody else. Enjoy life. Be happy. Be content. And, yes, we did have a good holiday in Turkey. Thanks for asking.'

'Who's sounding bitter now?'

The silence stretched for an eternity. The haunting emptiness of a previous undying love, now gone badly wrong. The invisible string on a violin that had stopped playing the joyful and harmonious note a long time ago.

'Please tell Yasmin and Karan I love them and that I'll see them soon.'

We both cut the connection at the same time. At least some synchronicity still remained.

Fernando stared at me through the bars of his cage.

The outer walls of my terraced house had not cooled down for a long time. They felt warm to the touch and the heat was clawing its way from the ceiling to the floor. I turned on the fan in the front room, went upstairs, had a cold shower and changed into a T-shirt and shorts.

As I was channel surfing on the television, feet up on the coffee table, enjoying a cold glass of Sauvignon Blanc and wondering what to eat tonight, my mother rang.

'Hello, *Beta*. How are you? Not heard from you for a long time.'

It was the voice designed to make me feel sorry for her and go running across to my parents' house. I apologised again for letting her down for the previous lunch appointment. I explained I was busy at work but would see them soon.

'Oh, don't worry about the lunch I had cooked. Gave your share to the man who lives next door. His wife was rushed into hospital with a suspected heart attack. Poor man, doesn't know how to cook.'

After a few more pleasantries, we said goodbye.

'Home sweet home,' I heard Fernando say, repeating the phrase I had said to him just before I had gone to meet Grace at The Omar Khayyam. I turned around and saw him staring intently at the television screen. It was a programme on one of the nature channels about the Amazon Rainforest. Turning up the sound — trilling birdsong, howling monkeys, the gushing of a waterfall — I heard the commentator say, 'And here we have a colourful and rather majestic macaw gliding through the canopies of the rainforest...'

'Hey, Fernando. A macaw. Could be one of your Scottish relatives with a name like that.'

I didn't expect him to laugh. But he didn't flap his wings or twirl on his perch as he usually did when I called him by his name. Instead, he repeated, 'Home sweet home.'

His head drooped and he lifted it slowly. His big, round, moist grey eyes fixed on the screen. Then he looked away.

CHAPTER 7

I came downstairs at some early hour in the morning, not able
to sleep much due to the heat and sweat. The small desk fan in
the bedroom did not provide much respite.

'*Olé!*' I said, as I whisked away the covering on Fernando's
cage.

He looked at me, then looked down.

'What? No *olé* for me, Fernando?'

He had not eaten his pumpkin seeds or the sliced apple and
pear. Despite the heat, his water tray was still full. A few
feathers, short and gossamer-like, lay on the old newspaper
covering the bottom of the cage.

'Oh, Fernando. What's the matter with you? Too hot? Eh? I
know you're lonely and want to go home. But where are you
going to go? This is home for both of us now. I can't let you
just fly away from here. It's a jungle out there, so to speak. The
kites, falcons and kestrels will make mincemeat of you before
you can say *shish kebab*. Come on, eat your food.'

He looked at me with his big, grey eyes. I opened his cage,
stroked his head and midriff, and placed him on my shoulder.
He pooped onto my fresh shirt.

'Oh, Fernando, why did you do that?'

After changing into a fresh shirt, I made some French toast
and sipped a mug of *masala* tea, wondering what to do about
him.

My mobile rang.

'Sorry to disturb you so early in the morning, Sir,' said the
male voice from the serious crimes division, 'but we've got
another body. Young woman. DS Nicholson's on her way. Ben

Carter and his forensics team are already there. The pathologist's been informed.'

The clear blue sky, the thin wisps of cirrus clouds, and the already blazing sun promised another hot and sultry day as I drove. A red kite swooped past my car and soared high in the sky, looking for unsuspecting prey. In the distance, the parched grass and scorched woodland screamed for rain.

The natural beauty and serenity of the location in which the body had been found hit me as I walked towards the bank of the river Soar. The vegetation was luscious, the trees, grass and bushes fed by a steady, but dwindling, supply of fresh water. The stillness was disturbed by the occasional whistle of a bird I didn't recognise, and I wondered whether the *plop* sound in the slow-flowing water in the middle was an otter diving, a species that had been reintroduced here recently. In the tall reeds a heron stooped, gazing at its still reflection, ready to pierce an unsuspecting fish with its long, razor-like beak.

The sounds of nature were replaced by the hushed voices of forensic officers and divers in black wetsuits and snorkels as I approached an old willow tree, bending in prayer over the river's edge, providing shelter to a profusion of pennywort. I nodded to all as Ben Carter pointed to the tall reeds, not too far from the bank. A young woman's naked body was caught in the vegetation, the arched back resting on the surface. The legs were bent at the knees and rested under the water. A gold belly button ring glinted in the morning sun. The rest of the body was hidden by the vegetation.

'Who found her?' I asked Grace as she approached.

'The two boys over there,' she replied, pointing to two teenagers standing in the distance, being comforted by their parents and an officer in uniform. 'They said they'd come here early for a day's fishing. It's a lovely spot for it. Then they made the discovery. They didn't touch anything and rang their parents, who came here to verify the situation. Then they rang us. They're all in shock.'

'Thanks, Grace. I'll speak to them once I'm done here.'

A moorhen with two chicks following glided on the water, skimming the surface with its rounded beak, while a tortoiseshell butterfly tried to ride on the non-existent breeze, clapping its gossamer wings furiously.

Ben and his team continued collecting any potential evidence from the surrounding areas, which were cordoned off by the usual crime-scene tape. Three police divers in the water picked up any evidence in the pennywort and in the tall reeds. Eventually, they approached the body, taking great care not to disturb anything and treating the dead woman with the greatest respect. One supported her back while the other two cradled each end.

As they came towards the bank, I turned towards Grace and asked her to check on where the pathologist was, and to inform the parents of the two boys that I'd like to speak to them soon.

She nodded, looked past my shoulder and gasped. Then she turned, ran a few steps, bent down and vomited on the ground.

I turned around.

The divers gently placed the body on the recovery sheet on the grassy bank. The head and both hands were missing. The gold chain with the small rose in the middle hung around the right ankle.

Hasina? Oh, God, please no. No, it can't be, I thought to myself.

After the post-mortem had been performed, all relevant tests conducted and their results looked at, the team met in the incident room. We started with the unidentified diver again.

I turned around in my chair as Ben Carter pressed a key on the computer. An image appeared on the monitor behind me.

'We believe this is a good likeness of our John Doe,' he said.

Anyone looking at the image of the man with the short hair, a receding hairline, brown eyes and gaunt cheeks would easily understand that it wasn't a real photograph. However, it was better than an e-fit.

I stared at the man, trying hard not to think about whether he had a family and how they would take the news of his death. But, sadly, that was still to come.

I broke the silence by asking Grace to upload the image onto the Police National Computer and to ask other forces for help in identifying the deceased, especially those on the coast. I also wanted the image circulated on social media and to the printed press, and I told her to ask whether any channels on television would give it some coverage on their news bulletins, both national and local.

I didn't hold out too much hope for the last course of action because if they agreed to all such requests, they would not have much time to report anything else. I also asked Grace to circulate the image to the Salvation Army, because they had a good track record in locating missing individuals.

'Oh, and circulate the image to the Coast Guard, too,' I continued. 'Just in case they've come across him.'

'We've run his DNA sample through the national database,' continued Ben, 'but we couldn't get a match. Either a direct match or a familial match.'

'Okay, thanks. Let's move on to our Jane Doe. What have we got so far? Apart from the fact that the killer, or killers, didn't want her face — or her fingerprints — identified?'

'The poor young lady was probably in her early twenties,' said Dr Malik. 'Her DNA samples indicate her origins were in the region of Afghanistan or northern Pakistan, with traces of Middle Eastern ancestry.'

I raised a quizzical eyebrow at him.

'In addition to the belly button ring,' he continued, 'she had a silver ring pierced through her left nipple. No outward signs of stab wounds or any other injuries to account for her death.'

'Apart from the missing head, Dr Malik,' said Grace.

'Yes, the missing head,' he replied tersely. 'But she could have been killed before the head was severed. Which brings me to the next point, DS Nicholson. The head and hands were removed swiftly using a circular saw or chainsaw. No hacking through muscles, bone and gristle. Clean cuts.'

Grace grimaced and looked away.

'The person or persons who did this knew what they were doing,' the pathologist continued. 'They also used a blood-coagulating drug, probably injected near death into one of the major arteries in the neck. That would stop profuse bleeding, allowing the saw to be used fairly freely without too much blood splatter. There were also trace amounts of alcohol and muscle relaxant drugs found in her bloodstream. Probably used while the victim was still alive.'

'Were they used voluntarily or forcibly?' asked Ben.

'Can't tell you that, of course. However, muscle relaxants are often used to facilitate various sexual acts. As is alcohol,' Dr Malik replied. 'Sexual activity took place not long before her death. There was evidence of semen in her vagina. Two types.

One from a Caucasian male, the other African-Caribbean in origin.'

'Any evidence of sexual violence?' I asked.

'Nothing apparent. No internal tears or bruises. Although there's one aspect which I don't fully understand. In addition to the semen in her vagina, we found traces of lubricating oil. The type used on condoms. Obviously the two men weren't wearing one. Unless they split.'

'I ran the DNA from the semen samples on the national database,' said Ben. 'No hits, either direct or familial.'

'Could she have been a sex worker?' I asked.

There was silence but for the whirring of the air conditioner and the cooling fan in Ben Carter's laptop.

'I know it's difficult to say. But any idea of the time of death?' I continued, grateful that Dr Malik hadn't made any inappropriate comments.

'You're right. Very difficult to say,' he replied. 'As I said before, whoever did this knew what they were doing. The body was dumped in the river. All external DNA would've been washed away. The corpse was also frozen for a few days at least. Maybe in a chest freezer. So, the time of death will be more difficult to ascertain.'

'Could our victim have been killed in the last two to three weeks?' I asked, thinking about Hasina.

'Oh, yes. Perfectly possible. But I wouldn't rule anything out.'

Definitely hedging his bets, I thought. *But who could blame him?*

'What about any forensic evidence, Ben? Anything significant?' I asked.

'Nothing, Sir. No tyre tracks or anything of consequence near the site. The body was obviously dumped somewhere else and it floated down, getting caught in the reeds.'

'The boys who found her didn't see anything relevant,' I said. 'Any other eyewitness evidence, Grace?'

'No, nothing, Sir. It's an isolated area. No witnesses. No houses, no commercial properties along the river. We did speak to the manager of the riverside inn and the boat mooring site upstream. But that's drawn a blank. Nothing from the Missing Persons Unit either. Sad that nobody's reported her missing. Family, friends. She must have some.'

'Thanks. We need to identify this poor woman, and try to recover the missing body parts if we can. But I'm not too hopeful about that.'

I asked Grace to approach all shopkeepers and commercial premises along the Golden Mile, especially near the road on which I lived, for their CCTV images of the day I encountered Hasina. I wanted to see whether a young woman dressed in a striking Middle Eastern outfit could be spotted. It had been a long time, but I was hoping the images would still exist on some of the hard drives.

I didn't say anything more about Hasina and her sudden disappearance. The ethnic profile, the height and body shape certainly fitted what I remembered of her. If she was a sex worker, her traditional outfit would have appealed to some punters.

'Grace, please do all the usual things. Send the information we have on the second victim to the National Missing Persons Unit. They can make all the relevant checks, maybe shed some light on her identity. Also, put out appeals on social media and the rest, leaving out the gruesome details. Contact the local radio station and British Asian stations and ask them to put out an appeal for information.

'I think our two cases may be connected. Both victims are unidentified, the man in the wetsuit and this young woman. Any ideas on how or why, anybody?'

They stared at me, then at each other.

'Oh, there's one more thing,' said Dr Malik. After seeking Ben's permission, he inserted a USB stick into the laptop.

Three images rotated on the large screen, one after the other. Close-ups of shrivelled skin with fine, dark scrawls.

'What the hell's that?' I asked.

'Looks like some sort of writing,' he said. 'Found three sets between each of the toes on the left foot of our female victim. It has been done in fine needle and permanent henna, like the ones used by South Asian and Middle Eastern brides. Water wouldn't have removed it.'

'And the writing? Is it Arabic?' I enquired.

'No, not Arabic,' replied Dr Malik. 'Some of the letters are. But not others. My knowledge of the language is limited. Don't read the Koran regularly anymore. Haven't done since I went to a *madrassa* as a child. Needs a proper linguist. Parts of it look just like Urdu, but some of the letters could be in Farsi, the language spoken by Iranians. Doesn't make sense to me.'

He had cost us time. I hid my anger. If he had mentioned this before, I could have arranged for a translation.

'The victim was obviously trying to hide the message,' said Grace, 'whatever it is. Must've been really painful doing that with a sewing needle, or any other sharp point. Tells us she was right-handed.'

'Yes, when she had one,' added Dr Malik.

CHAPTER 8

It was late morning. The bright sunlight streamed through the windscreen as I tried to navigate the Mercedes along the busy road near police headquarters leading out onto the motorway. Grace was with me. Traffic was heavy in both directions, and the late-Victorian terraced streets and the shops were similar to where I lived. There were shops selling sarees, gold jewellery, cheap carpets and second-hand furniture, and fruit and vegetable stalls on the pavements. An area for the dispossessed and the poor. An area for the haggard and care-worn, and now arrivals from Latvia, Romania and Bulgaria, dreaming of a better life but instead surviving in overcrowded, squalid conditions. More shattered dreams.

We turned a corner and crept past the local hospital. In the distance, the university buildings dominated the skyline, the grounds shared with the magnificent concert hall built more than a hundred years ago.

'You think it's her, don't you? Hasina?' said Grace, interrupting my thoughts.

'Yes, I do. But I've got no firm evidence to suggest it is her. Apart from the ankle chain, that is.'

'It wasn't your fault. You know that, don't you?'

I looked at her. She smiled comfortingly and I caught a scent of orange blossom and sweet spices.

'Why do you think Dr Malik's like he is, Grace?' I asked, changing the subject. 'His comments are often highly inappropriate.'

'I agree,' replied Grace. 'I've thought about it, too. Perhaps it's a defence mechanism. He chose to work with dead bodies, but it must be soul-destroying, so to speak. They're not going to wake up and say, *Boo!* Not like having a living patient in a hospital ward you can have a laugh and a joke with. Can't be much fun cutting up corpses, weighing hearts and livers, looking into dead eyes and examining the smelly contents of stomachs and colons. Still, it must be gratifying to work out how a person died.'

'Yes,' I agreed. 'Perhaps he says all of those things to maintain an emotional distance from what he does. Maybe he tries not to think of them when they were alive. If he did, would he be able to use a circular saw on the skull? Or a pair of rib cutters?'

Grace remained silent. Then she said, 'The dead can speak. If you ask the right questions.'

I parked the car in the university car park and we walked towards the eighteen-storey tower block, resembling a cheese grater. This was the university where Professor Sir Alec Jeffreys, as a relatively young researcher in genetics, had developed the techniques of DNA analysis in the mid-1980s that cleared an innocent man of the murder of two teenage girls and helped convict the real killer. This work had changed crime detection forever throughout the world. This was also the university that had been closely involved in the identification of the bones of Richard III, which had been found under a council car park, causing an international sensation.

The lift eventually brought us near the top, where we were met by Dr Izad Khorram, a researcher in Indo-European languages.

'Good to meet you, Inspector Sharma and Sergeant Nicholson. Hope I can help. It's lucky we could meet — not many of my colleagues are present, it being the summer holidays. And I'm due to return to Teheran soon.' Dr Khorram appeared to be in his late thirties and looked athletic. He shook my hand vigorously with both of his.

We went into his office. I switched on my laptop and showed him the photographs of the tattoos on the dead woman's toes. He stared at each picture in turn, zooming in and out as he tried to make out the writing. His brow furrowed beneath his thick, wavy hair, his dark moustache showing early signs of grey hair.

After a while, he said, 'This is in *Pashto*. It's a national language of Afghanistan and is spoken by about sixty million people there, mainly in the east, south and south-west of the country. But it's also spoken in eastern Iran and northern Pakistan. In lesser numbers, it can be found in India and in Tajikistan. And, of course, migrants in the West speak it too.

'Pashto is written in the Roshani script,' he continued. 'It has forty-one letters, not like the twenty-six of the English alphabet. It's relatively new as a language, only about five hundred years old. It has twenty-eight letters of Arabic and thirteen new ones, which were dreamt up by Pir Roshan from Waziristan —'

'Please, Dr Khorram. What does the writing say?'

'Oh, sorry, I was getting carried away. You're not my students. Very sorry. It's difficult to say with certainty, given the condition of the script. But the letters between two sets of toes say *Loy Bagh*, which is a small village in Helmand Province in Afghanistan. The remaining set spells out *ina*, which could be the ending of a woman's first name. Highly unlikely it's a family name. Could be *Rosina, Mahsina, Tamina, Mohsina*, or some such name.'

My heart sank.

'Since the village is small, you could ask the police or village elders if one of their daughters is missing. Thing is, they often don't want to talk about missing girls. Many end up as child brides, and they don't want outsiders asking questions.'

Before leaving, we thanked Dr Khorram and confirmed with him that he would keep this enquiry confidential.

As we drove off, Grace was unusually subdued. I gazed at the scorched grass of the big park as we drove along one of the roads which skirted it. It was full of laughter, of teenagers playing, boys and girls shouting, and courting couples reclining on blankets, sipping cold drinks and eating ice creams.

It was a park where I'd come to play cricket as a child a lifetime ago. Where, as a sixteen-year-old, I'd bumped into a girl from the sixth form that I'd had a crush on. We'd sat down on the grass, talked in soft tones, laughed and held hands as we'd lain staring at the clear blue sky, dreaming of all the things we would do in our lives. She'd made a daisy chain for me and placed it gently around my neck. Then she'd kissed my cheek and smiled, sending my raging hormones into a wild orbit.

CHAPTER 9

'This really is finger-lickin' good, Dad. Thanks for bringing us here,' said Yasmin. She had inherited my dimples in her tanned cheeks.

It was early evening and we were at one of the colonel's restaurants in a cinema complex on the outskirts of the city. We had seen an updated version of a Disney film, with a mixture of computer-generated imagery and real human beings. Karan, four years younger than Yasmin, had enjoyed it and his sister had certainly laughed in all the right places.

The bright lights and the cheap plastic tables were not my idea of eating out, but the kids had said they didn't like 'ethnic food'. It disappointed me that they were denying part of their identity, but they didn't get much food of Indian origin with Faye and Pierre, and I had made little effort to help them speak Gujarati. They should have been bilingual and they weren't, and that made me feel bad.

The heat in mid-August was suffocating and the air conditioning was much welcomed. Three orderly queues had lined up, facing the long counter.

Yasmin stared at the queue nearest to our table, pulled the plastic straw away from her mouth, being careful not to catch it on her braces, and said, 'I'm sorry you don't have a sister anymore, Dad. There are lots of brothers and sisters here.'

'Yes, I do miss your auntie Maya, especially at this time of year with Brothers' Day not too far away. I often think about how she would have come to me and tied the string bracelet round my right wrist. Then she'd have placed a sweetmeat to my lips, hugged me, and thanked me for being her brother. But, sadly, it is not to be.'

'We're sorry, Dad. What was she like?' asked Karan.

'Well, she was only three when she was kidnapped. And I was five. But she was a sweet child, always laughing and smiling. She had dimples, just like you, Yasmin, and mischievous eyes. She always wanted to play with me.' I turned away, trying to stop the warm tear from sliding down my cheek. 'You would've liked her.'

'And what about Fernando?' asked Yasmin.

'Oh, he liked her, too.'

'No, I meant how is he?' she said, smiling and biting into a chicken drumstick.

I returned her smile and then explained how worried I was about him — how he didn't eat very much, was unusually quiet, and was leaving plucked feathers at the bottom of his cage.

'He must be lonely, Dad. Stuck in the cage all day, with nobody to talk to.'

I confessed to them that I didn't know what to do. I had looked up his condition online and had spoken to a vet. Both concurred that he was distressed, hence the loss of appetite and the plucking of the feathers. What could have set him off was watching the David Attenborough programme, which had shown grey parrots in their natural habitat in the West African tropical forest. 'Home sweet home,' Fernando had kept repeating. The vet had informed me that unlike other African greys, who were hatched from an egg in the United Kingdom, Fernando had been born in the wild and given to my parents. He must have had a residual memory of life in the forest. And, quite naturally, he was yearning to return. I knew how he felt. But where would I return to? My head was in one part of the world, my heart in another. Just like the African greys born here, my children wouldn't have the same problem as me and Fernando.

'How about keeping his cage outside during the day? In the back yard?'

'I've thought of that, Karan. But the local cats would try to get him. It would terrify him. He'd probably have a heart attack.'

'How about hanging his cage from the bedroom window at the back?' said Yasmin.

'Mmm … maybe,' I said. 'Will think on that.'

'We've got a big garden, Dad. We could look after him during the day, since it's the school holidays,' offered Karan.

'Thanks very much, son. But your mother wouldn't approve. She'd say to me, "What d'you think this is, Rohan? A care home for depressed parrots?"'

We all laughed.

'Hey, Dad,' said Karan, proffering his iPad, 'it says online here that there's a place in Lincolnshire that looks after macaws. They look like parrots, but a bright blue colour. It says they let their birds fly for a little while in the day. They always come back 'cos they know they'll get food and water. You could try it with Fernando?'

'We could, I suppose. Let me think some more,' I replied.

We carried on eating. I pinched Yasmin's cheek, ruffled my son's hair and told them I loved them. They said they loved me too and thanked me for taking them out. We drove back to the house in the suburbs where we'd once lived as a happy family.

It broke my heart to say goodbye to them.

CHAPTER 10

'And where did you say you found this, Inspector Sharma?'
asked Dr Jenny Tyburn, the curator of the local museum,
which had a well-known collection of Middle Eastern
antiquities. She smiled at me. She'd only recently returned from
her summer holidays, so I had had to wait several days after
the visit to the university before she was back. In her mid-
thirties, she was a renowned authority on a wide range of
antiquities, especially those from Syria, Iran and Iraq.

'I didn't. Somebody gave it to me. She didn't say where it
came from, or how she'd got hold of it.'

'You can't ask her?'

'No. Afraid not. What can you tell me about it?'

Dr Tyburn's long, delicate fingers held the small statue which
Hasina had thrust into my palm. She caressed it as she turned it
around slowly in her hands. Still staring at the statue, her hand
wandered down and opened a drawer below her paper-laden
teak desk. She pulled out a large magnifying glass, and then was
silent for a long time.

The dirty whitish-grey statue, probably carved from bone or
ivory, was about eleven centimetres long and six centimetres
wide, a perfect fit in my palm. It depicted an antelope lying on
its back, hind legs supine, head looking up, surrendering. A
lioness sprawled over it, its long tail curling under its hind legs,
its strong, muscular jaws clenching the antelope's neck. The
inlaid eyes of the lioness were dirty blue, while the eyes of the
antelope were reddish-brown. Both animals were sculpted on a
thick base, the statue carved out in one piece. A diamond

pattern was etched around the base and the antlers of the antelope had traces of a fading yellow material.

Dr Tyburn put the statue down on the cushioned pad in front of her.

'Well?' I asked.

'I don't want to get carried away until we've done some more tests — carbon dating and so on — to verify its age and to get a second opinion about authenticity. But if this is what I think it *may* be, then it's an important archaeological discovery.'

I looked at her smiling, tanned face as she tried to hide her excitement. Her fingers trembled.

'This piece is carved from ivory, as you may have guessed. All one piece, not three bits stuck together. The skill involved is breath-taking. It will have taken a lot of time and patience to carve it. In my opinion, the eyes of the lioness are lapis lazuli and those of the antelope could be carnelian. Both are semi-precious stones. The colours would have looked fabulous when the stones were first inlaid. And I think the diamond shapes in the base were inlaid with gold leaf. The antlers look as if they've been embellished with gold leaf, too.' She paused, then looked at me. 'And you can't tell me how it came into your possession, Inspector?'

What would I say? That a young woman of Middle Eastern origin, a complete stranger, had thrust it into my hands one morning a few weeks ago?

'Sorry, Dr Tyburn, I'm afraid not.'

'Oh, please call me Jenny.'

I smiled at her. 'Rohan.'

'I think this little statue might have been carved about eight hundred years before the Common Era. So, eight hundred years before the birth of Christ. And why do I think that? Because two similar carvings were found in a well in the palace of Ashurnasirpal in northern Iraq. We know the location more commonly as Nimrud. Those two are of a lioness killing a Nubian boy. One of the carvings is in the British Museum in London. The other is in Iraq.

'I've seen and studied both. The subject matter in this carving is obviously different, but the style is similar. It was probably carved by the same person, and probably looted from the same well. But we didn't know it existed. If verified as genuine, this statue could get the academic and archaeological world buzzing with excitement. If it ever came on the open market, it could fetch a lot of money.'

I wondered how the hell Hasina had got hold of it.

'If it's genuine, Rohan, people will want to know how it was discovered,' Dr Tyburn went on.

So would I, I thought.

I made Dr Tyburn promise she would undertake the tests in secret and not say anything to anybody. I intimated the statue was part of a criminal investigation. She was only too delighted to accept my conditions.

She knew that her eventual academic paper on the subject, along with a picture of her and the statue, would make her famous. A few weeks or so of silence was a small price to pay.

'Do you know much about the current antiquities market? The international scene?' she asked.

I shook my head.

She glanced at her watch and said, 'I know a good pub that serves food. Why don't you buy me a late lunch and I'll tell you?'

A little while later, we sat at an outside table on the canal bank at one of the local inns. The large parasol provided welcome relief from the bright sun. In the distance, a handful of industrial units, with their tall chimneys and lorry yards, stood on either side of the canal. A barge with brightly painted watering cans on the bow and a television aerial on the roof chugged past, the bargee seemingly oblivious to the long, bluish-brown diesel stain trailing behind him on the surface of the water.

I had little idea of the world Jenny Tyburn described to me — of the wholescale looting of Mesopotamian antiquities from war-torn Iraq and Syria, the crumbling museums of Egypt and the lawless desert sands of Libya, especially after the Arab Spring. She'd told me that such antiquities had ended up in legitimate and illegitimate markets in London, Paris, New York and Rome, to name but a few. Unscrupulous dealers had a growing number of unscrupulous buyers, especially the *nouveau riche*, from Russia, China and India, and millions of pounds and dollars changed hands, largely without trace. And this market, of course, attracted organised crime from all over the world — not only the Mafia in Italy and the United States, but also the Triads in China, the *Narcos* in South America and the various gangs based in India, Dubai and Hong Kong. All were looking to launder money from drugs and prostitution and to broaden their sources of income. The world's heritage, going back to the dawn of human civilisation in the Middle East, was being plundered to satisfy this greed.

'It really is heartbreaking, Rohan. All that history lost, never to be seen again. And for what? It belongs to all of us.'

I looked into Jenny Tyburn's eyes. It was clear she was badly affected by this situation. *So should all of us be*, I thought.

'But it's wonderful to come across a piece like you brought in today,' she said.

I tried to ignore her foot brushing my leg under the table, as well as the golden strands of hair being pushed back every so often, and the fluttering eyelids. She pulled her chair into the sunlight and bent her neck backwards, exposing white lines of skin which hadn't tanned on holiday.

'Isn't this wonderful?' she said. 'The weather, I mean.'

I agreed.

She pulled out a pair of designer sunglasses with gold rims and said nothing for a long time.

As we parted company late in the afternoon, she shook my hand, held it for a second longer than she needed to, and said she hoped we would meet again soon.

'Oh, I know we will,' I replied. 'You've got my statue.'

She laughed, turned and walked away, with one more backward glance.

Perhaps I was misreading the situation.

CHAPTER 11

I returned to HQ and met up with Grace. She told me we had been given permission to contact the Afghani police in Kabul and, hopefully, they would contact their colleagues in the district of Loy Bagh, the name of the village in Helmand Province that had been tattooed on the dead woman's toes. She had already tried to make contact through the usual international channels and had offered to send the victim's DNA samples to Afghanistan, if her superiors agreed. However, given the state of the country's technology infrastructure and other problems, she told me that contact with the police had been difficult. She had also tried the embassy in London, but nobody had got back to her yet. She also informed me that none of the shopkeepers on the Golden Mile had any CCTV images of Hasina. It was highly likely that Hasina had come to my house through the back streets so she would not be seen by anybody.

I finished updating my report on the investigation so far for Superintendent Breedon and headed home. It was early evening, and I wondered what it would be like to finish work at five o'clock for once.

As I emerged from my car, the smell of communal drains, long deprived of rainwater to wash away their excesses, hit me. I tried to ignore it and instead lingered on the aroma of hot cinnamon, cloves and cardamom that wafted under my nostrils from a nearby kitchen. Two small boys played football near my parked car, but my stern gaze had the desired effect on them. Bhangra music blared in the distance, while cars honked their horns, drowning out the incessant chatter in Gujarati and Punjabi.

Before I could open the front door, I heard a voice.

'Hello, Rohanbhai, how're you? Haven't seen you for a while.'

I looked up to see the young Indian couple, my neighbours from a few doors down who had looked after Fernando while I'd been on holiday. That seemed like a lifetime ago now.

I exchanged pleasantries with them, then the man asked, 'How's Fernando? I saw his cage the other day, hanging from the iron bracket near the back bedroom. Is everything okay?'

I explained briefly that his mood had changed, and that he had become withdrawn and didn't readily make quips and wisecracks like he used to.

'Oh, we know what you mean,' said the wife. 'Always had something to say when he was with us. Or a wolf whistle. Loved watching films with us on television, especially Hollywood films from the thirties.'

'And some modern ones too,' added the husband.

'Yes, and some modern ones.'

I told them about my conversation with the vet, that fresh air and seeing other birds might be good for him. But I wasn't sure it was working. And I couldn't leave him outside all day in the searing heat.

'I'm sorry we can't look after him,' said the wife, 'since we're both at work all day, too. Have you tried taking him to the countryside, to let him fly a bit?'

She was the second person to have suggested that to me. I began to wonder whether to take the risk.

Inside the house, a subdued Fernando stared at me. He had eaten a few of his seeds, and there were splashes of water and fresh bird poo on the newspaper. He flapped his wings wearily and a few feathers, plucked today and lying on the bottom of the cage, floated into the air.

'Oh, Fernando. Why're you doing this to yourself?'

His big, round eyes blinked. He looked away from me.

I changed into a T-shirt and shorts, poured myself a glass of chilled Pouilly-Fumé, marinaded some chicken drumsticks in a ready-made tandoori paste and enhanced the flavour with natural yogurt and lemon juice. I then left them for half an hour before baking them in the oven while I prepared a salad. Once my food was ready, I sat down with a tray on my lap, keeping the television on mute.

The breeze from the fan felt good on my perspiring body, and the cold wine went down smoothly. I ignored the images on the television and played some of my favourite music.

I looked at Fernando as I took a long sip of wine. 'You really are lonely, aren't you? I don't know what the answer is, Fernando. You don't want to stay here. But I can't let you go. Please tell me what to do.'

He just looked at me.

'Think about me too, Fernando. I was born in East Africa. I've never been to the place in India where my family came from. And I only have vague memories of Kenya. And you? You were born in Fernando Po, an island off the west coast of Africa that was once a Portuguese colony. It's now called, oh, I've forgotten. Something else. You were brought across Africa, west to east, to my father's shop. And then you ended up in Leicester with me, via Kenya. We're the same, Fernando. Where do we belong? Where would our souls go if they had a choice?'

I took another sip of wine as Harry Chapin sang 'Cat's in the Cradle', a song about a father who was always busy and didn't have enough time for his growing son. And when the father became old, sadly the son was too busy for him. The circle of life.

'And why the hell do I feel guilty all the time, Fernando? I feel guilty about you. I feel guilty about letting my mother down. I feel guilty about my kids growing up without me. I feel guilty as hell about what happened to Hasina. If only I'd done something to help her. But what? What could I have done, Fernando?'

I took another bite of my drumstick and another long drink.

'And most of all, I feel guilty about my little sister. If I hadn't sneezed all those years ago while we were hiding, maybe the gang in Kenya wouldn't have found us. And Maya would be here with us now.'

I drank some more wine, staring at the programme on the television. People were laughing at something I couldn't hear.

Through the sound bar, Melanie Safka sang about wanting another long-haired man to help her make her bed; then Leonard Cohen thanked the two sisters of mercy, not sex workers but complete strangers he had picked up on the street who had willingly spent the night with him.

'Leonard was handsome. He could do that, Fernando. An example of sex without guilt. With me, though, it seems to be guilt without sex.'

Lata Mangeshkar sang about running towards her lover in the middle of the night in the pouring rain, while Mohammed Rafi ached for one to run to.

'The perennial human condition, Fernando.' My eyes were beginning to glaze over. 'If you were a dog, we could go out for a walk. But no, even if you want to, you cannot cross the Rio Grande. Not like that Abba song with your name. No, you'd get arrested by the Americans for being an illegal alien.'

He was nodding off.

I tried to focus on the television screen, but just then, my mobile pinged.

It was a text from Superintendent Breedon: *Important developments. Please see me tomorrow. 8am.*

I stopped drinking.

CHAPTER 12

The soles of my black shoes rested on the deep maroon carpet. I sat opposite the teak desk and looked through the window of Superintendent Breedon's office. The bright sunlight at eight o'clock in the morning sparkled in the drops of dew on the double-glazed window.

The heavy, wooden door behind me opened.

'Ah, Rohan, sorry to keep you waiting. The briefing with the Chief Constable overran.'

I stood up. He indicated for me to sit down again.

'Now, before we go any further, can you update me on the investigation you're working on? In case I missed anything in your report.'

This probably meant he had skimmed it at best.

I told him that the two victims were currently unidentified and that appeals had been put out, but we had no promising leads so far. I wondered if the two cases could be connected, but didn't have any firm evidence to link them yet. And the statue the female victim had given me outside my home was probably a genuine one, dating back thousands of years. We were awaiting carbon dating results.

'Don't jump to conclusions about the two being linked, Rohan. No evidence for that.'

I nodded as his piercing blue eyes under trimmed eyebrows stared back at me. The wrinkles on his forehead danced and his expensive scent — a mixture of lemon, sandalwood and ambergris — floated into my nostrils. His starched, dark uniform with shining shoulder epaulettes was immaculate.

'The media are beginning to put pressure on us to get results. Not to mention other, shall we say, interested parties. The young woman was probably not an Asian. Your community's not jumping up and down.'

Be cool, be cool, I told myself.

'What do you mean "my community", sir? Oh, you mean the community of Leicester.'

He stared at me, looked down at his paper-free desk and decided not to say anything further. He pulled out a manila folder from his leather briefcase, shuffling the few pages in his hands.

'Well, we have further developments which may, or may not, be linked to your cases. The French National Police have been in touch with the National Crime Agency. And the NCA, in turn, have been in touch with us. Apparently, the French have been tracking a gang that supplies Class A drugs, mainly heroin, from Afghanistan to some of the big cities in Europe. This includes us. They're also involved in trafficking people, mostly young women from the war-torn areas of the Middle East, who are then forced into sex work. They then launder the money by buying Mesopotamian and Egyptian antiques, for which there is a growing and lucrative market. Many of the rich and super-rich in various countries want such items. Not to mention that many of the museums, some of which are household names, don't ask too many questions when trying to acquire a unique piece of history. Of course, trafficking cultural property is an international crime. The French police and Interpol have been working closely on all of this over the last year.'

I shifted uneasily in my chair, my mind going into overdrive. I thought of Hasina and the statue. How had she got hold of it? Had she stolen it from the gang? She had told me it could fetch a lot of money.

'The French police and Interpol managed to turn one of the men involved into an informer,' continued the superintendent. 'He was from Afghanistan and hoping to come to the UK in search of his younger brother and sister. They paid a lot of borrowed money to be smuggled here, but the brother lost contact with them in transit, so to speak. He transported heroin from Afghanistan through Iran and Iraq and then to the Turkish border, sometimes into Istanbul. On the way, he picked up antiquities for the gang from Iraq. He managed to steal some of the artefacts to finance his life, to find his brother and sister, and to make life better for all three. But the gang found out. Poor man was burned to death in Northern Syria. He was carrying a listening device for the French to monitor and to keep him safe. But sadly, they couldn't.

'There was also a Turkish man the Afghan had named to the French. Lorry driver. He was going to transport a large consignment of heroin and antiquities hidden in his container lorry. The French managed to bug his apartment in Istanbul. Again, he wanted a piece of the action, a share of the pie. He decided to keep a few of the artefacts for himself. Not a good idea. He was found in his apartment with multiple injuries to his body; both hands were cut off, and his tongue was cut out and placed on his groin. They used anti-coagulant drugs to stem the blood flow after death. Poor man wanted money to pay for his sister's chemotherapy and her son's school fees.'

Superintendent Breedon paused. We both looked at each other, and then I asked the all-important question.

'Why did the NCA contact us, Sir?'

'The lorry drivers don't use just one European port. They go to Calais, Rotterdam, Zeebrugge, and maybe others.

Sometimes, the gang pay off corrupt customs officers to let the containers through on the nod. Other times, the drugs and antiquities are taken off at the ports and then transported in high-powered boats to various parts of our coast. The Turkish lorry driver often delivered his container to a lorry park on the outskirts of Peterborough. Another driver — an Iraqi — then picked it up. He then delivered the payload to a rich Asian guy's warehouse on the outskirts of Leicester. We have no idea who this guy is. The NCA is relying on us because of our local intelligence and, obviously, because it's our patch. They tried to muscle in. But I kept them at bay.'

He was obviously searching for glory and good media coverage, which was what he'd got when I caught Shiva the Destroyer.

'So, it's a highly sophisticated operation, Sir. With a lot of cogs and wheels. Whoever's in charge must have excellent information to keep tabs on everyone involved.'

'And they're ruthless, Rohan.'

The whirring of the air conditioner interrupted the long silence.

After a while, Superintendent Breedon said, 'Hasina and the statue are probably linked somehow to what I've just told you. And maybe — *maybe* — the dead diver.'

'So, what now, Sir?'

'Oh, yes. You're going to work with the French National Police, with an Inspector Laurent.'

The thought of seeing the Eiffel Tower, of walking along the Champs Elysée, of gazing at the Arc de Triomphe and visiting the Paris Opera House was irresistible. The excitement of trying to solve this case also came rushing to the fore, now that we had new information and new partners. But then a thought struck me. Who would look after Fernando while I was away?

CHAPTER 13

Several days later, I gazed at the Eiffel Tower behind Inspector Laurent's head. There were lifts taking tourists to the top and then down again. The nearby fountains gushed on laughing people as they tried to keep themselves cool. It was late afternoon, and the shadows were getting longer.

Inspector Laurent looked at me and said, 'I'm sorry, I was expecting somebody else.'

'Pardon?'

'When your boss said your name was Rohan, I thought of Rowan Atkinson. You know, Mr Bean. And when he told me your name was Sharma, I thought of Simon Schama, the English professor. So, I was expecting a white Jewish man called Rowan Schama.'

We both laughed.

'Well, I'm sorry to disappoint you, Inspector Laurent.'

'Please call me Nicole. And no, I'm not disappointed.'

The inspector, who looked to be in her early thirties, smiled at me from the computer monitor. We were just beginning our encrypted conference call.

My superiors had decided that since much of the work was going to be based in this country, there was no need for me to go to France, and Inspector Laurent's bosses wouldn't release her to come here. This had been relayed to me late one evening by Superintendent Breedon as he was about to travel to Heathrow to board a flight to Toronto to present a lecture to the Royal Canadian Mounted Police about the challenges of policing in a multiracial community. I'd had to brief him on the most pertinent issues before he'd set off.

'Hope you like the background, Rohan. It's a live feed of the Eiffel Tower.'

I said I did and hoped to visit before too long. It had been a while since I had been to Paris.

She nodded and smiled again.

Just then, there was a loud wolf whistle behind me. My face reddened. I explained it was Fernando and pointed the camera to his cage. Inspector Laurent laughed.

'He's been a bit depressed recently. Sometimes he perks up, like now. Other times, he's quiet for hours on end.' I explained how I had put his cage outside, but to no avail.

'Oh, poor bird. A friend of mine is a doctor. She worked in Sierra Leone during the Ebola crisis. As a thank you, some of the locals in the village where she worked gave her a parrot, just like yours, as a present. It became depressed too, here in France. But she played him some African rainforest jungle sounds. Pretty soon, he was fine. But he still gets moody if he doesn't hear them. Perhaps you should try that.'

I told her I would.

'Well, since we'll be working closely together, let me give you an update,' she said. 'As you know, Interpol's involved, too. But before I go on, do you know much about the antiquities market and how it's become a target for organised crime?'

'I'm learning fast,' I replied.

She then expanded a bit more on what Superintendent Breedon had already told me. 'And,' Nicole continued, 'organised crime in South America is involved, too. Have you heard of the fire that destroyed the National Museum of Brazil in Rio in 2018? The second of September, to be exact?'

'Yes, I do remember hearing something on the news about that.'

'The museum housed about twenty million artefacts. Twenty million! Can you imagine? That's about two for every person living in London. There was a fire which the authorities blamed on the air-conditioning system. Faulty, old wiring. Destroyed just about everything. Another blow to the history of humankind. But some people believe the fire was started deliberately by organised gangs in Rio. Many historical antiquities from central and southern America ended up on the black market. If you reduce supply, the demand for others around the world will go up. They worked with crime bosses in Europe who promised them a cut from the Middle Eastern market. So, as you can see, Rohan, there are many powerful forces at work. And they're not to be messed with lightly.

'So that gives you an up-to-date summary of the situation. Mix in drugs and the sex trade — maybe other contraband — and you have hardened criminals with millions to lose. And don't forget warzones also attract dealers in the arms trade. We're looking into this as well.'

She confirmed that hard drugs, antiquities and human beings were being trafficked to the UK, to Leicester or nearby. A rich South Asian businessman was involved, but somebody else may well be the mastermind.

I was impressed with Nicole's knowledge, but I suddenly became concerned for her safety.

'Oh, I'll be fine. Got plenty of protection here. But there's one particularly nasty gang member who's been involved in our cases. Both the lorry drivers who died — one in northern Syria, the other in Istanbul — were being tracked through listening devices. Sadly, we couldn't save them. Both suffered terrible deaths — they were beheaded and their hands and tongues were chopped off. We've analysed the recordings using state-of-the-art technology. Although the voices are muffled, we know two of the killers are men. The third is a woman. Her voice is not always clear because we think she wears a scarf around her face. Some of our informers have confirmed her existence, but many are too frightened to talk about her. Nobody knows her true identity. However, one informer said she was known as The Scorpion.'

'The Scorpion?' I said. 'Now, that rings a bell.' I thought hard, trying to remember where I had heard the moniker before.

'Anybody who sees her face usually dies,' continued Nicole, 'like the people who saw Medusa in Greek mythology. We don't know much about her, but we think she's probably an Arab woman. She's very cruel and she may have been part of ISIS, fighting in Syria. She's able to move around different countries quite freely, so she has important allies. And money.'

'And several passports,' I interjected.

'*Oui*. Something to go on. But not a lot.'

I then explained about Hasina, and a memory fell into place. 'That's it!' I said. 'Hasina referred to *Bichchoo*, the Hindi word for "scorpion" when I bumped into her outside my front door. She was afraid The Scorpion would kill her. But The Scorpion wasn't in the UK at the time — according to your recordings — so she couldn't have killed her. It must have been somebody else.'

Nicole listened and agreed. Since I had no evidence to connect the diver to this case, I left him out. I didn't want to muddy the waters.

'So, where does this leave us?' I asked.

'Well, we can't discuss it over a glass of wine,' she said, laughing. 'But the trail leads to Leicester and to you. And you also need to be careful, Rohan. Very careful. Because these are dangerous people.'

She said they felt pretty bad about not being able to protect their Afghani informer, Ghulam Barakzai, and were trying to trace his family through DNA. They wanted to give them some money, but given the problems in Afghanistan it was proving difficult to contact the police, or any other local authorities who could help. We agreed to catch up when there were new developments.

I waved to Nicole and said goodbye. I then stared at the blank screen for a long time, lost in thought.

Fernando was quiet.

CHAPTER 14

I contacted all relevant officers who had experience of the drugs scene and of gangs, including the county lines network involving teenage drug mules, and asked whether they could help with our enquiries. They could name individual dealers and pushers, and some of those involved in the sex trade, but they could not throw much light on the identity or role of a wealthy South Asian businessman, or on the smuggling of antiquities. Most were of the view that it had to be a clandestine operation, maybe relatively new, which was backed by wealthy but anonymous individuals. The whole set-up must have been meticulously organised and monitored. In all probability, other contraband was being traded too. In my discussions with them, a familiar name kept cropping up.

At about nine o'clock in the evening, as the cooling sun cast its pale rays over the slow death of another day, I drove an old, unmarked police car into the area where I'd lived as a child. I decided that my white Mercedes Coupé would draw too much attention in this poor, deprived neighbourhood of grimy Victorian streets lined with back-to-back brick houses and littered with fast-food wrappers, plastic bottles and fading newspapers. The wrinkled and prematurely ageing faces of the residents betrayed their hard lives. Children who should have been at school were pulling wheelies up the road on bicycles. The tall, grey steeple of St Saviour's Church stood majestically, dominating the skyline for miles around, having given up its battle to promote Christian values a long time ago. It now looked upon the shining, golden domes of mosques, each topped with the crescent and star. Further away stood a Hindu temple, its white marble carved by skilled artisans who had come over from India and then gone back again.

I parked the car behind some ancient garages that were scrawled with brightly coloured graffiti in English and Urdu. They stood near a decaying council estate that had been constructed in the 1970s. Not far away was the secondary school I'd attended, built above the Victorian workhouse where Dr Frederick Treves found Joseph Merrick, the so-called Elephant Man.

I got out of my car and walked slowly towards the dark hatchback parked in the distance. An Asian man in his late twenties was about to get in, having passed a small plastic bag to the driver of another battered car as it crawled away.

'Hey, Bobby. How're you?' I asked.

He was startled.

As I walked towards him, I wondered why some young Asian men preferred to Anglicise their first names. They were invariably called Joe, Jack or Bobby. Perhaps they ought to have changed their surnames to Kennedy.

'Hello, Mr Sharma. What you doin' here, bro?'

'I came to ask you the same question, Bobby. And I'm not your bro.'

'Okay, what you doin' here, Daddy-o?'

'Not watching too many old *Dirty Harry* films, like you seem to have done.'

The roller door to the lock-up where he was standing, patches of dark paint blistered and exposing the rusting metal underneath, was partly open. A used syringe lay on the cracked tarmac, dried blood on the needle. A dandelion at the bottom of the brick wall stood erect, its bright yellow head flicked by a momentary breeze.

'Up to your usual tricks, Bobby? Don't you ever learn?' I continued.

'I'm not doin' no tricks, Mr Sharma. It's the hookers roun' here who do that,' he said, staring at a used condom not too far away. 'Somebody's husband sees them, on his way home to a nice meal and a nice wife. And then he reads a fairy story to his young daughter when she goes to bed.' He stared at me for a while. His black hair was combed back, the hairline receding. 'Me, I'm lookin' for another kind of pussy,' he continued. 'My cat ran away. Must be hidin' somewhere roun' here. What 'bout you, Mr Sharma?'

'My pet parrot's depressed. He needs a therapist. Thought I'd find one here.'

Bobby laughed. 'Look, Mr Sharma, I'm clean these days.'

'That so?'

'After my last time inside, I decided to be a gardener. I feed and weed these days. Eat a bit. Smoke a bit. That's all. No dealing.'

I forced a smile and said I wasn't after him, but wanted some information. He looked uneasy, shifting his weight from one foot to the other. His wide, dark eyes darted up and down, and from side to side.

I asked where his supply came from and whether he had any connections to a wealthy businessman. I didn't mention his ethnicity. I told him that if he couldn't remember anything, we could always carry on with the interview back at the police station over a cup of tea or coffee.

Bobby looked at me for a long time. A fast train along the nearby London line screamed past, and then he finally said, 'Look, Mr Sharma, I don't know no names. My deliveries are dropped off at an agreed location by a Rasta bro. All I know about Mr Big is that he cooks and feeds.'

'You mean he makes heroin from raw opium? That's the cooking part, right? And then he feeds the habit to the junkies?'

'Please, Mr Sharma, I know nothin'. My life wouldn't be worth livin' if anybody knew I'd spoken to you. I'd end up as mincemeat.'

'You should be a poet, Bobby.'

He didn't respond. He looked genuinely scared. After trying to get a name, and him denying he knew it, I gave up.

As I walked away, I thought I caught a furtive shadow, head flashing back behind one of the garages. Maybe I was mistaken, because dusk was beginning to snatch the daylight.

'Mr Sharma!' Bobby called out.

I turned round.

'I hope you find a shrink for your parrot!'

CHAPTER 15

I visited numerous pubs in various areas of the city to find out whether anyone could help me identify the mystery man, Mr Big. We had exhausted the usual 'grasses', with many claiming to their handlers in the Intelligence Unit that they couldn't help or were too frightened to talk. I shouldn't have been seeking out this information on my own, but time was of the essence and many informants wouldn't speak to an unknown handler — especially since their usual handlers were usually white. Taking Grace with me was a definite no-no. An Asian guy with an attractive white woman could only mean one of two things: that she was a sex worker or a copper. I explained this to Grace, and she reluctantly agreed with my point of view.

Several evenings after my meeting with Bobby, I was parked up in a side street in a downtrodden neighbourhood again. Not having had much luck in sleazy pubs, I now focused my attention on the sleazy clubs. Not the more upmarket ones with soft carpets, pole dancers and high-class call girls, but those with torn vinyl flooring, scarred by cigarette burns and filled with hungry sex workers who were scarred by their habits. These clubs in quiet backstreets next to industrial units were often open all day, meeting all the needs of customers.

I watched the comings and goings of one of these clubs through the dirty windscreen of my unmarked police car, innocuous in this neighbourhood. It was late evening and I had visited several pubs and clubs earlier in the day and well into the evening. I had not had much luck in acquiring any new information.

The club was two terraced houses knocked into one. It tried to melt into the background, but the barred windows, frayed curtains and blue lighting told a different story. No music was audible from the outside, and the battery of CCTV cameras above the front door and on the sides of the walls warned off uninvited visitors. Occasionally, a bouncer, invariably a big, burly Black guy with muscles pumped by steroids, stood at the door or peered out from inside.

I got out of the car, knocked on the door and was admitted through the outer door. I then signed in and paid my one pound to be an exclusive member of the club. I wondered whether I would meet Shah Rukh Khan, the famous Bollywood actor who was also apparently here, if the name in the members' book was anything to go by. The inner door opened and I walked in. A hush fell over the room, and the pool players stopped and stared, palming the twenty-pound notes on the edge of the table. The bartender looked up from the beer pump.

'I'll have a coconut water,' I said, and regretted it almost immediately.

There was sniggering behind me.

Some of the older men played dominoes, again with large amounts of money. By the side tables, a couple of Eastern European women in short leather skirts and pale, protruding T-shirts sat uneasily with three men. Two middle-aged white men drank cocktails with two much younger Asian men, no one in any doubt about their sexuality, or whether any money was changing hands for services rendered.

I told the barman I wanted to see the owner, flashing my badge surreptitiously. The room went quiet again.

The owner, Mr Khosla, eventually appeared from upstairs. 'I'm sorry, Mr Sharma, I really can't help you with anything,' he said.

'Look, Mr Khosla, I just want some information. About one man.'

He looked at me. I could hear the sound of footsteps upstairs, mixed with soft music, the occasional laughter of men and women, and the sound of a television set.

'Okay,' I said. 'Let's go upstairs. Perhaps we can have a better chat in one of the quieter rooms.'

As I darted up the stairs, Mr Khosla followed. 'No, please. I have nothing to say.'

I barged into a large room with dark curtains, subdued lighting, old settees, a scattering of beanbags, low tables and full ashtrays. The wall of smoke, the finest Jamaica or Colombia could offer, hit my nostrils. About half a dozen men and women stopped what they were doing when they saw me. The large, wall-mounted television screen showed three men — two white, one Black — with two women, both white. All were naked and trying various positions graphically illustrated in the more upmarket publications of *The Kama Sutra*.

I did not recognise anybody in the room and walked out again.

'You know I could have you closed down, don't you?' I said to Mr Khosla. 'I could get you for all sorts of offences. Drugs and living off immoral earnings, for a start. Not to mention illicit gambling.'

'Please, Mr Sharma. Please don't do anything.' His frightened eyes widened and his thick, greying eyebrows danced.

He and I went into a quiet room and I pumped him for information about any guy dealing hard drugs and other contraband. He claimed not to know, but said he'd keep an eye out for me.

'It's not just your eyes I'm interested in, Mr Khosla. More importantly, I'd like to know what you've heard.'

'Okay, okay. But it must never get back to me.'

That was the second time I'd heard that in a few days. People were definitely scared. I gave him my card.

'I don't want to end up like a shish kebab,' he said eventually. He looked at me for a long time.

As I walked out, I heard somebody say, 'Hey, there goes the coconut kid. Brown on the outside, white on the inside.'

'Nah, he ain't no coconut kid. More like a Bounty bar.'

Further laughter.

I arrived home quite late and was famished. But I had to see to Fernando first.

'Sorry, Fernando. I know you've been home by yourself all day. I was hoping to pop in during the day, but I couldn't.'

He looked at me while I cleaned his cage, chopped apple and pear and grapes for him, sprinkled some pumpkin and sunflower seeds, and topped up his water. He looked at the small, round mirror in his cage. He would have blown a wolf whistle at himself before. Not now.

'I'm sorry I couldn't leave you outside. The neighbourhood cats would make your life hell. Birds of prey might swoop towards your cage too.'

He flapped his grey wings and I could see some dried blood where one of the wings joined his body. He had been pecking himself again, a sure sign of his unhappiness.

'Oh, Fernando, I wish you wouldn't,' I said as I rubbed some antiseptic cream onto the wound. His big, sad eyes blinked at me.

I might have to try Nicole's therapy before too long, I thought to myself, as I poured a cold glass of Pouilly-Fumé and prepared a snack. It was too late to cook a meal. I turned on my streaming device while searching for food in the kitchen. The rich voice of Sonu Nigam filled the lounge, singing about the futility of war. The song was from the Bollywood film *Border*, which was about the recent Indo-Pakistan conflict and was one of the greatest anti-war films ever made. After a while, I decided it was just a bit too sad.

I pressed the remote and Don McLean singing 'And I Love You So' from his album *Tapestry* lifted my mood. I sang along to it, thinking of the long-forgotten loves of my youth, while stuffing two warm shish kebabs into a wholemeal pitta bread and chopping up some salad. I also made some cucumber raita with a mint chutney to accompany it.

As I sat down on the settee to eat, my dinner reminded me of Mr Khosla's words: 'I don't want to end up like a shish kebab.' Bobby had said that he 'would end up as mincemeat.' Was it just a coincidence? Or did it mean something? I thought about it for a while and decided I was probably reading too much into it. Shrugging, I bit into the stuffed pitta bread, savouring the different flavours.

As I stacked the dishes into the dishwasher, looking forward to going to bed, my mobile rang.

'Sir, I know it's very late,' said the member of the support team back at HQ, 'but we've received some important information about one of the cases you're working on.'

I listened. It sounded like a major breakthrough.

'Oh, Fernando, you beauty,' I shouted to him, trying to contain my excitement, but he was nodding off.

I rang Grace and told her we had a positive ID on the dead diver, and that we were going to the seaside tomorrow.

'What, with a bucket and spade?' she asked.

'No, to meet the guy who's ID'd him,' I replied.

She laughed as we hung up.

CHAPTER 16

'Didn't know you liked Carole King,' I said to Grace as my Mercedes Coupé purred east out of the city along the A47. It was nine in the morning, and we had set off slightly later to miss the morning rush hour. I had picked her up at HQ after she had downloaded and printed the relevant information for us.

'How did you know?' she asked, slightly surprised.

'Heard it in the background when we were on the phone last night.'

She paused and then said, 'Didn't like it at first. Now I think it's fantastic. Her album, *Tapestry*, was a present from an old boyfriend. He was into that sort of old music.'

'Well, I like it and I'm not that old,' I said, and smiled.

She smiled back and pulled the visor down as we headed east.

'And I love *Tapestry* by Don McLean, too,' I continued. 'He's the guy who sang "American Pie" and "Vincent", the song about Van Gogh. Some wonderful tracks on there. Strange that their albums should have the same title.'

Grace didn't say much to my musings about the two singers. We passed the time making small talk and stopped for a comfort break near Peterborough. Just over two hours later, we arrived in the small coastal town of Hunstanton in Norfolk.

Soon we were sitting on the rotting deck of a static wooden caravan that should have been knocked down ten years ago. In the distance were the choppy waters of The Wash and the North Sea. The man we were meeting, Gordon Priestley, looked to be in his mid-forties, with short ginger hair he had clearly trimmed himself and a stubbly beard. His sunken cheeks and sallow skin told their own story.

'Yes, that's Raze all right. Poor bastard,' said Gordon as he handed the photograph of the diver back to Grace. It had been sanitised so that there were no maggots on the victim's face. Gordon had seen the image on social media and had contacted our HQ.

'Raze? Don't you mean Fraze? You told our people his name was Peter Fraser?' I said.

'He were known as Razor. We joined the Royal Marines together; we was only kids. We had to pass tough physical tests and were told not to think too much. Follow orders. Jus' follow orders. After a coupla years, we applied to join the Special Boat Service — y'know, like the SAS. Have to be a hard bastard to do that. Both mentally and physically. Kill or be killed, that sort of thing.'

Gordon paused and stared into the distance, the swell of the sea and the lapping water on the beach seeming to bring back memories. We didn't interrupt his thoughts. He scratched a long, angry rash on his forearm and flicked a scab.

'You fight for your country. You're ready to lay down your life. And what d'you get? A bloody wooden house that could blow down in a sudden gust. Or any kid with a box of matches could have his fun in the middle of the night.'

I tried not to think of my grandfather, who had been conscripted into the British Army in Kenya in the 1950s to fight the Mau Mau nationalists. My grandfather, who had served to protect the lives, lifestyles and profits of the wealthy white farmers, but who hadn't been allowed to drink with them in their whites-only bars and clubs.

'Raze and I both applied to join SBS,' Priestley continued. 'He passed and I didn't. Had to do tests for combat fitness, swimming, gym, parachuting, carrying heavy loads for miles around the Brecon Beacons in Wales. Also, there was jungle training in Belize and Borneo. Some died, just in training. All was kept hush-hush.

'We went to Afghanistan, Iraq, all them places. He were involved more in special ops. Worked with the SAS sometimes. Navigation, demolition, reconnaissance. Raze got his nickname 'cos he razed everything to the ground. Even houses with women and children inside. Machine guns, bombs, flame-throwers. Used to have a Rambo knife. Cut the heads off the bloody wo—' He paused, looked at me, then continued, 'Cut the heads off them first. Interrogated them after. We called him Razor Fraser.'

Grace looked at me, shifting uneasily, probably trying not think of the atrocities that had been committed by our dead diver. She took off her dark blue jacket and hung it on the back of the flimsy plastic chair. Her big, round sunglasses hid much of her face. Gordon stared at her chest.

'And what about family and friends?' I asked. 'Can you tell us anything about them? Is there anybody we can contact?'

'He were a loner, always. Didn't say much about family. He once told me he was adopted and didn't have much to do with his adopted family. Don't know if this were true. Sometimes told porkies, did Raze. The only friends he had were in the army and the SBS. After we was discharged — they didn't want us no more — then … then we slowly lost touch. He went his way and I got stuck here. A little money, an even smaller pension — at my age, too. I was thrown on the scrap heap. Couldn't get a job anywhere, so I came back home. But there was nobody to come back home to.'

He looked at Grace. I wasn't sure whether his rheumy eyes were watering or not. She looked at me and then towards the sea.

'I heard from him now and again,' Gordon continued. 'Used to boast about doing security work in Iraq, Libya, Syria, Sierra Leone, the Congo. Sometimes he went back to Afghanistan. He said rich Nigerians wanted to keep their families safe from Boko Haram kidnappers. He worked in Mozambique against ISIS, did special ops for the Saudis in Yemen. He said he made a lot of money, that he had a house in Brittany, and another in Lincolnshire. Also one on the coast here. Not sure of that, 'cos he wouldn't tell me where exactly. Sounded an exciting life. Always thought he wouldn't make old bones … thought he'd die in action in some far-off place. Not end up dead in a forest in Leicestershire.'

Gordon asked about the cause of death, and we told him as much as we could. I asked whether he had heard from Peter Fraser recently, about what kind of work he had been involved in, but he couldn't help.

'Once I were working undercover in Basra in Iraq and he was with the SBS in Afghanistan. He said he were involved in an operation that changed his life. *Operation Diesel*, he called it. Said he made a lot of money after that. Once let slip he worked for a rich Asian guy in Leicester with contacts all over the world. He said he were working with somebody else who was once in the SAS. Both served in special ops together. He wouldn't say much more.'

We'd got as much as we were going to get from him. As we stood up to leave, the hot sun making me perspire as the loud cackle of seagulls grew more strident, Gordon apologised and offered us a drink.

'Got a good single blend from Scotland.'

We declined, thanked him, gave him our card in case he remembered anything else, and headed to the nearest pub for lunch. We sat in the garden, away from the growing number of tourists and day-trippers.

'At least we've got a positive ID,' I said to Grace as I bit into a smoked ham sandwich, full of French mustard and salad. 'Contact HR at the MoD in London and get them to confirm Peter Fraser's ID, please. Send them the photo. See what else you can find out about him, and also Gordon Priestley. And see whether they can name anybody who's willing to talk to you about any special ops in Afghanistan. It was a long time ago, so they might. Stress that we're looking into an unexplained death. And see if there's a house in Fraser's name on the Lincolnshire coast. It's a long shot, I know. If he had one, he probably paid for it in cash when money-laundering regulations were not as tight as they are today. Anyway, see what you can find, please.'

Grace nodded as she sipped her fresh orange juice, the ice clinking against the glass. Under a clear blue Norfolk sky, a large flock of starlings flew past. Blackbirds became more brazen and snatched scraps from nearby tables. Two scrawny seagulls fought loudly for a piece of dry bread on the parched, brown grass. The birds were free, flying, feeding and breeding. I thought of poor Fernando back at the house, in his cage. I had to make a decision soon about what to do with him.

'I still don't get it,' I eventually said as I sipped a glass of cold, sparkling water. 'If Fraser was living this adrenalin-filled life in foreign places, making a lot of money in security or as a mercenary, how come he wound up dead in the middle of our patch?'

'And *how* did he die?' Grace added. 'We still don't know for sure. If he was pushed from a plane, then why? And by whom? And how did he even get onto the plane? Then there's the diving gear and the rich Asian guy on our patch. Who's he? What's he involved in? Drugs? Prostitution? People trafficking? Or something else?'

'All part of the tapestry in a detective's life, Grace,' I said. 'All part of the tapestry.'

Back in Leicester, I got the grapevine working again to identify the rich South Asian guy. Apart from the usual informers we contacted, I asked the drug squad to lean heavily on the local street dealers and pushers to see what they knew. I also asked constables on the beat and community support officers, particularly those of Asian origin, of which there weren't many, to see what intel they could pick up from the streets, shops and markets. I even asked my mother and father whether they knew anything, but they couldn't help.

It seemed to me that because the Hindu community was one of the first to be established in the city — mainly made up of immigrants from East Africa but also from India — it was the one where wealth was concentrated. Some were highly prosperous, owning large supermarkets, car dealerships, jewellery shops, restaurants, accountancy firms and estate agencies, among other enterprises. Other communities with origins in the sub-continent, such as the Muslim community from Pakistan, Bangladesh and Somalia had come much later. Some owned large warehouses selling cash and carry goods, or they were involved in the textile trade, but they were not in the same league as some of the wealthy Hindus.

I waited for the intel to come in, to see where it would lead. After several days, one name in particular kept being mentioned by different sources — a man who had initially owned one restaurant and now had a burgeoning business empire which had blossomed in a short time. I had to be careful with this information, because I knew the close-knit communities were often driven by jealousy of the success of others. I decided to test out the name with an external source who was not part of the internal politics of the various South Asian communities.

CHAPTER 17

I bit into the cold, stuffed vine leaves, a starter for my meal at The Omar Khayyam.

'Mr Rahimi,' I said, 'your chef is absolutely wonderful.'

'Yes, she is, isn't she?' he beamed, sitting opposite me at a small wooden table, legs crossed. The pink, cream and blue silk drapes fluttered in the cool breeze from the air conditioning vents and the ceiling fan. A faint aroma of sandalwood floated through the air, as did the smooth, soft music of the zither and accompanying flute.

'Please give her my compliments,' I replied as I put a spoonful of aubergine puree onto one of the vine leaves, picked it up with my fingers and put the end of it into my mouth. We sat in a quiet corner of the restaurant, away from the handful of customers. It was still early in the evening and not yet busy. As the front doors opened and closed, the slow drone of traffic, the occasional honking of a car horn and the voices from many parts of the world entered the restaurant, like uninvited guests.

'I know you've been in the business a long time, Mr Rahimi. And you know everything and everyone in Leicester to do with it. But what can you tell me about Mr Parekh, the owner of the Rajasthani Rasoi chain?'

'Are you asking me as a police officer or as a friend?' he asked.

I thought about it a while and said, 'As a friend. I promise nothing will come back to you.'

'Well, I know his rise was — what do you say? — meteoric. Started with one restaurant, which was okay — oh, not like mine,' he said with a smile. 'Nothing to write home about, as the British say. Very soon he opened two more, one in Nottingham and another in Birmingham. Then three more in London — Wembley, Southall and Tooting. All in Asian areas. There is some money to be made in ethnic food. But you only make a few pennies selling each shish kebab. And maybe a pound or two per main course. Certainly not the kind of money he seems to have access to. Perhaps he has a very understanding bank manager who knows more about this business than I do,' he finished, with eyebrows raised.

I pulled the silver serving dish towards me and helped myself to the cod loin cooked in a tahina sauce. It was served cold and was something I fancied on this sultry, suffocating evening.

'So, how do you think he made his money?' I asked.

His bright, brown eyes looked at me for a long time. The wrinkles on his forehead grew more pronounced. He shifted on his cushion, easing his crossed legs. 'Mr Rohan, you really have to promise this won't get out.'

I nodded between mouthfuls of soft, white flesh, licking the sauce from the corner of my lips.

'Only rumours. Cannot tell for sure. You know the car park not far from his restaurant? It's raised above ground level and has a drystone wall. Nobody driving or casually walking past can see what's going on. I've been told it's used for selling hard drugs — that he or his associates supply them. It's a thriving business all hours of the day. There're plenty of other locations too, I've been told. In different parts of the city and country. Check it out yourself.'

I knew of Mr Anand Parekh and his restaurant chain, but hadn't really given it much thought. I had eaten in his restaurant a couple of years ago and, as Mr Rahimi had said, there was nothing remarkable about the quality or the taste of the food.

'The money he made, and I don't mean from the food,' continued Mr Rahimi, 'was used to set up a string of gold jewellery shops. About five in different parts of the country. Twenty-four carat gold is expensive, Mr Rohan, so you need a lot of money to buy the stock. Not many in India or Dubai are going to extend credit facilities on that scale.' Mr Rahimi smiled and then added, 'Maybe he has an understanding bank manager after all and I've heard all this wrong.'

We were silent for a long time, while the air-conditioning unit hummed and spluttered occasionally. If Mr Rahimi knew what was going on, then so would my colleagues in the drug squad.

'Now, if you'll excuse me. Hope to see you again, Mr Rohan. And bring your pretty friend with you again next time. The one you brought before.'

I smiled, shook his hand and asked for the bill from the approaching waiter.

I also wondered whether Mr Rahimi had found a replacement for the one who seemed to have disappeared.

CHAPTER 18

After leaving The Omar Khayyam, I strolled along the Golden Mile. It was late in the evening, but the brightly lit shops would be open until darkness fell. I looked at the window displays, admiring the sarees in bright pinks, reds and blues, embroidered at the edges with gold thread and modelled by pale mannequins with long, black hair. I stared at the gold jewellery in barred windows: necklaces, rings, pendants, bracelets and chains, all waiting to adorn some excited bride. People hurried past me on the pavement, the high-pitched laughter of young women, some arm-in-arm, toddlers being pushed along in their pushchairs, happy teenagers licking ice-cream cones. The sound of popular Hindi songs from Bollywood films and traditional *qawwalis* sung by Rahat Fateh Ali Khan floated out of shops and cafes. Loud rap music came from black hatchbacks with throaty exhausts as they drove slowly along the road.

I entered one of my favourite music shops and went down into the basement to look at their selection. Though I had recently relented and started streaming songs, I still preferred to have my own collection of CDs. I bought a double compilation of classic Hindi songs because it featured one song in particular which I didn't possess.

As the sun started to set, I parked my car at the bottom of the quiet street, a short distance from the car park Mr Rahimi had identified. There were no streetlamps nearby and as the darkness of night took hold, I stared straight ahead. A young man emerged regularly from a dark, battered hatchback at the top of the car park near the restaurant, speaking into a mobile phone — no doubt a pay-as-you-go one. Every few minutes a car would appear, stay in the car park for a while and then drive off. This carried on for a couple of hours and numerous cars came and went. There was absolutely no doubt about what was going on. A good set up for a highly lucrative evening's work.

I turned on the ignition, performed a three-point turn and headed home. I remembered to switch on the headlights once I was back on the main road. As I drove, I thought it impossible that the restaurant owner and his staff would *not* know what was going on in the car park.

I was trying hard not to think about my colleagues and what they might or might not have known. The drug dealing in the car park was so blatant that some of the officers in the serious crimes unit must have been aware of it, but they had not closed it down. Were they on the take?

My phone rang. 'I'm sorry to ring so late, Rohan,' said Jenny Tyburn. 'Just to confirm, the statue's been carbon dated. Took longer than anticipated because people are away on holiday. And then there was a mechanical problem. But it's the genuine article.' I could hear the excitement in the museum curator's voice. 'We'll have to get together to celebrate sometime.'

'Yes, would be good to celebrate sometime. But remember, it's part of an ongoing criminal investigation. So please don't say anything to anybody.'

There was a pause at the other end of the line.

'I need that statue back as soon as possible, Jenny. As I say, it's an important piece of evidence in our investigation.'

'Of course. Let's meet up soon.' We arranged a time for me to pick it up from her before I hung up.

Even though it was late, I dialled Grace's number, thinking that she may as well get used to the fact that in police work your life is not your own. She picked up quite quickly. I confirmed with her that the statue was genuine, explained what I had been doing that night, and arranged for her to come with me to interview Mr Parekh tomorrow.

'Thanks for the update, Sir. I followed up with the Ministry of Defence in London. I was going to tell you tomorrow. Someone in HR only offered to talk to me once they'd confirmed my identity with Superintendent Breedon, and they insisted on a video call so they could see I was at HQ. They confirmed Peter Fraser's identity after I'd sent them his photo, and they also confirmed the identity of his friend, Gordon Priestley. Both were honourably discharged. Fraser was involved in a special operation to kill a Taliban leader near Bahram Charin Helmand, and a bit later he was involved in an operation to rescue Italian hostages captured by them.'

'What about *Operation Diesel*? Anything?' I asked.

'Reluctant to go into too much detail. But it was a Special Forces operation. Heroin worth more than fifty million pounds was seized, and factories and poppy fields were destroyed. More than twenty insurgents killed. Don't know why they were so cagey. Fair amount of information about this operation online.'

'Really?' I replied. 'Anyway, Priestley said Fraser made a lot of money after that. Worked with a rich Asian guy on our patch.'

'Yes, Sir. Think I know where you're going with this. Fraser probably turned before, or after, his discharge because of the amount of money to be made. He would have become involved with warlords farming opium and then pushing the heroin to the West. They would've valued someone like him, wouldn't they?'

'They would indeed. Good work, Grace.'

CHAPTER 19

It was mid-morning and yet another bright sunny day. I stopped my car in front of the tall wooden security gates, pressed the button and spoke into the intercom. A security camera blinked, undoubtedly taking a picture of my face. Another camera swivelled towards my car. Moments later, the gates opened slowly, the cast-iron hinges groaning with the weight. I pulled the car forward slowly along the half-mile drive, immaculate rose beds on either side. The pinks, reds and yellows were a vivid contrast to the green grass. In the distance, the well-tended grounds were punctuated with mature oak, elm and pine trees. The thick green foliage of a silver birch had been shaped into an umbrella, while mature magnolia trees with cream and white flowers bowed down to the ground. At the front of the large Georgian mansion, in the centre of the circular drive, stood an ornate fountain with two sculpted dolphins, a steady stream of water spouting from each long mouth.

Grace and I got out of the car and approached the heavy teak door, another security camera blinking its red light above. I lifted the large cast-iron knocker in the shape of a great white shark and thumped it twice on the metal base. The sound reverberated under the cream-coloured porch supported by four concrete columns.

The door opened and a young Indian woman looked at us.

'My father's expecting you. Please come in,' she said. We were led through a wide marble hallway. On the high, pale walls hung paintings by Jackson Pollock and Grant Wood, he of *American Gothic* fame. Through the doors at the back, we were led into an enormous glass conservatory. My house could have fitted into it. Outside, I could see two horses grazing in the paddocks.

The unexpected cool air, a welcome relief, slapped my face as we walked in. The young woman nodded to us and slipped away, and then Mr Parekh entered the room.

'Ah, Inspector Sharma. I've heard so much about you. Pleased to meet you at last,' he said. He beamed and shook our hands after I had introduced Grace. He then placed an unwelcome arm on my shoulder as he led us further inside. His wavy black hair was carefully combed back, and the unmistakable scent of expensive cologne wafted in the air.

'I saw you admiring the Pollock and Grant Wood paintings. All copies, of course. Sadly, I can't afford the real ones.'

I had my doubts about that.

'Now, you were very cagey on the phone when you asked to meet me. What exactly can I help you with? I will of course do my best to help the police.'

Grace pulled out the photograph of Peter Fraser from a manila folder and asked, 'Do you know this man, Mr Parekh?'

He studied the photograph intently for a few moments and then handed it back to Grace. 'Poor man looks a bit anaemic. Was he ill when the photograph was taken?'

'Do you know him, Mr Parekh?' Grace repeated. 'His name's Peter Fraser.'

He shook his head and said, 'Frasier, Frasier … the only Frasier I know is the guy on the American comedy programme. He's very funny. You should see it sometime, if you haven't done so already.'

'Peter *Fraser*, Mr Parekh. *Fraser*,' I said.

Parekh looked thoughtful. 'No, I can't say I know him,' he said finally. 'Although I once went on holiday to Fraser Island, off the coast of Queensland, Australia. Wonderful place. I love warm, tropical lands and their flora and fauna.' He smiled. His teeth had clearly cost a lot of money.

Around us in the temperature-controlled conservatory were orchids from various parts of the world. The bird of paradise flowers, in different sizes and colours, reminded me of the iridescent heads of crowned cranes. The intoxicating smell of jasmine floated in the air. I recognised a mimosa sapling, and hibiscus and commelina flowers.

'I see that you too like tropical plants, Inspector. This here is a Venus flytrap. Insects are attracted to it because of its intoxicating nectar and before they know it, they're glued to the sticky liquid on the inside. The barbed trap closes. No escape. Gradually, the plant digests its prey.'

I met his penetrating gaze. 'We have reason to believe you and Mr Fraser were acquainted, Mr Parekh,' I said.

'Like I said, I don't know him. Although if I saw him, I would advise him to see a doctor. His face looks a bit pale.' He smiled at Grace as he said this.

Her right hand formed a fist. She unclenched it slowly. 'He was once a soldier, Mr Parekh,' said Grace. 'Highly successful at what he did in the forces. Do you know any other soldiers?'

The sudden downturn of his lips betrayed his seething anger. 'No,' he eventually replied.

'Don't know if you've seen the press and social media coverage recently, but Mr Fraser was found dead in Charnwood Forest not long ago. We're treating the death as suspicious. If you did know him, Mr Parekh, it'd be in your interests to say so.'

The bright, brown eyes stared back at us. The dark pupils were now pinpricks. 'Let me be clear, I have never seen him before. Please give my condolences to his immediate family.'

'The car park near your restaurant,' I said.

'Yes, that is something I do know, since it belongs to me.'

'Can you explain why it's so busy with people who don't always go into your restaurant?'

'It's for my customers. If others use it to go shopping, I can't stop them. But I sometimes have a security guard at the entrance during busy times.'

After a pause, I said, 'I must congratulate you — a chain of successful restaurants all over the country, jewellery shops…'

'I cook and feed, Inspector. Cook and feed. Got lucrative contracts supplying my food to the big supermarkets. I've worked damned hard for my money. Used to be an accountant and made slightly more than you probably do now. Well, it wasn't good enough for me. I used the profits to open jewellery shops. And for the record, I'm also involved in importing and exporting goods. Some of the profit margins are very high. But being a public servant, I wouldn't expect you to know much about that.'

I clenched my teeth. A trickle of sweat ran down my back, despite the cool air of the conservatory. Mr Parekh had also finally lost his cool.

'And I'm not sure what the hell you're both doing here. I'm a law-abiding citizen with good connections. So, if you don't mind, I've got other things to do.' He pressed a buzzer.

His daughter appeared within a few moments and led us out.

As we drove through the front gates, Grace said, 'He's guilty as hell. He knew Peter Fraser.'

'Of course he did. And did you hear what he said to us? "I cook and feed, Inspector. Cook and feed." A street dealer said the same thing to me not long ago: "All I know about Mr Big is he cooks and feeds." Our rich Asian cooks heroin from raw opium, then he feeds the habit to the junkies.'

Then it hit me. The food references: Mr Khosla didn't 'want to end up like a shish kebab' while Bobby had feared becoming 'mincemeat'. Had they both been trying to tip me off by making references to Mr Parekh's restaurant empire? I resolved to speak to them both again.

Grace didn't say much as we drove back to HQ. She stared out of the car window at the fields of north Leicestershire, lost in a world of her own.

CHAPTER 20

The magnificent central dome of the Basilica of Sacré-Coeur, built with pale travertine stone, was brightly lit in the early Parisian evening. The massive church overlooked thousands of houses in the Montmartre district of Paris.

Nicole Laurent sat at the dining table in her kitchen, looked through the window and said, 'Wonderful, isn't it?' She then turned back to the camera.

I nodded, thinking not just of the church, which reminded me of the Taj Mahal, but also of the many famous artists who had lived in its shadow in times gone by. Renoir, Modigliani, Matisse, Degas and Van Gogh, one of my favourites.

'Not a screensaver this time, Rohan. I'm so lucky to be living in this top-floor flat, with a view of Paris to die for. No wonder they call it a city for lovers.'

I wanted to pack my suitcase and go straight there, to the Louvre, to the top of the Eiffel Tower, to the many nightclubs catering for every taste, and to the many restaurants doing the same. But it was not to be.

We were on our secure video conference call, keeping each other informed of developments. I wanted to know if the French police and Interpol could shed any further light on my case.

'First things first, Rohan. And this is really important. Where's your glass of wine? Mine's here,' she said, lifting a full glass of undoubtedly excellent red wine. 'St Émilion,' she added, as if reading my mind. She was wearing a white blouse and her long brown hair was immaculately groomed.

I poured a large glass of white wine, a good Sauvignon from the New World. We both raised our drinks to each other and took a sip.

'Now,' she said, 'something really important. How's Fernando?'

At the mention of his name, Fernando came to life behind me. There was a fluttering of wings and a squawk.

'He seems to be in a better mood at the moment. Why don't you ask him yourself?' I pointed the screen towards the cage.

When she asked the question, Fernando whistled and said, 'Rohan wants to be … bad, Nicole. Rohan wants to be bad, Nicole.'

'I'm really sorry,' I said with a blush, feeling awkward.

She laughed. 'I've been told worse things.'

I wasn't sure what to make of that and let it drop. 'The last time we spoke,' I said, changing the subject swiftly, 'we talked about Hasina, the dead Afghan woman. At least that's who we think she is, because of the gold chain on her ankle. You told me about the looting of antiquities and how this could be tied up with drugs, the sex industry and people trafficking.

'I think we've identified the Indian guy here in Leicester who may be the ringleader. But it's going to be difficult to pin evidence on him. We're working on it.' I explained what we had so far, including my conversations with Bobby, the street dealer, Mr Khosla, the owner of the sleazy club, and the interview with Anand Parekh earlier that day. I also expressed my concerns about whether members of the drug squad were being paid off. 'And we've identified the dead diver whose photograph I've emailed to you. Still not sure how he ended up in the middle of a forest in Leicestershire.'

'I'll circulate the photo to my colleagues here and at Interpol,' said Nicole. 'See whether they have any information on him or can throw any light on his death.'

We agreed to have another conversation soon. As we said goodbye, Nicole said, 'It's not good for Fernando — or any other living creature — to be locked up. The cage could be made of iron, or it could be mental — one we make for ourselves. It traps us. I know. I've been there. Play Fernando the sounds of the jungle. They're the sounds of his heart, of his spirit. And if that doesn't work, then it's time to set him free.'

Although late in the evening, the daytime heat from high summer had penetrated deep into the brickwork and the roof tiles of my house. It was hot and the partially open windows brought in warm air and traffic fumes, rather than any cool respite. My floor fan oscillated at high speed from left to right. It blew the pages of my newspaper on the coffee table and the magazine resting near the television set. The scent of fried *methi* seeds and fresh coriander wafted from the kitchen. I sipped the dregs of my Sauvignon Blanc, which had accompanied my light meal earlier on, trying hard to cool down. I was feeling melancholy when one of my favourite films, *Sleepless in Seattle*, started on one of the movie channels. I was sure it would lift my spirits.

The phone rang, so I paused the film.

It was Yasmin. After the usual pleasantries, she said, 'Well, Dad, you said in your text you knew what to do with Fernando.'

'Yup. One of the things we talked about was letting him listen to some African jungle noises — even other parrots and birds. Could make him happy. But I can't do that for the rest of my life. Or his.'

'Why not, Dad? David Attenborough's done it all my life. And most likely yours!' She giggled.

'Good one,' I replied. 'I've given it a lot of thought. I think the best solution is to give him to London Zoo. They've got an excellent reputation for keeping tropical birds. I'm sure he'll be happy there with the other birds. And he'll have a *des res* address.'

'But Dad, you're exchanging one cage for another. And he'll be hounded by hundreds of visitors every day. Some will make stupid noises at him, getting him to mimic them. He'll become stressed and unhappy. Might be all right for the birds born there. They don't know any different. But Fernando is ours. He's a member of the family.'

I paused. I had thought I had found a compromise to ensure that he would be well looked after and would have company. It took a thirteen-year-old to state the obvious.

'Dad, please don't do it. Why don't we take him to the countryside and let him fly for a bit? I'm sure he'll come back. The woman who looks after the macaws in Lincolnshire said they always returned.'

'Thanks, darling. Let me mull it over for a bit.'

'It's that special day today for Indian brothers and sisters, isn't it, Dad?' Yasmin went on, changing the subject. 'I've seen boys and men wandering around with string bracelets tied to their wrists.'

'Yes, it is. And you should do that for your brother, too.' It being *Rakhi* day, I was missing my sister. The feeling became stronger and stronger as the months and years went by.

'I know, Dad. Wish I knew more about your traditions.'

'Not mine, Yasmin. Ours.'

She fell silent.

'I'm sorry, darling. I didn't mean it to sound like that. I'm sure it must be difficult for you and Karan.'

We then talked about what they had been doing, about the school holidays ending soon, and what she was going to do before then.

'Tomorrow's Saturday,' she said. 'Mum and Pierre usually go to the supermarket in the afternoon to do the food shopping. Why don't we — you, me and Karan — go to Rutland Water for a picnic?'

'Sounds great to me, darling.' My mood lifted immediately.

'That's wonderful, Dad. Oh, by the way, bring Fernando with you.'

CHAPTER 21

It was late morning as I put Fernando's cage on the back seat of my car and then sat in the driver's seat. Turning round, I said, 'Okay, Fernando. We're going to a really nice place today. Give you a chance to fly for a while. But promise me you'll come back.'

He balanced on his perch, staring at me with those big, round eyes. It had been a long time since he had been in a car.

'You fly. You come home,' I said.

'ET phone home,' he replied, remembering watching the film a long time ago.

'No, not ET phone home. You come home,' I said, pointing at him and then the cage.

He scratched his neck and two short grey feathers fluttered to the bottom of the cage. 'Come home,' he said after a moment.

'Good boy, Fernando. Yes, you come home.'

I drove across the city and pulled up outside the house in the suburbs that I had previously shared with Faye and the kids. I waited a few minutes and then honked the car horn to let them know I was waiting. Pierre appeared at the lounge window. A few years younger than me, and originally from Martinique, he was dark, lithe and handsome. He looked at me, smiled nervously and disappeared. I didn't return his smile. I could understand why Faye had gone for him and I tried to rationalise that he was innocent — he just happened to work at the same school as Faye. But part of me could not forgive him either. He had the choice of saying 'no', but he went along with the destruction of a marriage and three other lives. But if he hadn't, perhaps another man would have come along. Who knew? I certainly didn't, but here I was, outside my old house, with another man sleeping in my old bed. Well, maybe they had changed that.

As I dwelt on these painful thoughts, which still cut deep despite the passing of time, the front door opened and Yasmin and Karan ran out, smiling and waving. Faye blew them a kiss, waved at me, and closed the door.

When Yasmin saw Fernando in the back seat, she asked to sit with him. Karan didn't often sit with me in the front and was glad of the opportunity to do so. They said 'hello' to Fernando, and the children chattered for more than half an hour before we reached our destination.

Rutland Water is a large, artificial reservoir on the eastern side of the county. Surrounded by over three thousand acres, the perimeter track is over twenty miles long. People from all over the East Midlands use it for many leisure activities, including birdwatching, sailing, fishing and canoeing.

The midday sun was high in the sky when we found a quiet picnic table near some ancient woodland. I brought over the hamper and Fernando's cage. I asked Karan to bring the cool box from the boot of the car, and two Tupperware containers with Fernando's seeds and dried fruit.

'Let's eat first,' I said.

The kids were more than happy to do so. Karan bit into a chicken drumstick and shovelled some crisps into his mouth. Yasmin munched a salmon and cucumber sandwich, put on her sunglasses, leant back on the bench and looked up at the sky. After a while, she retrieved her mobile from her rucksack. Fernando's cage was on the table with us. I put some of his food into it and he ate it without fuss. Once I had seen to all of them, I dipped a slice of pitta bread into hummus and ate it, followed by a green olive stuffed with pimento. Fernando picked up a large cashew nut with his claw and put it into his sharp, dark beak. It was one of his favourite foods. Periodically, he stopped and looked at each of us in turn. He ate dried apricots and some sunflower seeds, then put his beak in the water tray and thrust his head back, quenching his thirst.

'Aaahhh, Fernando. Good boy,' said Yasmin.

The waters of the reservoir were well below their usual levels, but what remained stretched far into the horizon. The surface shimmered as the vast blue sky, with occasional wisps of cirrus clouds, reflected in the water. There was not much wind for the sailing boats, but the canoeists and kayakers rowed furiously, trying to race each other. In the distance, the pleasure cruiser, full of day-trippers, chugged through the middle of the reservoir.

We did not say anything for a long time. On the water, coots and great crested grebes swam along, beaks plunging below the surface every now and again. A lapwing flew past. A fisherman on the banks reeled in a struggling trout.

When we had finished eating, Yasmin fanned herself with the lid of a plastic container and Karan put a cap on his head. Sweat trickled down my temple.

Even though I didn't want to, I eventually said, 'Okay, kids. Let's get this out of the way.'

I opened the cage. Fernando hopped out and perched on the side of my hand. Yasmin and Karan took turns to stroke his soft head. His grey feathers looked dull and lifeless.

'Time for you to fly, to soar and be free. But remember to come home. Fernando, come home.' I pointed to the cage.

His round, dark eyes blinked as he looked at each of us in turn.

I stretched up my hand as far as I could, pulled it down slightly, then jerked it hard upwards. Fernando's wings flapped a couple of times, his claws digging into my hand. He stared at me, then looked up as his wings flapped hard and he flew unsteadily away from my hand.

He soared towards the tall trees, wings flapping furiously, his long grey tail turning left and right, a rudder trying to direct his body. This was the first time he had flown any meaningful distance.

As he flapped away, the three of us ran after him, shouting, 'Not too far, Fernando! Not too far!'

He carried on towards the woods, with tall trees and thick foliage — a bit too far and out of reach.

'No!' I cried. 'No, Fernando! Come back.'

We ran after him, shouting his name.

'Come home, Fernando! Come home!'

But he was gone.

My heart raced. We ran towards the woods, the kids struggling to keep up behind me. There was panic in my voice.

'Come back, Fernando! Come back!' God, what had I done?

'Please, Fernando. Please come back,' pleaded Yasmin as she caught up with me.

'Dad,' said Karan as he came up behind us, gasping, 'he hasn't gone … has he?' His eyes filled with tears.

Why did I do this? Why? I kept asking myself.

I tried to sound calm. 'Let's go back to the table and wait. He could've flown anywhere. He'll be back,' I said, trying to console both them and myself.

As we walked back to the picnic table, my mobile vibrated in my back pocket.

I looked at the number and thought, *What the hell do they want?*

'Sorry to disturb you on a Saturday afternoon, Sir,' said the male voice from HQ, 'but the body of a man's been found. Sergeant Nicholson was shopping in the city centre and is already making her way to the site. And the usual support staff are there, or on their way. Somebody said you knew the victim.'

He told me the location, but said he had no idea who the victim was.

Shit, I thought. *Must find Fernando. Please God, if there is a God, please don't let anything happen to him.*

We sat at the table. I paced up and down. The kids were agitated. I thought Yasmin felt guilty about having suggested we bring Fernando out here. She was quiet and played with her mobile, crossing and uncrossing her legs.

After a while, she said, 'Dad, I've been looking at a map of this area on my phone, to see where Fernando could've gone. Can't work anything out. But did you know this is a special area for breeding ospreys?'

Fuck, fuck, I thought. Giant birds of prey with razor-like talons that were once an endangered species. Fernando would be a mere morsel for one of them.

'No, I didn't know.' My voice faltered. 'You two stay here. I'll go back to the woods and see if he's in one of the trees.' I sprinted towards the woodland.

I looked up at the trees, shouted his name and left cashew nuts on the ground for him. Nothing happened.

I couldn't leave him here, but I had to get to the crime scene. *Please, Fernando*, I thought. *Please come home.*

CHAPTER 22

The long, white bonnet of my car gleamed in the hot sunshine, the engine purring as we drove back to the city. Bugs splattered on the windscreen as I started breaking the speed limit. We were all quiet, lost in our own thoughts. I felt as if a part of me had been torn away and was lost forever. Fernando had always been with me. Growing up as a young boy in Kenya, I'd chuckled at his mimicking, fed him, and talked to him every day. My parents had brought him to Leicester despite all the paperwork involved, and I'd laughed with him every day during my teenage years. Then my parents had given him to me and Faye during our married life. Along with my two children, he was part of the family and always had been. And now, he had gone and I was shattered.

The silence in the car was deafening. Occasionally, the kids tried to comfort me by saying he would be back. I had asked the staff who worked at the reservoir to look out for him and to let me know if they spotted anything. At first, they were incredulous at my story, but then they gradually became sympathetic. I asked them to try to entice him into the cage with cashew nuts and other seeds that I left behind. I offered to pay for their services and was hoping they would do their best, since the area was a bird sanctuary as well. However, I feared for Fernando because of the presence of ospreys, red kites and falcons. He would be an easy target. He had no idea how to survive in the wild.

I dropped off my children and made my way to the crime scene, driving along a line of abandoned, red-brick Victorian terraces, not that different from the road I was living on. This one was not far from the railway station, and the street was scheduled for demolition to make way for modern energy-saving flats with solar panels on their roofs. I parked the car and walked along the cracked, uneven pavement to the house. The front door and windows had been boarded up with rusting, corrugated sheets. I noticed a parked ambulance and nodded to the support staff and uniforms standing outside. Ben Carter helped me with my forensic suit and, as we walked to the back of the house through the broken gate at the side, he explained what we would find inside.

We entered through the warped, wooden door, barely hanging onto its hinges, which led into the kitchen, now trashed. The wash basin was stained brown, the taps were missing, and the old, white gas cooker stood in the corner, its iron rings rusted and rotting. I trod carefully, avoiding the crushed, empty beer cans, used syringes and the small rectangles of aluminium foil on the floor.

I struggled to breathe through the forensic mask as thick dust rose in the clawing, humid air. We went into the derelict front room. Four bright arc lights on stands bathed the room in a sanitised white glow, making a mockery of the devastation in front of us. Three forensic investigators in white suits stood aside. The bare, uneven floorboards, covered in dead flies and rat droppings, creaked as Ben and I approached. In the middle stood an old office chair. A man sat in it, facing away from us, his arms behind his back and bound with plastic cable ties at the elbows. There were two bloody stumps where the hands should have been, and his feet were also tied at the ankles. He wore a pale blue T-shirt, and congealed blood ran down his shoulders. One of the forensic investigators gestured for us to stop. She walked to the chair and turned it towards us. A long kitchen knife had been thrust through his heart, the thick, dried blood on his chest swarming with flies.

He had been decapitated and his head had been placed on his lap carefully, his blue jeans now turned mostly red. His cheeks were heavily bruised and his mouth, partly open, front teeth smashed, was covered in dark blood.

'No mistaking the cause of death,' said Dr Malik, the pathologist, from behind one of the forensic masks. 'The tongue's also been cut out. No sign of it. Still, he won't be needing it anymore.'

I looked at the scene a few moments longer, wondering how one human being could do this to another.

'Who discovered the body, Ben?'

'Local woman — she's being looked after in the ambulance outside. She's in a bad way, as you can imagine.'

I went outside and entered the back of the ambulance. A young woman with short, bleached blonde hair and streaks of mascara down her cheeks was being comforted by a paramedic. They sat on the wheeled stretcher, her body wrapped in a hospital blanket. She let out periodic sobs, her hands trembling.

I introduced myself and asked whether she would answer a few questions. She nodded. I stayed with her for half an hour, asking questions gently, with her bursting into tears now and again. However, I eventually managed to gather as much information as I was going to get.

She said her name was Jane; she was a sex worker and had been using one of the rooms she rented by the hour, not far from the station. The man she had been with was a regular customer and had told his wife or girlfriend that he was off to the football. He'd just wanted a bit of diversion first, which she provided. Afterwards, she needed a fix and came to this house, as usual. The addicts would come in through the back, inject themselves and stay while the drug ran through their veins. *And through their lives*, I thought. Anyway, she'd arrived just after the start of the football match and entered this room. That was when she had seen the body and screamed, running out as fast as she could. She had screamed for help outside, and eventually a passer-by had rung the police. No, the passer-by hadn't come into the house. He probably hadn't wanted to get involved. No, she didn't know who he was.

I thanked her and told her someone would be over to take all her details. I also asked her to contact us in case she remembered anything else. I asked the nearby officers for Grace's whereabouts and was told where I would find her.

She was sitting on a low brick wall in the back yard of one of the adjoining houses. It looked as if it had once been a flowerbed, a ray of vibrant colour in a dull, grey and brown existence. She looked at me as I approached, not trying to hide the pool of vomit near her feet.

In the old days, the quip would have been, 'Welcome to homicide.' But in this day and age, I immediately thought of post-traumatic stress disorder. I smiled and sat down next to her. She tried to smile back through red, swollen eyes. We sat in silence for a long time.

Eventually, I said to her, 'Come on Grace. We can't stay here all day. If you need to speak to anyone, please ring me. Or ring the twenty-four-hour helpline which HR have set up. Don't try to deal with this by yourself.'

She tried to smile again and stood up.

'I'm sorry, Grace, but we need to put out requests for information,' I said. 'Get the uniforms knocking on doors and asking questions. Speak to the sex workers and junkies we know in this area. We may not get much, but we need to do it. If you don't feel up to it, I'll ask somebody else to do it.'

'No worries,' she replied. 'I'll get to it.' After a while, she asked, 'Do we know who the victim is?'

The victim's bruised and bloodied face crashed into my mind's eye.

'Yes, I'd met him before. The last time I saw him, he wished me well in finding a shrink for Fernando.'

She gave me a quizzical look.

'His name was Bobby — the street dealer I mentioned after we visited Mr Parekh. I was going to speak to him again.'

I asked her to notify any immediate relatives and to get family liaison involved.

As I drove away, I tried not to think of Bobby's face. God, had I been responsible for his death? Had somebody seen me talking to him? Or was he involved in something else, something I didn't know about?

I tried not to think of Fernando, but to no avail.

Maybe I needed a therapist as well.

CHAPTER 23

The next few days were a maelstrom of conflicting emotions for me. I felt sorry for Bobby, but I wasn't surprised the drug dealer had met an untimely end, even though it was particularly gruesome. The manner of his death reminded me of what Nicole and Superintendent Breedon said about the beheaded lorry driver in Istanbul. Hands and tongue sliced off. Ears, too. And, of course, our female victim had been beheaded. Same general pattern, maybe the same killer.

While these thoughts swirled through my head, Fernando and his plight were never far from my mind. I had flyers printed with his photograph and the number of a pay-as-you-go mobile which I'd bought recently. The kids and I distributed the flyers one afternoon and a few kind rangers pinned some laminated ones to tree trunks, fences and to the walls of the rural centre. I had offered a reward of one hundred pounds for Fernando's safe return. I rang the staff at the reservoir about any possible sightings, stared at the stand in the front room that had held his cage, and avoided the kitchen cupboard containing his packets of seeds and dried fruit. The kids rang me now and again, trying to comfort me and asking to go to the woods again to look for him, but I said there was no point. If the staff couldn't find him, then our chances were slim. Even Faye rang to ask how I was and for any news about Fernando. My parents, too, were devastated. But life had to continue.

'It's highly likely that the victim was tied up first. Then his tongue was cut out using a sharp knife,' said Dr Malik at the briefing session I called when all the evidence surrounding

Bobby's death had been collated and analysed. 'Would've stopped him screaming.'

Grace, sitting next to me, fidgeted with a pen. She had rightly referred herself for post-traumatic therapy after seeing the mutilated corpse.

'No sign of hard drugs in the body,' the pathologist continued. 'But we found traces of cannabis and nicotine in the bloodstream. A pinprick in each eyeball was probably caused by a syringe containing sulphuric acid. Poor bugger. Slow, painful — very painful — death. I think the beheading would have been a welcome relief for him.'

The quiet humming of the air conditioner in the early afternoon broke the silence. I looked at Ben Carter.

'The killer — or killers — didn't leave much forensic evidence for us,' he said. 'No fingerprints on the knife handle, so they were probably wearing gloves. Many footprints on the floor, but they could belong to anybody — if we could identify the shoes, that is. Sorry, Sir. Not a lot to go on.'

'And I suppose,' said Grace, 'there was overkill. With all the injuries and mutilations. The message must be "hear no evil, see no evil, speak no evil". Something like that.'

'Yes,' I replied. 'The killer left a message. Don't mess.'

I recalled the furtive shadow, the head flashing back behind one of the garages when I had spoken to Bobby. Whoever it was had seen us together, and had perhaps overheard our conversation.

Grace then told the group what I already knew: appeals for information about the killing and the victim had drawn a blank. Given the area and the circumstances, it didn't surprise me.

On Saturday evening, a week after Fernando's disappearance, I was sitting at home, staring listlessly at the television screen and trying to ignore the silence and loneliness. My mind couldn't focus on any programme, and I didn't have my best friend to talk to. I sipped my third full glass of a cool Chilean Chardonnay and remembered a Bollywood song from my childhood, the one I had found on the double compilation in the music shop the other week. I put it on and listened.

The song was allegorical and could have appealed to children as part of a fairy tale, or it could have been interpreted as a parable for adults. It went like this: there was once a nightingale that sang sweetly to a red rose in a luscious garden. The rose loved the lilting singing of the nightingale and looked forward to it all day, and it started falling in love. This went on for a long time until one day the nightingale didn't appear. A hunter had captured it and caged it so he could listen to the nightingale by himself. The rose grieved and pined for its friend every day. On hearing the rose's cries, the nightingale smashed through its bamboo cage and returned to the garden to sing for the rose. The moral for adults was that if you fall in love, then love freely like the rose and the nightingale.

I thought of failed past loves, of Faye, and of Fernando as the song ended.

The ringing of my landline phone disturbed my thoughts.

Not many used that number and I knew who it would be. After the usual pleasantries — asking if I had eaten, if I was looking after myself properly — my mother eventually said, 'Why aren't you happy, Rohan? Why don't you find another woman? Settle down, have some company. It's not right for human beings to live on their own.'

'I'm fine, Mum.'

'I'm your mother. I know you're not fine. I just heard about a poor woman whose husband was killed in a car crash some time ago. She's on her own. Just a bit younger than you. She'd be good for you. And you'd be good for her.'

'Please, Mum. Not now.'

'When, then?' She sounded terse. 'You work too hard. You drink too much. You don't look after yourself or others. Look what you did with Fernando. And we lost your sister all those years ago.'

This was the first time she had alluded to my responsibility for Maya's kidnapping. If I hadn't sneezed, maybe we wouldn't have been discovered in our hiding place.

'And your children — what about them? Living with another man — a Black man —'

'Mum!'

'Well, it's true, isn't it? And they're growing up not knowing our language or culture. And they don't even eat our food. Other people are also saying this.'

'Please, Mum. I don't need this.'

'You always destroy the things you love. You could've fought for your wife and children. You gave up too easily.'

'Mum, she left me! I'll ring you some other time.' I put the phone down.

As I gulped down the rest of the wine, I acknowledged that some of the things she'd said were true.

But what do you do if you're trapped by a hunter, real or imagined?

CHAPTER 24

The bees swarming in my head competed with the persistent sound of my mobile phone vibrating. I stared at the bedside table from under heavy eyelids. I didn't want to speak to anybody. The daylight penetrating the gaps in the curtains caused a sharp pain inside my head. I sat up, ruffled my fingers through my matted hair, and tried to suppress a yawn.

'Hi Jamie,' I said when I'd accepted the call. My tongue felt furry.

Jamie Shriver, the head of the IT unit, apologised for ringing me at ten o'clock on a Sunday morning. 'We've been monitoring Mr Parekh's online activities, as you requested,' he went on. 'He uses the dark web a lot. The signal bounced around many computers around the world, also encrypted. But my team's managed to keep tabs. Last night, he arranged for a large shipment of cobalt to be transported from Kampala in Uganda to Hong Kong.'

'What?' I said and waited for the buzzing in my head to stop. 'Cobalt's used in electric batteries, isn't it? Strange thing for the owner of a restaurant and jewellery shop empire to be dealing with.'

'That's what I thought, Sir. I did a bit of digging around online. You're right. Cobalt's used for batteries in electric cars, mobile phones, laptops, tablets. Even space rockets. Demand for it is going through the roof because of the Green agenda and climate change. The price has rocketed, if you'll pardon the pun.'

'Mined mainly in Central Africa, right? The Congo?'

'That's right, Sir. About three quarters of the world's supply comes from there, almost one hundred thousand tons. It's mined mainly by children, and they're paid about a dollar a day, often less. They have terrible working conditions — mine roofs collapse, and many children die because of the dust they breathe in. They also suffer chronic health problems.'

'But it's not a crime to mine cobalt, is it?'

'No, Sir. But the UN has laid down guidelines on how much to mine and how much to export. The world's major multinational companies — household names, many of them — ignore these. While we charge our phones and laptops and electric cars, young children die mining the stuff.'

I didn't want to feel guilty on a Sunday morning. 'Why Kampala to Hong Kong, Jamie?'

'It's easy to evade scrutiny in Uganda. It's next door to the Democratic Republic of Congo. Corruption's rife. A lot can be exported from Kampala, no questions asked. Mr Parekh's family came to Leicester as refugees from Idi Amin's Uganda in the 1970s. I gather he's established business contacts back there now. The cobalt's taken from Hong Kong to China, where they make the electronic batteries and computer hardware. Highly lucrative. Another big mark-up from its sale in HK. May not be illegal, but it is highly immoral and unethical.'

'So, it tells us that Parekh's got no principles. Can't get him on that.'

'True. But get this. He was paid for the shipment into an offshore account in the British Virgin Islands. More than half a million pounds. It may or may not be illegal, but it's sailing close to the wind — which I suppose you can do on a yacht in the Caribbean Sea.'

'Thanks, Jamie. Great work.'

'Sir, before you go — I know you've been working with the French, who are working with Interpol. Our capacity to track the dark web any deeper is limited by our technology and staffing. I know the French have an excellent team that specialises in this. Since you already work with them, maybe they'll help some more. Better than starting from scratch with our National Crime Agency.'

I thanked him again.

I drank three cups of strong Fairtrade coffee, took two paracetamol tablets and stood under the shower for a long time. I turned the water to hot, as hot as I could bear, and after a few minutes, I turned it to cold. Then I repeated the process.

As I did so, the cobwebs in my brain started pulling apart and dissolving. I thrust my head backwards, and the water stung my closed eyelids.

Some things were becoming clearer. I knew Anand Parekh was buying and selling drugs. He was a key player, and was possibly involved in Bobby's death since Bobby had been seen talking to me. He'd wanted to send a message to others not to talk. He probably laundered the drugs money into antiquities. And now we had evidence that he was buying and selling cobalt, almost certainly breaking UN guidelines. Was it another money-laundering exercise? He obviously wanted to keep his involvement secret, hence the payments to an offshore account.

As I came down the stairs, the silence in the house was deafening. I craved Fernando's company; I wanted to see him, stroke his soft grey head and talk to him. I tried hard not to think about whether he was safe, but it wasn't easy.

I knew Jamie was right about how to proceed. I wanted to use Grace as a sounding board, but she was still too fragile. I did not want to speak to Superintendent Breedon on a Sunday morning. He'd probably have said he was off to church, which I would have doubted.

I texted Nicole: *Sorry to trouble you on a Sunday. Can we talk? Would help me a lot.*

Sorry, Rohan, came the reply. *We're going for a walk in Montmartre. Having lunch at a favourite café on the banks of the Seine. Can chat later. Please give a time to suit.*

This was the first time she had referred to 'we'. It would have been great to have Sunday lunch on the banks of the river Seine, under a warm summer sun and with a soft breeze blowing.

I put the thought out of my head.

CHAPTER 25

'I'm sorry about asking you to work on a Sunday. Did you enjoy your lunch, Nicole?' I asked at four o'clock when we had re-established contact. The scenes of Montmartre on a bright summer's day looked wonderful through the kitchen window behind her.

'*Oui*, it was really good. We enjoyed it.'

I tried not to think of Nicole and her boyfriend walking along the banks of the Seine, hand in hand. 'Serious?'

'Yes, it was a serious lunch.'

'No, sorry. I meant is the relationship serious? Just being nosey. You don't have to answer if you don't want to.'

'No problem. We've been together three years. We would like to get married, settle down, and have a couple of children when we're ready. Hopefully soon.'

I smiled and wished them both well. I then related what Jamie and his team had found out about Mr Parekh and his activities. I explained our investigations could be limited and asked whether she and, if necessary, Interpol could help us further. She said she had expected to.

'But first you need to know a bit more about the Panama Papers,' she said. 'You and your team need to look into them and search for local connections, since there's a link to the British Virgin Islands. I'll also ask my cyber team to look at them again. We'll liaise more with Interpol.'

'Panama Papers… Panama Papers… Rings a bell, Nicole. Oh, you don't mean the Pandora Papers, do you? They were mentioned on the news recently, but I haven't had much time to follow the story. Millions of leaked financial documents exposing the secret wealth and dealings of the rich and famous around the world, including world leaders and prominent politicians.'

'No, I don't mean the Pandora Papers. Too recent. We're going through the information contained within them at the moment. They will be a treasure trove. No, the Panama Papers are from Panama in Central America. Some time ago, more than eleven million documents from a legal firm called Mossack Fonseca were leaked. The documents contain the financial transactions of more than two hundred thousand offshore companies and individuals. Some of the documents go back twenty years or more. It's possible Mr Parekh and maybe his associates were using the services of this law firm over a few years. The firm was wound up some time ago. But the damage to them and their clients was done.'

'I do remember something about this,' I said. 'Didn't the Panama Papers mention the activities of politicians and film stars too?'

'Yes. If I remember rightly, one of your ex-Prime Ministers was mentioned. So was a famous Hollywood actor. In all, hundreds of celebrities, businesspeople, current and former world leaders and other wealthy individuals were mentioned. From almost all the countries of the world. Good place to use if you want to deal secretly. Although the documents were leaked some time ago, many countries are still taking action against the individuals mentioned. Those involved in illegal activities, that is.'

'More than eleven million documents, you say? That's a lot to go through!'

'Oh, we have lots of software that tracks individuals and different types of data. It's time-consuming, but not difficult. Your IT unit should be able to investigate them. Please give me any more details about Mr Parekh and any of his associates. And the contact details for your IT team. I will get our cyber team and the one at Interpol to look into it too.'

'Thanks, Nicole.'

'You're welcome. We're a team.'

I smiled.

'Oh, by the way, I forgot to mention earlier,' she said. 'We think we've worked out how your dead diver ended up where you found him.'

'What? Why didn't you mention this before?'

'Sorry, Rohan. Once we started talking, I lost my thread, as you British say. Strange expression that, don't you think? I wonder where it comes from?'

I was drumming my fingers on the table, but tried not to sound impatient. 'Maybe when Theseus was in the labyrinth looking to find and kill the minotaur. He tied a piece of string at the start so he could follow it back. Please tell me what you know about the dead diver.'

'Well, I asked for information from the officers of the Directorate here and from officers working at Interpol. Seems there was a case like this in Australia a while ago. You're in the middle of a heatwave, aren't you? Lots of forest fires and so on, yes?'

'Yes, yes, Nicole.'

'They had the same problem in eastern Australia. New South Wales, not far from Sydney. Large forest fires, stretching for miles and miles. Destroyed hundreds and hundreds of acres of vegetation. Millions of wild animals were killed, not to mention sheep and cattle. Many houses and farms were burnt. The fire crews didn't have enough water from the rivers and lakes to douse the fires. They used helicopters fitted with large metal buckets that could hold hundreds of litres of water. The buckets are dropped into the sea and then flown to the fires. The water's then released.

'In one sad case, a scuba diver was swimming in the sea. One of these buckets lifted him up with the water and carried him a long way. Then he was thrown from a great height onto the fires. Poor man. He was in full diving gear and was wearing an air tank. He was reported missing by friends but wasn't found for a long time. Then he was identified through DNA and dental records. The only theory which made sense was this chance in a million. Many people don't believe this story, but it's been confirmed by our Australian colleagues. As they say, when your time's up, it's up. *C'est la vie.*'

I paused and thought about this. What Nicole said fitted all the known facts.

'I know you find it hard to believe, Rohan. But how else can we explain it? Now, what was it Sherlock Holmes once said? "When you have eliminated the impossible, whatever remains, however improbable, must be the truth."'

'Nicole, you really are something else. Thank you. I'll ask a few more questions about what he may've been up to. Now we've got a possible explanation of how he ended up there.'

She smiled. Through the kitchen window behind her, the central dome of the Basilica of Sacré-Coeur sparkled in the late afternoon sun.

'The nylon string around his waist means he was pulling something behind him,' she said after a while. 'It got cut by the plunging metal bucket. Might've been pulling a submersible, possibly full of drugs. They often use a vacuum pump to remove as much air from the submersible as possible. Helps when taking it underwater. Maybe his boat engine was broken.'

'So he was diving underwater and pulling this thing along, full of drugs or whatever. Wouldn't be detected.'

'It's possible. I've asked the Coast Guard here and in Belgium to look for a drifting boat and any submersible — anything washed up on the coast. Would be good if you asked your Coast Guard and Border Force people to do the same, just in case.'

I said I would.

'As you know,' she continued, 'we're also tracking other things, like arms dealers. Most in Europe are — how do you say it? — legit; they work with companies that have licences to sell arms. They have proper end-user certificates, which means they're being sold to different governments and their authorised agencies. But as you can imagine, some arrive in their country of destination and disappear. They end up on the black market, then are sold to opposing sides in places like Syria, Iraq, Central Africa, South America. Other arms are also sold by Russia and China. Billions of *euros* change hands every year.' She leaned sideways and then asked, 'Where's your bird? The parrot? He made me laugh.'

I explained what had happened and she said she was very sorry. She was sure he would come back. They were intelligent creatures. She knew that from her friend who had one.

I so hoped she was right.

We agreed to catch up again after we had done our homework.

CHAPTER 26

Just over a week later, I was sitting in the incident room with Jamie Shriver. It was early morning. He looked tired, his dark hair unkempt, dark pouches under his eyes.

'Sorry, been up all night, Sir. Tracking cyber accounts and activities in different parts of the world. Needed to monitor activities in real time, so the various time zones have played havoc with my body clock.'

'No need to apologise, Jamie. I'm grateful to you and your team for all the work you've done.'

He smiled, the dark stubble on his top lip showing flecks of grey. 'Thank you, Sir. We've delved deeply into the Panama Papers, worked with cyber teams from France and also with Interpol, as you suggested. Our Mr Parekh is an enthusiastic user of the dark web. Managed to track his movements eventually. Well, most of them — not sure we know all of what he does. He uses many aliases, one of them being under the company name APEX Enterprises. Obviously the first two letters are his initials. He's set up many offshore accounts on the British Virgin Islands, Turks and Caicos, and the Cayman Islands. Also, there were payments into Swiss bank accounts and also accounts in Singapore. Interpol were very good at identifying those in particular, given their connections.

'Anyway, we identified payments made from his accounts to people in Syria, Iraq and Afghanistan. There were also transfers to an account in Odessa in Ukraine, as well as payments into accounts in Kampala in Uganda.'

'That could be for the cobalt,' I said.

Jamie nodded. 'The individuals receiving the money,' he continued, 'could be real or they could be fictitious. But there are addresses linked to the accounts, which seem to be real. Could be easily tracked down if we wanted to do so. Would need help from Interpol.'

'Hold on, Jamie. Let's go through that some more. The payments to Syria and Iraq could be for arms or stolen antiquities, couldn't they?'

'Both could be possible. But they're more likely to be for stolen antiquities, because we're talking payments of several hundred thousand pounds over short periods of time. Or they could be payments for the supply of heroin from Afghanistan. Again, the size of the payments would indicate that. Armaments could run into millions, depending on what was purchased.'

'But small arms and ammunition could account for the figures we're talking about, couldn't they?'

'Could do, yes. But we've also got sizeable payments going to two individuals in Cairo and one in Alexandria in Egypt. There's no large-scale fighting, arms trade or major players we're aware of in Egypt. More likely to be for stolen antiquities from the Valley of the Kings, from Libya and from the Cairo Museum. The museum was ransacked a few years ago during the Arab Spring and many treasures disappeared.'

I recalled what Dr Tyburn had told me about the wholescale looting of Mesopotamian antiquities from museums in war-torn countries.

'What about Odessa? Any ideas about the connection there?'

'Odessa's always been dodgy. If you want anything on the black market, you can get it delivered there. It's a port on the Black Sea. Corruption's a way of life there. Goods arrive there, no questions asked. Then they're transported to Europe, the

Middle East, anywhere in the world really. It's also an important staging post for the heroin trade in Afghanistan.'

'What about Singapore?'

'Not sure about that. We're working on it. Mr Parekh's got several accounts on the British Virgin Islands. Considerable sums have been deposited into them from three accounts in Singapore. We tried to dig deeper into those accounts, but their firewall is really good. Couldn't break into it.'

'Is that legal, Jamie?'

He looked at me with bloodshot eyes, then shrugged.

I didn't probe any further. There was probably some legal loophole in money-laundering cases which allowed us to do this. I would look into it when I got a chance.

'I got Her Majesty's Revenue and Customs to give me his tax returns and other relevant information,' I said. 'Had to get a warrant. They confirmed the turnover from Parekh's restaurants and jewellery shops runs to a couple of million pounds. He pays the appropriate level of tax on his declared profits. The modest profits do not explain his apparent wealth, the house and the rapid expansion of his business. I also got in touch with the relevant financial authorities. He's borrowed some money in the past, but not the amounts needed to expand his business empire. The funding had to come from somewhere else.'

'Well,' said Jamie, 'he's got access to millions in his offshore accounts. It all comes in from different accounts in different parts of the world. It's a sophisticated money-laundering operation.'

'What about moving money from this country to another country? How difficult could that be?'

'Not that difficult, Sir, according to the officers from Interpol that I spoke to. International banks in the City of

London operate in such a market and will transfer money fairly readily. No problem at all. The bigger the amount, the greater the commission for them.' Jamie looked at me, then went on, 'There's one account that doesn't quite fit in with the rest — payments of several hundred thousand pounds over several years to an account holder in the UK. The address is Hunstanton in Norfolk, and the name of the account holder is Pietro Francisco.'

'Peter Fraser? Our diver?' I asked. Gordon Priestley had stated that Fraser had a house on the coast, but he had claimed not to know the address. Grace's enquiries about it had drawn a blank so far. Not surprising, given the change in name.

Before Jamie could respond, my mobile rang.

'Sorry, Jamie,' I said as I saw it was Grace and accepted the call. 'Good morning, Grace. What you got?'

'Well, I chased up the Border Force people and the Coast Guard in Norfolk, as you asked. BF found a boat drifting in the North Sea some time ago. No idea of its identity or owner. Towed it into harbour, and it's currently moored in Lowestoft. Further north, the CG found a pale blue craft floating in the sea. It was difficult to see in the sea, given its colour. It was mostly airtight, they said, so difficult for it to sink. It was not far from Mablethorpe in Lincolnshire. They brought it in and found packets of heroin and cocaine worth a fortune. Again, they had no idea where it came from. They did confirm there was a nylon string attached to it — cut in half or a quarter or whatever. If it's the dead diver's submersible, then the forensics team should be able to match the serrated cuts of the string with each other.'

'Good work, Grace. Thanks very much.'

I turned round and said to Jamie, 'Think I've answered my own question.'

I was about to explain what Grace had just told me when the pay-as-you-go mobile phone rang in my briefcase. I fished it out.

'Hello, is that Mr Sharma, the man who's lost his parrot?'

'Yes, it is.'

'My name's George,' the voice at the other end said. He sounded young. 'Think I've found him.'

My heart leapt with excitement. 'Where?'

'In the woods. Near the north reservoir.'

'Grey feathers, white near the neck and head, big round eyes?'

'Yes, he looks like that.'

'Is he okay?'

'I don't think so. He don't look too good.'

'Why?'

'His head's missing. There's blood all over his body.'

I rushed to my Mercedes in the car park. Why on earth had I released Fernando? Oh God, why had I done it? He was my one loyal friend — somebody who had been with me all my life. And now he'd been killed. *Please forgive me, Fernando. Please.*

Other officers in the car park stared at me as I ran past, breathing heavily. Sweat poured down my scalp in the mid-morning sun.

I wanted to take a police car, blue lights flashing. Other traffic would have given way. But I knew I couldn't — this wasn't official business. And, in the clear light of day, there wasn't anything I could do to save Fernando. My car would have to do.

I drove at speed along the busy dual carriageway, past the hospital and university and finally onto the main arterial road leading out of the city. I was breaking the speed limit, but I was hoping that if any traffic officers saw me, they would recognise my car and assume I was rushing to a crime scene or some other emergency.

Please forgive me, Fernando, I kept thinking. Fernando, whom I had looked after all my adult life. The one who made wisecracks. The one who mimicked Faye having an orgasm. *Oh, God, please Fernando, don't go*. But I knew it was too late. My chest felt heavy. The rush of blood pounded in my eardrums.

Cars coming in the opposite direction were one long blur. The bright sun on the horizon reflected off my windscreen. I pulled down the visor and leaned down to get a better view of the road. Cars blared their horns as I performed risky overtaking manoeuvres. I hit the speed dial number for the park ranger at the reservoir, hoping she could get to Fernando and let me know what had happened. No reply. I rang George again, who said he was waiting. He wanted to know if he would get the hundred pounds reward money I had offered for further information about Fernando's whereabouts. I said I would honour the offer of a reward. I kept trying the ranger's number, but the voicemail kept cutting in.

Thirty minutes later my tyres squealed as I turned a corner and headed to the car park nearest to where Fernando had been sighted. I hit the brakes. My body lunged forward. I flung open the car door and ran towards the woods in the distance. An ambulance, blue lights flashing, sat in the car park. Sweat dripped down my temples, my armpits and along my back. My chest hurt as I fought to breathe. I ran as fast as I could, my legs getting heavy. A young boy stood near the first clump of trees, clutching the handlebars of an electric scooter, and waved to me. I struggled towards him. To the right, a young woman in a brown ranger's uniform jogged towards me.

'I'm Gill,' she said. 'George alerted us to the problem. You must be Inspector Sharma.'

I nodded.

'Sorry, couldn't answer your call. Had an emergency on the pleasure cruiser. One of the passengers had a suspected cardiac arrest. Had to perform CPR. The paramedics are now looking after him. Hopefully, he'll make a full recovery.'

I hobbled towards George, bent down and introduced myself. 'Where ... where ... is ... he?'

'Over there, under that big tree.' He pointed.

I ran towards it, my lungs hurting, the shade of the large maple tree making it difficult to see anything. As I approached the parched brown grass, I saw bloody grey feathers, a long grey tail. The body was emaciated. Poor Fernando. The boy was right, the head was missing. He'd obviously been killed by a bird of prey and then the head had been devoured by a fox or some such wild animal.

My heart ached. Why had I let him go? Why?

Then I thought, *I have nothing to take him home in. No shoebox, no bag. He deserved better.* I turned to Gill. She knew what I was thinking.

'I'll be back soon,' she said. 'I'm sure we have some disposable gloves and something to wrap him in.'

The boy stood next to me. He had freckles, ginger hair, and pale blue eyes. 'I'm sorry, Mister. Sorry about your parrot. You must've liked him a lot to come straight here.'

'I loved him, George.' I tried not to let him see the tears in my eyes.

Gill arrived back not long after. I put on the disposable gloves while she held open a large plastic Tupperware box lined with tissues, the clip-on lid underneath.

'Left by somebody on a picnic,' she said, and offered a comforting smile.

I squatted down and my knees cracked. I tried to hide the pain. I stared at the body before picking it up and standing. I held the body in my right palm, turned it over and saw deep red claw marks on the chest. It was almost weightless. The feet were curled tight in rigor mortis and looked like two small, dark trowels.

I looked at George, then at the ranger. 'This isn't Fernando,' I said. 'It's a pigeon.'

CHAPTER 27

Grace and I were sitting in my car, some distance from Anand Parekh's house. It was very early in the morning — just past five o'clock. The rising sun's rays warmed the side of my face.

'What're you thinking about?' asked Grace.

I felt a hollow pain in my chest. It was a question Faye had often asked after we had made love and we were in that relaxed, floating mood where nothing else in life mattered.

I turned round and looked into Grace's eyes. There were early signs of crow's feet at the edges. She smiled. I smiled back.

I wanted to tell her that the sun's rays in the early morning would often form two dancing shadows on the bedroom ceiling. They had reminded me of two dodos staring lovingly at each other.

'Hello? Is anybody there?' she asked, nudging my bare arm with hers.

'Oh, sorry, nothing significant, Grace,' I replied.

'I know that means the opposite of what it's meant to mean.'

'Isn't it sad when bad things happen to good sentences?' I replied, and laughed.

She joined in, then asked, 'And what about George? Did you pay him the reward?'

'Well, I was in a bit of a quandary about that. Since it wasn't Fernando, thank God, I didn't pay him the full amount. I gave him twenty pounds for his trouble. He seemed happy with that.'

'It was good you'd put up flyers in the area. Certainly helped.'

My eyes rested on hers. Her dark brown irises reflected the pale morning sunlight. She suppressed a yawn.

I eventually said, 'Yes, it was, wasn't it?' I then turned back to face the house.

I had asked Superintendent Breedon to secure a warrant for us to search all of Parekh's properties, and he had reluctantly agreed. I asked for another senior officer to lead the search of his restaurants and jewellery shops and requested help from other forces with Parekh's properties in various parts of the country.

I had contacted the Planning Department of the council to secure the design of the building, but I could remember much of it from when I'd last visited. I briefed the team in detail. The firm that monitored the security cameras had been forewarned not to alert anyone in the house. Behind me was a police van with six armed officers in full protective gear, including body armour and helmets. In front of us was another van with a further six officers, similarly dressed and equipped. Two specialist officers with sniffer dogs were in an estate car not far away.

It was important that all the raids were co-ordinated at the same time. I was equipped with a body camera and encrypted radio to collect evidence and to synchronise the bust.

'Strike! Strike! Strike!' I called over the airwaves. My voice reached all the teams around the country.

The armoured van drove slowly to the front of the imposing wooden gate. The bumper rested against it and the driver skilfully nudged it, inch by inch. There was a loud crack as the inner crossbars gave way and the two doors were breached. The van then sped along the tarmac drive, the other van and estate car behind. Within moments we were at the front door. Officers jumped out of the van, two with a red metal battering ram taking turns to break down the front door, while a few shouted, 'Police! Open up! Armed police!' The wooden door came crashing down, splintered from the frame. The great white shark door knocker rested at my feet. Somewhere within the house, the burglar alarm shrieked.

We rushed in, breathing heavily. I ran upstairs with two officers and kicked the bedroom door. My foot hurt. I then turned the doorknob, opening the door. A large king-size bed was to the left. Light streamed through the partially open curtains. Anand Parekh sat on the bed, trying to put on his underwear. Under the cotton sheets, the pale brown face of a young woman cowered.

Parekh turned round. 'Sharma, what the hell are you doing in my house?'

'Calm down, Mr Parekh. We've got a warrant to search this place. And everywhere else you own. Looking for contraband, drugs, anything illegal.'

'You're a real bastard, Sharma! Got no idea what you're talking about. Everything's legit. I'm going to get you for this.'

'Now, now, Mr Parekh. Wouldn't threaten a police officer if I were you. Got plenty of witnesses.'

'I was referring to your job.'

Yeah, like hell, I thought.

'Get your girlfriend here to get dressed. And you, too. Seen better sights than that. And while my officers search your house, you can both stay put.'

He glared at me. The young woman covered her head with the sheets.

CHAPTER 28

The faint rumbling and the occasional horn of the morning commuter traffic could be heard in the distance as we continued searching the large house and its grounds. Anand Parekh sat in one of the reclining chairs in the spacious reception room at the back of the house, a wall of bifold doors looking out over the immaculate lawn and swimming pool. A blackbird landed on the rim of the marble birdbath, dipped its beak in the water and stretched back its head as the warming sunlight bathed the day. A solitary magpie hopped under a lush rhododendron bush.

'Y'know what they say about seeing one magpie, don't you, Mr Parekh?' I said, as I strolled into the room. 'One for sorrow, two for joy.' The two officers standing guard near the door moved to one side.

'Is that the best you can do, *Mister* Sharma? A stupid English song for children? Haven't found anything, have you?'

Black curly chest hair, mixed with grey, poked out of the top of his dark blue silk dressing gown.

'Oh, but we have. We found the young woman with you. And we haven't finished searching yet.'

'What, you mean Salma? Syrian, hardly speaks English. But she's skilled in the language of love.' He smirked.

'But she's somebody's daughter. Somebody's sister. Doesn't that bother you?'

He shrugged.

'She may not speak English,' I continued, 'but she speaks fluent French. As does one of my officers. She told us she was in a refugee camp in Jordan; she went there to escape the fighting in Syria and was promised a good job and a great life in the UK. She was smuggled here, and what happens? She was locked up, and now she doesn't see anybody apart from a few other young women, all living in the same room. They're not allowed out, apart from to service dirty old men like you.'

'And what was she going to do in a camp in Jordan? Rot with the others. At least here she's got a bit of money and nice clothes. She gets to meet nice people and eat well.'

'What money? What nice people?' I shouted. 'She's a slave! She's doing time on the cross. Just like Jesus did while dying a slow, painful death.'

'My, my! A Hindu man talking about a Muslim woman and referring to a dead Jew. Got problems with your identity, have you, Mister Sharma?'

'We're taking her away from the likes of you, so she can have a decent life.'

'What, and end up in a homeless hostel with other refugees and asylum seekers? She'll be raped and abused. And for what? For nothing. Who'll protect her there?'

I didn't answer. 'Where're the others?' I eventually asked.

He shrugged. 'Don't know what you're talking about.'

'We'll find them, Mr Parekh. We'll find them. Along with the drugs and the stolen antiquities. Got plenty of evidence against you. And she's told us she knew Hasina.'

The mask slipped for a second or two. Then he said, 'I like to laugh, too. *Hasina* means to laugh, doesn't it?'

Before I could say anything more, Grace walked into the room. 'Sorry to disturb you, Sir. But we found something you'll be interested in.'

'What on earth are you talking about?' asked Anand Parekh, as Grace and I walked out of the room. His voice was not as confident as before.

In the corridor, Grace placed the item in the palm of my hand. There was no doubt about what it was, and I put it into my pocket.

I waited half an hour before finally going back into the room, letting Parekh sweat a bit longer.

'What've you found?' he demanded as I walked in.

'Thought you said there was nothing to find. Why're you so worried now?' I pulled up a chair in front of him and looked straight into his soulless brown eyes. 'Look, Mr Parekh. It's best if you come clean. We've got financial records showing you paid off unsavoury characters in Syria and Afghanistan. We know these payments were for stolen antiquities in Syria. Also, there were payments to well-known warlords in Afghanistan who own poppy fields and manufacture heroin — good chance the drug money was used to pay for the antiquities. And you're also involved with the sex trade here.'

Parekh laughed. 'What financial records? What warlords? You've got to be joking. I run restaurants and jewellery shops.'

'Yes, you do. But that's a front. We've seen your tax records from the HMRC. You wouldn't be able to buy a house like this on what you declare. I know there's no mortgage on this property.'

He stared at the floor.

'Heard the name Pietro Francisco?' I continued. 'With the account in Hunstanton? We know you made substantial payments into that account. We can easily find out his real name. And we know you've made payments to people in Egypt — definitely for stolen antiquities there. Egypt isn't known for growing opium.'

'That's for perfume bottles and papyrus drawings. Tourists love that sort of thing. They want to buy them here, too.'

'What, for hundreds of thousands of pounds? Where d'you sell them? None of your shops do.'

'Online.' He shuffled in his seat.

'And what about the cobalt, moved from the Democratic Republic of Congo to Kampala in Uganda to Hong Kong?'

'Nothing illegal about that. I told you before, I buy and sell anything that makes me money.'

'Nothing illegal, I grant you that. But highly immoral and against UN guidance. There're specific limits on how much can be exported. It leads to the deaths of hundreds of children.'

'Oh, they wouldn't have lived long anyway. You know Africa. Disease and starvation would've killed them eventually.'

I clenched my fist.

'Go on, punch me. Just do it!' he shouted.

'Be careful what you wish for, Mr Parekh.'

'You've got nothing on me,' he said, smirking. 'Just vague references to financial records you may've forged. And slanderous assertions. Since there's nothing here, I insist you leave my property. And I'll sue you for all the damage you and your officers have caused.'

'Not so fast, Mr Parekh,' I replied. 'A lorry driver was murdered in Turkey in a nasty manner. Very cruel. We believe you were involved in his death.'

'You have got to be joking!'

'And you will be extradited to Turkey to face a murder charge. You know what those Turkish prisons are like. You wouldn't survive long. You'll be locked up for the rest of your life. And just imagine the things other prisoners will do to you. They're very imaginative with broom handles.'

There was a momentary hint of panic in his brown eyes.

'And we know an Afghan lorry driver was brutally killed in Syria as well. We can link these deaths to you and your accomplices. We also think you were involved in the killing of a local drug dealer named Bobby. And you know what, Mr Parekh? Your friends don't trust you. Look what we found in your conservatory: a microphone hidden in one of the plant pots.'

'You planted it there,' he replied.

'Yeah, in a plant pot. Watered it regularly, hoping it would grow.'

'Look, Inspector Sharma. I had nothing to do with murder. I've no idea who killed Bobby. I liked him. I saw him around. And I have no idea about the other two deaths you're talking about.'

'Well, we can go to the station and talk further, if you like. Or we can talk here. You heard of the Panama Papers?'

He combed back his thick hair with his manicured fingers, now realising where some of our information had come from. The Panama Papers revealed traceable bank accounts. 'I swear to God I didn't know anything about Bobby's death. I heard about the one in Turkey and the one in Syria. Well, I heard The Scorpion was involved.'

I looked up. Nicole had also mentioned the female gang member in connection with the two lorry drivers' deaths. 'What can you tell me about The Scorpion?'

'It lives in the desert, mainly. Has a sting in its tail.'

'This is no joke!'

'She's a woman. Bad piece of work. Kills at will. I believe she's an Indian woman from Kenya. She was kidnapped as a child and grew up in Somalia, then joined the jihadis in Syria. She's supposed to be pretty and has a birthmark on the back of her neck. But I've never seen her, so I can't say for certain. That's all I know.'

The blood drained from my face.

CHAPTER 29

I followed the convoy out of the main gate. Salma sat in the back of my car with Grace. We were going back to HQ, and then we would process the documentation so she would be properly looked after, either in a safe place for asylum seekers or in a women's refuge. The officer with a good knowledge of French had explained this to her and she'd smiled. She'd asked whether she could make a phone call to Jordan and Syria to let her family and friends know she was safe. I said that wouldn't be a problem.

As we drove along the outer ring road towards the city, she looked in wonder at the tall buildings, the traffic and the houses. She had been locked up during most of the day, and at night she had been taken to various places to sleep with men. I tried to hide my anger at the thought of this.

I dwelled on what Anand Parekh had said about The Scorpion. No, it couldn't be. It had to be a coincidence. It felt as if my heart was being squeezed. I switched off the car's air conditioner and opened the windows a few inches. I felt the warm air on my face, breathed in deeply and slowly breathed out again.

No, it just couldn't be, I thought. The irony would be too cruel.

I saw Grace staring at me in the rear-view mirror. She smiled as she put a comforting arm round Salma's shoulder.

My phone rang and I answered. Ben Carter's voice echoed in the car.

'Sir, we found a DNA match for the semen sample taken from our female victim. Remember, the African-Caribbean sample? Not a direct match, but from familial DNA. You'll never believe who it belongs to. A well-respected teacher! Somebody you know.'

Treacherously, my mind went straight to Pierre, Faye's partner, though I knew that was unworthy of me. I sped towards HQ as Ben updated me on the situation.

After leaving Salma in the capable and comforting hands of the team responsible for vulnerable people, Grace and I made our way to the large academy on the southern outskirts of the city. It was late August and schools in Leicestershire were open again for the autumn term, well ahead of other schools nationally. The school holidays here were still governed by the closures of factories and mines dating back to the nineteenth century.

I drove slowly up the long drive leading to the academy's reception area. Trees lined either side of the tarmac road and the grassy areas were weed-free and well-tended, despite the lack of rain. An occasional bright yellow dandelion drooped near the edge of the tarmac. The front office area was busy with an assortment of staff and students, one of whom was being looked after by the school nurse. We introduced ourselves to the receptionist, surreptitiously showed our identity badges and were informed that the member of staff we needed to speak to was on the playing field, observing a class being taught aspects of health and emotional well-being. He was pointed out to us from the large window and the receptionist offered to fetch him, but I said it wasn't necessary since she was obviously busy.

As we approached, we could hear the teacher talking to a student who had been taken aside: '…and when I feel lonely and depressed, Jason, I always speak to my partner. Quite often, her daughter, not much older than you, tries to help too, and she hugs me.'

'Really, Sir? Don't think of you feeling down. You're always so happy.'

'We all feel down sometimes, Jason.'

'Thank you for talking to me, Sir. Don't know many people I can trust.'

'You're welcome.'

'Good afternoon,' I said.

David Griffiths, the academy's principal, looked round at me and then Grace. He smiled in recognition. 'Inspector Sharma? My PA didn't tell me you were expected. Didn't think we had another careers talk from you today.' He turned to Jason and asked him to join the rest of the class. 'Just observing and helping the newly qualified teacher, Inspector Sharma. First few weeks of teaching.'

David shook my hand. I introduced him to Grace. He was tall and athletic, elegant in his starched white shirt and pale blue tie with a red paisley pattern. His widow's peak was immaculately groomed.

'How are you? And what're you doing here? You haven't come to arrest me, have you?' He laughed.

'Shall we go to your office, David?'

'Sounds serious. No, here's fine,' he said, looking around.

'Not here to arrest you, David. But that's still a possibility.'

'What on earth are you talking about?'

'Do you know a young woman called Hasina?'

'No.' His hands trembled. A thin trickle of sweat ran down his temple, and a drop rested in the oval-shaped, pitted scar of a childhood injury. He yanked out a handkerchief and wiped his forehead. 'Hot, isn't it?'

'Hasina was the young woman found dead in the river a few weeks ago, or so we believe. You must've heard about it.'

'Jesus Christ,' he said. 'Was that her name? You don't think I had anything to do with that, do you?'

'David, I think it would be best if we went to your office and talked about this.'

'No, I'm fine here.'

'Okay, as long as you're sure.'

He stared at me and shook his head, his smooth dark skin glowing under the perspiration. He wiped his brow again.

'Sir, Sir!' shouted a student, running towards us. 'Sharon's calling me names.'

'I'm sorry, I'm busy, Leanne. Please speak to your teacher. I'm sure she'll sort it out.'

Leanne stopped, stared at Grace and I, then wandered off.

'Your niece Jessica was caught drink driving a few days ago,' I said.

'Was she?' He paused. The raucous sound of teenagers playing happily, laughing and shouting, could be heard from the far side of the field. 'I didn't know. Anyway, what's that got to do with me?' he asked.

I looked at Grace.

'When people commit a serious crime,' she said, 'like your niece did, we take a mouth swab, get a DNA sample. The results are registered with a national database. If that person commits another crime, we can usually match any DNA traces to them.'

'Yes, but I haven't committed a crime. I haven't had a mouth swab.'

'You may not have given a swab, Sir, but with the rapid advances in technology, we can now match DNA samples to members of the same family. This is known as familial DNA.'

David Griffiths licked his top lip. His ivory-white teeth flashed momentarily, and he stared at Grace and then at me.

'We found samples of your DNA, through your semen, in Hasina's vagina,' Grace continued. 'It had been placed there not long before she died.'

He looked at the uneven concrete ground below his feet. 'Jesus Christ,' he said. 'What if my wife finds out?'

'David, at the moment, that's the least of your worries,' I said. 'This is a murder investigation. We need to know your role in all of this. Let's go to your office. Tell your PA you're not to be disturbed.'

He nodded.

CHAPTER 30

David Griffiths sat behind his dark wooden desk in front of a large window with white venetian blinds. 'You have to believe me when I say I didn't know her real name,' he said.

Grace raised an eyebrow. I waited for further explanation. Students laughed as they walked along the corridor outside.

Eventually, he went on, 'All the women were named after flowers, depending on where they came from. One was called *African Violet*, another was *English Rose*, *Buttercup* was Chinese, *Marigold* was Indian. There was the *Afghan Daisy*, the *Asian Bird of Paradise*, *Blue Passion Flower*, and the *White Rose* from Syria.'

'How did you contact them?'

'On the dark web. Easy to find. There are photos of the women, along with what they could help you with.'

'Who did you liaise with?' I asked.

'She's known as the *Fairy Queen*. She makes all your dreams come true — anything at all. But I'm not into the kinky stuff.' He looked at Grace and tried to smile. She frowned.

A framed photograph of his wife and young daughter stood in one corner of the desk. Both were smiling and hugging each other under a leaning palm tree on a tropical beach, looking straight at the camera. I tried not to think of their future heartache.

'I swear to God, Inspector Sharma, I had nothing to do with her death. I met with her, stayed with her for about an hour each time and then I left. She was always glad to see me. She said she'd not been with a Black man before. She asked if I was a Muslim because of … well, I won't go into the intimate details.'

'Where did you meet her?'

'Always in a hotel room. And the hotels kept changing. Never the same place twice.'

'How about payment?'

He paused and looked down at his desk, trying not to look at the photograph. He cleared his throat. 'Online account, believe it or not. Well-known company. You probably use it. Once the payment was made, you were sent a text message by the *Fairy Queen* telling you the name of the hotel and room number. You had to book at least a day in advance. For the kinkier stuff, you went to isolated farmhouses, where you couldn't be disturbed.' He reached into the side drawer and jotted the name of the website and a phone number onto a notepad. He handed me the notepaper.

'Our tech team will be able to track down the *Fairy Queen* through the phone number and the IP address of the website,' I said.

'Look, please, you've got to believe me. The last time I saw her, I met her in Room 315 and was with her for an hour, and then I went. You can check with the hotel. I was on my own.' He named the hotel.

'Oh, we'll check. They'll have CCTV cameras everywhere,' I said.

'She liked to see me,' he continued. 'She thought I might be able to help her. She said she'd been smuggled into Britain from Afghanistan with her brother. They were forced apart in the middle of the night when they landed here. She didn't know what had happened to him. She couldn't escape. She wanted me to go to the police on her behalf.'

'But you didn't. And look what happened to her.'

'God, if only I'd known, I would have. But I thought she was exaggerating. And then I had my position to consider. Didn't want that compromised.'

Grace gave him a scathing look.

'She really did like me… She even let me do it without a condom. Against the rules, but she said she was given precautions in case the condom burst.'

The lingering silence hung in the cool air.

'At the moment, David, you're a suspect in a murder investigation. It seems you were one of the last people to see her alive.'

'I had no reason to kill her. God help me, it's true. I couldn't do anything like that. I'm a schoolteacher.'

I tried hard not to respond to the hypocrisy.

'Did you see anyone else, either before or after you went to see her? Another man? Caucasian?' asked Grace.

'No. Why're you asking?'

'Not to worry.' She looked at me.

'Given the seriousness of the situation, David,' I said, 'you'll have to come to the station to make a formal statement. We're not charging you with anything because there's no evidence yet to link you directly with the murder —'

'What do you mean "yet"?'

'— and you didn't withhold information,' I continued, 'because you didn't know who the victim was. Or so you say. But you're a person of interest. Once you make a statement, we'll release you on police bail, pending further investigations.'

He looked at me, wide-eyed. 'Please don't do this to me. My career. My family.'

Should have thought of that before, I thought.

CHAPTER 31

Three days later, I pulled off the main road, drove into a wealthy village south of the city, and then entered a circular drive leading to a large, opulent house. Grace pulled up in her car behind me. Jamie Shriver and his team had worked round the clock to identify the various accounts and find the addresses they were linked to in the UK, Singapore and the Caribbean. We had to threaten senior executives of the UK headquarters of the online payments' company that if they didn't co-operate with our enquiries, then we would get a warrant to search their records and could also charge them with more serious matters relating to their possible role, however unwitting, in murder. They relented.

The gravel beneath our feet crunched as we walked to the black wooden door with a brass knocker in the shape of a winking Tinkerbell and an obvious spyhole through the open eye. The red light of a security camera blinked high above my head. I rang the doorbell and heard the loud chimes in the hallway. A few moments later, the security chain clinked, the Yale lock was turned, the key to the mortice lock squeaked and the door handle pointed down.

An immaculately groomed middle-aged woman with shoulder-length blonde hair opened the door.

'Well, you're not wearing a dark suit,' she said, looking at my expensive summer suit, 'and you're not carrying a copy of *The Watchtower*, so you're not here to convert me. But whatever it is you and your friend are here to sell, we don't buy at the door.' She tried to close the door, her bright red nail polish glimmering in the sun.

I put my foot out. 'Are you Mrs Hardcastle? Felicity Hardcastle?' I asked.

'Yes, I am. And who exactly are you?'

We showed our badges.

'My husband's not been caught speeding again, has he? I'm really sorry. He'll be back soon.' She brushed back her hair, a heavy gold bracelet falling down her wrist.

'Don't know about that, Mrs Hardcastle. It's you we've come to see.'

'Why? What's this all about?'

'I think it would be best if we came in to discuss things with you.'

Her blue-grey eyes flicked from me to Grace and then back to me. She pulled the door back and led us into a magnificent lounge with shag pile carpets and expensive furniture.

She pointed to a settee, where Grace and I sat down. She sat opposite, crossing her legs. She then lit a cigarette, put the gold lighter on the side table next to her and said, 'I know it's a bad habit, but I need to.' Her fingers trembled as she put the filter tip between her lips and drew in the smoke. She took a long drag before exhaling. I looked away, towards the open French doors.

'Do you know a Mr Griffiths?' I eventually asked.

'Never heard of him.'

'Well, he knows you. Or of you, shall we say?' said Grace.

Her eyes pierced Grace. 'How does he know *of me*?' she asked.

'Are you also known as the *Fairy Queen*?'

After an eternity of silence, Felicity Hardcastle said, 'Oh, I see. The online account details. He told you how he made payments. And then you dug around.'

We didn't answer.

'Look, I know why you're here. But I've done nothing wrong. They book online and make a payment. Then they're allocated numbers, they go to the hotel, the girl or girls are there and that's it. No money changes hands. I don't know who the clients are.'

It reminded me of a scandal I'd read about whilst at university. High-powered figures, including judges, politicians and Cabinet Ministers in a previous Conservative government had paid for services using luncheon vouchers issued by an upmarket brothel in south London. Any taste was catered for.

'Mrs Hardcastle, we're here because we're investigating a murder.'

'What? You got to be joking.'

'We never joke about death,' replied Grace.

She took another puff of the cigarette and flicked some ash into the heavy, frosted Lalique ashtray. 'The girls were provided by Mr Parekh. I assume you know him. It was his idea to set up a website with different passwords for different levels. It depended on how the clients wanted to be serviced. All were straight. All were adults. Didn't deal with, shall we say, more exotic preferences.'

'How did you choose the women?'

'They were brought to some warehouse or industrial unit in the middle of the night, usually in a lorry. Many were in a filthy state, having travelled for days or sometimes weeks. They had to be cleaned up, fed and looked after. The doctor checked them over. They were told what was expected of them. His heavies beat up any that refused to co-operate. They all did, eventually. Some did live action on webcams — this was a good little earner on the side, too.'

I stared at her. She had given a clinical description, showing no remorse. I tried to focus.

'Ever heard the name Hasina?' asked Grace.

'No. They were all given names. Pretty, colourful flowers. Never knew their real names. Best for me not to know, if you see what I mean.'

'No. I'm sorry, I don't,' I said. 'I can't imagine what those poor girls must have gone through.'

'They were better off here than in their own rat-infested and diseased countries,' she barked. 'At least they were properly looked after and kept in various safehouses.'

Time on the cross, I thought again.

'Anyway, no, I don't know who this Hasina is. But I'm sorry she's dead.' The eyes looked down at the carpet — a sure sign she wasn't telling the truth. 'Different girls came and went. I didn't ask any questions. If any disappeared, it wasn't that unusual.'

'You must've heard of the body found in the river? The one without a head or hands?'

'I heard about it but didn't give it any thought. It wasn't her, was it?'

Grace ignored the question. 'How did you meet Mr Parekh?'

'At a gala dinner in a plush hotel in Park Lane, London. It was during the days when my husband was a successful businessman. We were there for a charity ball. Anybody who was anybody was there.'

'And? Your involvement?'

'I used to run a dating website. I was having difficulty securing clients who'd pay for an exclusive service. With my husband's business collapsing, one thing led to another. It was easy money.'

She inhaled the cigarette smoke deeply, held it in, then threw back her head and blew it towards the ceiling. A white gold chain with a diamond pendant sat easily on her pale neck. It glittered in the sunlight streaming into the room.

'What about the money? What happened?' Grace asked.

'I transferred the money, minus my fifteen per cent, from the online account to the offshore account in Singapore. From there I transferred it to the British Virgin Islands, or wherever it was required. All offshore. All under an assumed name.'

'Which is?'

'APEX Enterprises. AP stands for Andy Parker.'

Anand Parekh, I thought to myself.

She took a final puff of her cigarette and stubbed out the end in the ashtray. Then she looked at me. 'Well, what happens now, Inspector?'

'Mrs Hardcastle, we're arresting you on a charge of living off immoral earnings. We also believe you're involved in the trafficking of people.'

She was wide-eyed. 'You Black bastard! I've done nothing wrong!'

I read her her rights. Grace asked her to stand up and quickly handcuffed her. She rang the patrol car waiting in a nearby street to take the suspect to HQ to be charged.

Felicity Hardcastle screamed and started kicking. One of the stiletto heels caught me in the shin and I tried to hide the pain.

My mobile rang just as we were struggling to get Mrs Hardcastle into the back of the patrol car. It was from an unknown number, but had stopped ringing by the time I slammed the car door shut.

We followed the patrol car back to HQ and I formally charged Mrs Hardcastle with the offences, and also said she was a suspect in others. She was still kicking and screaming and spat in my face as she was led into the custody suite.

It was early afternoon before Grace and I arrived at Anand Parekh's house. A patrol car was stationed nearby, just in case.

After announcing ourselves into the intercom system, we drove through the heavy wooden gates, which had undergone temporary repairs after the damage caused the other day. We pulled up at the end of the long drive outside the main doors.

'I'm not sure what I can help you with,' said Anand Parekh, as he led us into the same spacious reception room we had been in before. 'I know I don't have a choice at the moment in speaking to you. You don't have any evidence against me. I'm still on police bail, which, incidentally, I've asked my solicitor to challenge in the courts. And I've also asked him to make a formal complaint against you for harassing me.'

I looked at him and said, 'Well, you're within your rights to do all of that, Mr Parekh.'

Through the bifold doors, at least ten sprinklers sprayed fine drops of water onto the green, luscious lawn. There had been intimations recently from the local water company about introducing a hosepipe ban for gardens to conserve water, but it didn't seem to matter in this household. There were no signs of any ground staff.

'Hope this doesn't take too long, Inspector, because I've got to get to one of my restaurants. I'm getting ready for the evening opening. You'll forgive me for not offering you and your colleague a chair.'

'Not found any bugs in the conservatory recently, Mr Parekh, have you? And I don't mean the flying variety either.'

His brown eyes squinted at me, the folds of skin between the eyebrows more pronounced. He didn't say anything.

I sat down on the settee. Grace sat down next to me.

'I suggest you do the same, Mr Parekh.'

'Look, say what you want to say. Then get out of my house.'

We didn't say anything. Eventually, he sat in the recliner opposite.

'Do you know a Mrs Hardcastle? Felicity Hardcastle?'

'Never heard of her.'

'Are you sure?'

'Are you deaf, Inspector?'

'What about the *Fairy Queen*?'

He stared at me.

'Mr Parekh,' said Grace, lifting her eyes from her notepad, 'I suggest you start co-operating with us. These are serious matters we're asking you about.'

He looked out of the wall of glass. Under one of the sprinklers, a solitary magpie hopped on one foot. It stood still and then ruffled its wet feathers, shaking off some of the excess drops of water. Anand Parekh watched it until it flew off.

'She took payments for the services provided,' he eventually said, a resigned look on his face. 'The money was transferred to an offshore account in Singapore and then to my account in the Caribbean.'

'The one registered in the name of Andy Parker?'

'Yes.'

'And you used that and other money to buy cobalt. Which was eventually sold off at a huge mark-up to the Chinese. Some of this money also financed drugs from Afghanistan and antiquities from the Middle East. All the trade in human misery helped finance this house and your lifestyle.'

He shrugged.

'Not much to do with restaurants and jewellery shops, is it?' I said. 'And then there's the matter of the murders and your possible role in them. If you co-operate with us, then the courts will look upon it favourably. Reduce your sentence.'

The magpie had returned, pecking at a ball of feathers on the ground. The magpie held it and shook it about; then I saw that a small bird hung from its razor-sharp beak.

Parekh looked at me, his long eyelashes flickering. He pouted, then eventually said, 'I really don't know anything about any murders. I had no part in them.'

'What about Bobby?' asked Grace.

'I liked him. Nice kid. Went astray.'

'Yeah, because of you,' I said.

'But, honest to God, I don't know who killed him. Or why.'

The air-conditioning unit just below the ceiling juddered.

'Any accomplices working with you, Mr Parekh?'

He licked his top lip. 'The only thing I can tell you is that he's known as The Boss. And one of the names he uses is Jim. He has properties everywhere. He also has a pilot and helicopter based at East Midlands Airport because a lot of his business is from around here. He uses it to fly across the Channel for his deals. Look for him in the Panama Papers, which is where you probably found the information about me. I was hoping it would stay buried in there, amongst the millions of other documents. He also uses the initials G.M. He gets in touch with me by phone — an encrypted pay-as-you-go mobile. He's the one who organises all the big deals — especially from Afghanistan and the Middle East. I take care of the rest at this end.'

Grace glanced at me and then continued scribbling, shifting her position on the cushion. She crossed her legs.

'How did you meet him?' I asked.

'I was propping up a bar a few years ago. He came in with a couple of his mates, or so I thought. We got talking. When he realised I was an accountant wanting to earn more money, he said I could be useful to him.' He looked at me and shrugged. 'The rest, as they say, is history.'

'And what about Hasina?'

'I didn't know her name. We had so many girls coming and going to different safehouses. But the one you're talking about — he ordered her to be taken out, as he put it. She kept escaping and was becoming too dangerous to the operation.'

'Who killed her?'

'I honestly don't know. Jim has contacts everywhere. He pays informers handsomely, and there are people who'll kill for a few thousand. But The Scorpion, now, she's different.'

'In what way?'

'Only life's experiences make you that cruel. It is something that is learned.'

A ripple of pain darted across my chest. I tried to gather my thoughts. Eventually, I asked, 'Is she here? In the UK?'

'I honestly don't know.'

'Any more?'

He shrugged and said that was all he knew. I said we would need to take him to the station to formally charge him.

He stared at me for a long time. 'Mind if I answer a call of nature first?' he asked.

I looked at Grace.

'No, she can't come with me,' he said, forcing a smile. 'Look, I'm not going to run away. Where d'you think I'm going to go? I've told you everything I know. And you can see the toilet door from here.'

I hesitated. 'Okay, Mr Parekh. But please don't take too long.'

He went through a door situated next to the room we were in. I waited outside and heard the sound of water splashing against the toilet bowl. Then the flush. Then the tap from the wash basin. The hand drier whirring.

After a few moments, the tap was still running.

I knocked on the door. I shouted his name and turned the handle. It was locked from the inside. I asked if he was okay and banged on the door, louder and louder. I kept shouting his name, crashing my body against the door.

The wooden frame eventually cracked and the door flew open. I couldn't believe what I saw.

'Should've gone with him after all, Sir,' said Grace, peering over my shoulder.

The small, frosted window was wide open. I ran towards it and looked out. The clicking sprinklers sprayed water onto the luscious lawn. Silver birch and mature magnolia trees dotted the gardens.

There was no sign of him.

I shouted to Grace to alert the patrol car waiting outside to look out for him, and to ask one of the officers to come into the grounds to help us search. I ran out, and Grace ran behind me, shouting into her mobile. We came out of the nearest door. I ran to the left into the large grounds, while she ran to the right. In the distance, an officer ran towards us from the main gates.

We searched everywhere. In the trees. In the hedges. The garden outhouses.

But there was no sign of him.

The officer on foot approached, breathing heavily. 'Sorry, Sir … no sign of … no sign of him anywhere. But we found an electric scooter near the outer perimeter fence. Under some bushes.'

Fuck! That was why he had escaped so quickly.

Grace bent down, panting, sweat pouring down her temples.

The patrol car drove into the grounds. The officer inside confirmed Parekh was nowhere to be seen in any of the streets nearby. Then he said, 'Hopefully, our drone will have picked him up.'

'What drone?'

'That one,' he said, pointing to the sky. 'Saw it circling as I drove up. It's one of ours, isn't it? You ordered it, didn't you?'

'Shit!' I replied, squinting at the drone as it turned sharply and flew off towards the horizon.

CHAPTER 32

It was late evening. I kept thinking about the events of the day.
We had lost a prime suspect and I should have anticipated
what he might have done. I knew Superintendent Breedon
would pull me up on that, but there was nothing I could do.
We just had to hope we would apprehend Anand Parekh
quickly, and then we'd engage in a damage limitation exercise.
Superintendent Breedon would be worried about the response
of the media, the perceived damage to the reputation of the
police force and his own position within it. He would talk to
the press about how lessons had been learned, procedures had
been tightened and it was unlikely that such an event could
happen again, but nothing could be ruled out. A good
diplomatic response. For me, it was a mistake that I had made,
and I would have to accept it. Human error, pure and simple.

I was more concerned about what Anand Parekh had told
me about the background of The Scorpion. Could it be her?
No, not my younger sister. She couldn't be a killer, could she?
No, definitely not her. But what if she was? Oh, shit. We didn't
even know if she was alive. How the hell could we have both
ended up on the streets of my home city? No, The Scorpion
must be somebody else, not Maya. I had spent a lifetime
longing to see her again, to make sure she was all right. But not
like this.

My heart raced.

My heart ached.

I took another long sip of Pouilly-Fumé and picked up the
phone.

'I'm sorry to ring late, Mum. I wanted to speak to you and Dad. Is he about? Can you put the speakerphone on?'

'What's the matter? You sound a bit … how d'you say … tipsy? Are you okay?'

'I'm fine, Mum. Just wanted to talk to you and Dad about Maya. About when she disappeared.'

'There's nothing more to tell, *Beta*. We've spent years talking about it. Have you eaten? Your father and I just finished ours. A late meal today. It's so warm in the house.'

'Please, Mum, just one more time. Make sure nothing's missed out.'

She sighed, then related the familiar, sorry tale. We'd hidden in the basement when the gang had arrived. The maid had been murdered. I'd sneezed. We'd been discovered. The money and Maya had disappeared forever.

'We went through all of this before,' my mother said wearily. 'When you caught that killer a while ago, the news reporters wanted to know about it. About your life story — our life story. And you told them. You know the facts. There's one thing I don't understand, though. I always wondered how the gang knew we had money in the house. Your father here spent the afternoon with his whore in a hotel room. He thinks nobody knew about her, but the whole town was talking about it. I was quite ashamed. But I couldn't leave him. Where would I have gone with two small children?'

There was an eternity of silence. My father said nothing. Then I heard the scraping of a dining chair and the slamming of a door.

I felt devastated. My father had visited a prostitute? My poor mother, having to cope with that in a small town in the middle of nowhere.

'Please, Mum. Don't call her a whore.'

'Well, it's true. Everybody knew that. Probably dead with AIDS or syphilis by now. Your father must have told her about the money. And she'll have told her boyfriend, who was probably part of the gang. Our family was ruined forever because he couldn't keep it in his pants. My poor baby, my poor Maya. I hope she's all right. I hope she is happy, wherever she is.'

I didn't say anything.

'Anyway,' she said after a while, 'why do you want to know again? Why go through it all again now?'

'Oh, no reason, Mum. Just wanted to know if I had all the facts. There's nothing else you haven't told me, is there?'

'No, that's it, *Beta*. That's all there is to know.'

I thanked her, wished her good night, although I doubted she would have one, and hung up.

I poured the final dregs of wine into my glass and took a long, slow sip. The image on the TV screen was not as sharp as it had been a couple of hours earlier.

Why were relationships so bloody difficult? Why was the balance between happiness and sorrow tilted more to one side than the other in my life? If Maya was The Scorpion, how in the name of God was I going to handle it? And then there were my children. I absolutely adored them. But they were growing up without me. And I was growing older without them. I looked at the empty space in the corner of the room where Fernando's cage usually stood. My best friend, gone. The silence in the house stretched. Gone were the wolf whistles, the quips, and the mimicry which I missed so much. My heart ached.

My phone pinged. I ignored the text message. It was late and there was nothing I could do for anybody at this time of night. I wanted peace and quiet.

After finishing the wine and putting the empty bottle in the recycling bin, I made my way upstairs to bed.

I floated into and out of a restless slumber, and at times my own snoring woke me up. I listened to the steady drone of traffic outside the bedroom window, and distant voices speaking in Gujarati and Punjabi. Ghostly shadows danced on the ceiling — long extinct dodos. I drifted off again.

The I heard the steady pitter-patter of raindrops on the rear window, getting louder and louder. No, it couldn't be raining; it was the height of the drought. I got up, went to the back bedroom and looked out. I wondered if the neighbourhood louts were throwing gravel at my window. No, there was nothing in the darkness. I went back to bed and dreamt I was waiting in the dark outside the house I'd once shared with Faye and my children. I was wringing my hands, overwhelmed by pain. Was it me? Or was it somebody who looked like me? Was it our house? Or was it the isolated house in Naivasha, where we'd lived as a happy family and where nothing would ever go wrong?

My tired eyes opened as the early morning sunlight broke through the gap in the curtains. The mattress and pillow were drenched in sweat.

CHAPTER 33

The late-night text was a summons to Superintendent Breedon's office first thing in the morning. *News certainly travels fast within the force*, I thought. I sat opposite him across his big desk, looking through the window behind him. The early morning traffic along the dual carriageway was heavy as usual.

His cold blue eyes pierced me as he said, 'Another late night, was it?'

'Sleepless night, Sir.'

He shuffled a few papers from his in-tray to his desk and asked his PA to hold his calls. 'Mr Parekh's solicitor has lodged an official complaint against you, for harassment of a prominent businessman and philanthropist. And he is suing the force for damaging his property. It will run into a few thousand.'

'Everything was done by the book, Sir.'

'Yes, including his escape, I suppose. What on earth were you thinking of when you let him loose?'

'It was a split-second decision. He wanted to go to the toilet. I didn't have another officer to accompany him, apart from Sergeant Nicholson, that is. And asking her wasn't appropriate. I didn't think he would escape. It seemed genuine. I didn't want him pissing in the patrol car. We would've been done for cruelty if that had happened.'

Superintendent Breedon raised both eyebrows at me. The wrinkles on his forehead were pronounced. 'Did he escape by himself or was he helped?' he asked.

'Don't know for certain, Sir. Found the electric scooter near the outer perimeter fence. There were fresh tyre marks on the dirt road near the fence. Could've been helped by people on the outside.'

'And the drone could've been sending pictures and sound to whoever was operating it, I suppose.'

I nodded.

'So, his place was being monitored by others. Others protecting their interests and their man.'

'Fair assumption, Sir. It would explain the bug we found in the plant pot.'

'Of course, this doesn't look good for us — letting a main suspect in a major case escape. The sharks will have a feeding frenzy. They're probably circling already.' He raised his left eyebrow towards his well-groomed dark hair and stared at me.

I didn't say anything. In the past I had been cast adrift, and I knew I couldn't rely on his support.

'No, doesn't look good at all,' he said after a while. 'Especially since you're one of the few detectives of colour we have. They'll question your competence.'

Won't be the first time, I thought. 'I'm sorry, Sir, but I'm not a person of colour. Strictly speaking, I'm brown.'

'Look, Rohan, I don't need a lesson on political correctness or on diversity. Had enough —'

'Neither do I, sir,' I interjected, saving him from saying something he would regret.

He paused. A tiny drop of sweat appeared above his top lip, under the well-groomed moustache. He tapped his forefinger on the desk, stared at it, then looked up. 'This is what we'll do,' he eventually said. 'We obviously need to apprehend and charge Mr Parekh as quickly as we can. If the press and TV bay for our blood, I'll explain that a proper evaluation of the incident has taken place, lessons have been learned, and procedures have been tightened.'

All bases were covered. Reputations would remain intact.

I looked at him, registered the use of 'we' and 'our' and nodded. I was relieved I would be protected from the circling sharks. But I also knew I would be fed to the wolves, piece by piece, if it suited him.

'Okay, Rohan, keep me posted.'

I closed the door behind me and walked down the stairs to the incident room, where Grace was waiting.

We went through the details of the case so far; I asked her to alert all forces about Mr Parekh and to circulate details about him. His restaurant websites were full of his photographs, so I asked her to download several of these and to post them on the national computer. Further appeals for his whereabouts, or any information about him, were to be made on social media.

'Are you okay, Sir?' Grace asked after a while.

'Yes, why?'

'Oh, you look shattered. First time I've seen you with a cut on your chin.'

'Accident with the razor early this morning, Grace. Wasn't paying attention,' I said and gently touched the thin line of dried blood.

My mobile rang — the same unknown number that had called me before, while we'd been arresting Felicity Hardcastle.

'Sorry. Should see what this person wants.'

I listened as the male voice said, 'I tried ringing you the other day, Inspector Sharma. But you didn't reply.'

'I'm sorry, been busy. Who is this?'

'I know who killed Bobby,' the voice said.

'What?'

'Yes, I know. And it's not who you think it is.'

The caller gave me his name and asked me to meet him at an agreed location later in the day.

My heart raced.

I did not say anything to Grace. I would brief her afterwards. She didn't ask any questions and got on with her tasks, while I updated our reports on the case.

CHAPTER 34

Daylight was fading as I leapt over the iron railings of the park on the eastern side of the city. I winced as my knees jolted. Traffic along the adjacent main road was beginning to thin out, while the greengrocers and an express supermarket nearby were closing for the night. The Indian takeaway and the fish and chip shop had a steady stream of customers, some coming in from the nearby pub.

The gathering dark clouds chased the dwindling daylight, streetlamps flickered on, and a bird trilled its last song for the day. I walked slowly along the darkening tarmac path near the shallow stream, the moorhens plopping and diving into the water. Mature trees lined the fence in the distance, while two giant oak trees stood majestically in the middle of the park. The thick, high branch of one grew parallel to the ground and then rose up to the sky. A few years ago, an Indian youth with all his life before him had come into this park one night and hung himself from that branch because he couldn't marry the girl he loved. I remembered seeing photographs in the local paper of the many colourful bouquets laid at the bottom of the tree.

As I walked, the ghostly headlights of cars bounced off the tops of the trees, with an occasional glint on the steel chains of the nearby swings. An owl hooted in the distance. Just visible on the horizon, bats swooped in the dusk and caught an unsuspecting insect before flying high up in the air again. I skirted the children's playground, which had a roundabout, climbing frame and seesaw.

Eventually, I arrived at the old wooden canopy, a long viewing area near the bowling green, and sat down on the end of the bench lining its length. I rubbed my knees and breathed out. I was not visible to anyone, except for those who knew where to look.

Footsteps approached and the bench creaked as the heavy body of a man planted itself a few feet to my left. He lit a cigarette. I saw his face in the glow of the match, and he blew cigarette smoke into the roof of the canopy.

'Bobby was my son, you know.'

'No, I didn't know,' I replied.

'Yeah, not many people know that... Ha, would you believe it? Isn't that what Michael Caine said in one of his films?'

'Mr Khosla, I'm really sorry about what happened to your son. I really liked him. And he was trying to get back on the straight and narrow, or so he told me.'

Mr Khosla, the owner of the club I had visited previously, turned his head towards me. The cigarette glow intensified, the embers a bright orangey-yellow. I remembered asking for coconut water in his establishment and the accompanying sniggers of the regular customers. He pulled the cigarette out of his mouth.

'I had him when I was quite young. His mother was a young English woman. We split up. She didn't want the responsibility of raising a child. I pleaded with her not to go, but she did. I couldn't raise him on my own, not while trying to run a bar like mine. My sister and her husband raised him. He even took their family name. I used to go round to see him as much as I could. He knew I was his father. But he thought his mother had betrayed him ... and I had abandoned him. He went off the rails at school, and this continued as he got older. He was just getting his life back together when...' He trailed off.

'Did he confide in you recently?'

'Said that bastard Parekh kept demanding more money. He accused the boy of short-changing him; then he had him tailed and threatened him. Bobby was scared. He rang me a couple of days before he died and asked me to help him. I told him to leave Leicester for a while and come back when things quietened down. But he wouldn't do that. He was spotted talking to you and was reported to Parekh. Bobby even rang me afterwards to say you'd been nosing around.'

'Mr Khosla, I'm really sorry. I would have offered him protection if he was willing to give evidence against Parekh. But I didn't know. I'm sorry.'

He went quiet. The embers flared again. He suppressed a cough, threw the stub on the ground and crushed it under his foot.

'You said on the phone that Bobby's killer isn't who I think it is. What did you mean by that?'

'You probably think it was Parekh, don't you?'

I nodded, then realised he could not see me in the dark. 'Well, he's the main suspect. And both you and Bobby tried to tip me off with comments about mincemeat and shish kebab.'

'I'm surprised you pay so much attention to inconsequential words, Inspector.'

'Are they inconsequential?'

We were silent for a while. There was a rustling sound from the hedge nearby. A half-moon appeared in the clear night sky and stars twinkled.

'I thought it was Parekh,' said Mr Khosla. 'And it could still be him. Maybe he'll confess to it. But the rumour on the street is that Parekh's controlled by somebody known as the Grand Master. A white man. That's your Mr Big. And he probably had my son killed.'

'What can you tell me about him?'

'Nothing more. Don't know where he lives, or even if it's in this country. Given his connections and wealth, he could be livin' anywhere. Sometimes he goes by the initials G.M.'

I remembered what Anand Parekh had told me the day he'd escaped: he'd said to look for the initials G.M. in the Panama Papers.

'Did they know Bobby was your son?'

'No idea. But it wouldn't surprise me. Sometimes Bobby said more than was good for him. I asked you to meet me here to play safe. If they knew, I'd be dead meat, just like a tandoori chicken leg. My club would be burnt to a crisp.' He lit another cigarette.

'I wish I smoked sometimes,' I said. 'Helps you relax, I understand.'

'Bad for your health, Inspector. Just like some people.' He took a few more drags. 'I'll let you know if I hear anything more,' he added, stubbing out the cigarette.

He stood up and disappeared into the darkness.

Back at home, I was restless, trying not to think of Maya, of recent events, of sorrow, of death. I so wanted to see Maya again, to hold her, to laugh with her, to love her. But what had she grown up into?

The low lighting in my lounge was accompanied by soft music, classical Hindi songs by Lata Mangeshkar and Asha Bhosle — my attempt to calm down, to reach some sort of equilibrium. But it was difficult. I paced up and down, a glass of mineral water in my hand. I sat down, then got up again, pulled back the curtains and stared out of the window.

Why did those who left always take a part of your heart with them? It seemed that life could only be complete on their return, but it was never as simple as that. It was like trying to repair the shattered image in a cracked mirror: joining the silver shards together would never make it whole again.

It was long past midnight. I closed the curtains and finally trudged upstairs, flopped into bed and tried to sleep.

My mind whirred. Thoughts tumbled: I caught them and then released them. They carried on tumbling down. I couldn't make sense of them.

The headlights of passing cars shone through the semi-circular gaps at the tops of the curtains, creating ghostly shapes on the Artex ceiling. Sleep came and went, along with memories of long-forgotten friends, of my childhood in Naivasha, and of the poor dead maid whose family I didn't even know. I thought of Mr and Mrs Mehta and their murdered daughter, Geeta, and of Ayan Suleiman — both young victims of the psychopathic killer, Shiva the Destroyer. And then I thought of Hasina and Maya.

There was a persistent tapping on the back window again. Bloody kids, throwing bits of gravel. I was just too tired to go and challenge them.

Eventually, I fell asleep for more than a few moments.

Tring, tring! Tring, tring!

Oh, not now, Fernando, I thought. *Please don't wake me up. I need to sleep.*

Tring, tring! Tring, tring!

Please, Fernando… Please stop your mimicking. I need some peace and quiet.

I looked up, rubbing my eyes. The early rays of daylight broke through the curtains. My landline phone was ringing. I stared at the bedside clock. It was almost six.

'Sorry to bother you so early, Sir,' said the male voice. 'I tried your mobile, but it's switched off or needs recharging.'

It took me a few moments to realise the voice belonged to Ben Carter, the senior forensic investigator.

'I got a call myself from HQ not too long ago,' he said. 'I'm at the crime scene now. Got a John Doe. Think it best if you get yourself here.'

'Any idea who it is?'

'No.'

'Age? Young? Old?'

'No idea.'

'You said John Doe. So, the victim's male?'

'Yes … think so.'

'What d'you mean "think so"? Oh, never mind, Ben. Ethnicity?'

'No idea.'

'Why not?'

'You'll understand when you get here, Sir.'

I forced my tired body out of bed, quickly washed and shaved and drove to the scene. I used the wireless charger for my mobile and rang Grace. She wasn't picking up — probably asleep, I thought. I left a message for her, pressed the accelerator and was there in under fifteen minutes. I parked my Mercedes, made a quick phone call to HQ, and rushed to where a growing number of forensic investigators were gathered.

CHAPTER 35

The hot, humid days of summer were slowly receding as a cool breeze ruffled my hair. It was now September, and autumn was taking over. Breathing heavily, I stood on the pavement near Bow Bridge in the west of the city, gazing at the modern skyline of the business district nearby, the morning traffic already busy, diesel and petrol fumes assaulting my lungs. The M1 and M69 motorways were close by and commuter traffic from other parts of Leicester, Coventry and Nottingham was building up.

The pavements on both sides of the bridge were cordoned off with the usual scene-of-crime tape. A handful of forensic investigators in full white suits were on their hands and knees, brushing dust, fibres and other materials into plastic evidence bags. I lifted one of the strips of blue and white tape and walked down the steps leading to the edge of the river. I waved to Ben Carter as I approached; he was directing the work of other staff on both sides of the river.

'Morning, Ben. What have we got?'

He shook my hand vigorously and pointed to the top of the bridge behind me. I turned and looked up. An awning had been erected, with two striped sides pulled out so nothing would be visible from either side.

Hanging from one of the four, black cast-iron pillars straddling the bridge, was the body of what looked like a man. A thin steel wire cut into his neck, a knot tied tightly to the decorative crown and sceptre at the top of the pillar. His head was covered in a black cloth mask, and dried blood had congealed on the front of his pale shirt. His gloved hands were tied behind his back with plastic cable ties. Dangling around his neck was a square piece of brown plywood, held by a piece of string in each corner hole. Blood glistened in the early morning sun on the front of his dark trousers, his polished shoes pointing down.

'Not had time to put an awning on top yet,' said Ben. 'Waiting for my team to bring one. Not easy to find. But one's on the way.'

'Now I understand why you couldn't tell me anything about his age or ethnicity,' I said to Ben. 'There's no visible skin at all. What about that board round his neck? Any ideas?'

Ben shrugged. 'When my team's finished on the ground, we'll cut him down,' he said. 'Dr Malik's on standby to conduct an initial examination of the deceased.'

'Thanks, Ben. I've asked our guys from Traffic to set up roadblocks and to divert traffic away from the area, so your team can get as much as you can.'

'Yup, we need to do that. Before you ask, he was found by that man over there. He was walking his dog. Thought it was a scarecrow or some such thing left hanging by the students from the university. It's the start of freshers' week, rag week and all that.'

I turned around and saw a middle-aged white man standing with a chocolate-coloured spaniel in the distance. While waiting for Ben and his team to finish, I thought I would go and speak to him.

'I'm sorry I'm late, Sir,' said Grace, gasping and perspiring as she ran towards me later that morning. 'Absolute gridlock round here … and I couldn't find anywhere to park. Left the car miles away.'

'Good morning, Grace. I'm sure that's an exaggeration, but I'm glad to see you. You look tired. Late night?'

'Just restless sleep,' she replied, looking away.

I pointed to the body and explained how it had been discovered. The dog walker hadn't really added anything of consequence. We were just waiting for Ben Carter's team to finish, and then we would lower the body.

My phone rang.

'Rohan,' barked Superintendent Breedon, 'what the hell's going on? Got hundreds of calls jamming our switchboard — drivers baying for blood because of the diversions you've set up. People are running late for work and the school run. Traffic round the hospital's also gridlocked with drivers trying to avoid the roadblocks. Got doctors and nurses who cannot get in. Office, university staff, all sitting in cars. Social media's going wild.'

I explained to him what he already knew. We had to preserve evidence. And I had told our media team to put out urgent messages on the diversions. I appreciated this was causing headaches, but people had to realise we were dealing with a serious incident.

'Well, hurry it up, Rohan.'

All very well for him to say from behind his comfortable desk with a cup of coffee in his hand, I thought. *He gets to come into work at a reasonable hour of the morning.*

'Do we know who the victim is?'

'No, Sir.'

I was just about to speak to Grace when Ben informed me that a commercial barge with a long wooden deck would be here soon. He had ordered it from a company upstream. The body would be lowered down onto it and all precautions would be taken to preserve evidence. I turned round to speak to Grace.

There was a high-velocity whizzing sound above my head, then everything happened in slow motion.

There was a muffled explosion against the iron railing. The steel wire was cut in half. The body fell onto the barge. Ben and Dr Malik were running along the barge. I saw a vanishing glint of steel from the rooftop of a nearby high-rise office block. Grace was frozen to the spot, wide-eyed.

I ran towards the high-rise block. Traffic was jammed along all the roads, blocking my sprint. I wove in and out of cars, taxis and lorries, avoiding cyclists and jostling pedestrians.

I knew it was no good. The sniper would be long gone.

I shouted to one of the traffic officers to run to the office block, too. Then I saw a figure in dark leathers come out of the service road at the back of the block. The motorcycle engine screamed, while a steel case was rapidly secured to the back seat. The rider wore a dark helmet, and deep brown eyes smiled back at me, lingering. The rider's head turned around. There was a tell-tale birthmark on the back of the neck, below the helmet.

'Maya!' I screamed.

She turned again and shot past through stationary traffic. She was soon gone.

I ran back to the barge, stood on the deck and bent over, breathing heavily. In between gulps of air, I shouted to Grace to contact HQ and ask any units in the vicinity to look out for the bike and give chase. But I knew it was futile. The escape route and eventual hiding place would have been well planned by the rider.

When I got my breath back, I asked her to organise a team of uniforms to go knocking on office doors, to take witness statements, ask for any CCTV images which could help us, and to put out a request on social media and other channels to all drivers in the area for any relevant dashcam footage.

The crumpled body, still with the hood over its head and the plywood square round its neck, had been straightened out on a blue plastic sheet. A white tent was already erected around the body, so nothing was visible to any onlookers, and an arc light had been connected to the barge's electrical supply. We all donned full forensic suits and gloves before approaching the body. Ben Carter went down on his knees, lifted the head and pulled off the plywood square. He looked at the reverse side for a few moments and turned it towards us. Both Dr Malik and I read the message on it.

'Any idea what it means, Inspector?' asked the pathologist.

I shrugged, but I now had an inkling of who the victim could be.

Ben then asked for a pair of surgical scissors from Dr Malik, who retrieved them from his Gladstone bag, and he slowly snipped away the hood covering the victim's head.

After a cursory inspection, Dr Malik said, 'Tongue's missing and both ears have been sliced off. The eyes were probably removed with an ice-cream spoon. Poor fellow died an agonising death. I doubt he was enjoying a Neapolitan at the time.'

We ignored the last comment. Ben said, 'Seems the message is clear. Hear no evil, see no evil, speak no evil.'

A phrase I had heard before.

I looked up and saw a magpie land on one of the bridge's iron pillars. Its dark blue and white feathers ruffled in the breeze. The long black beak rose skyward, seemingly in triumph. 'Well, Mr Parekh,' I said. 'Definitely one for sorrow.'

The other two looked up at me, but didn't say anything.

CHAPTER 36

On the evening of the next day, I had a FaceTime conversation with my kids. They were back at school and bored already. They were trying not to be too sad about Fernando. I had tried not to think of him too much because it only upset me. It was a form of bereavement, losing a beloved pet. It had been many weeks since he'd disappeared. There had been no sightings of him, apart from the false alarm with the pigeon, and I feared the worst. A bird of prey could have got him, or he could have died of starvation, not knowing what to eat or where to find it. Poor Fernando. Loyalty bound him to me, apart from the one mad moment on his part when he had made a bid for freedom.

The screen on my laptop came to life, ending my melancholy reverie. Montmartre was bathed in a radiant evening glow below a dome of bright blue sky. Hundreds of people moved like tiny ants along the narrow streets and broad avenues. I thought of Vincent Van Gogh traipsing the streets of Paris, hungry and cold.

Nicole Laurent smiled at me, looked behind her and said, 'It's good, no?' Her dark, glossy hair fell onto her shoulders and pale yellow T-shirt.

I replied that I could never tire of it and then we got down to business. I explained what had happened yesterday, how we hadn't managed to track down the sniper. The receptionist in the office block had been completing a long nightshift and hadn't thought too much of a dark-skinned woman under a motorcycle helmet who'd carried a case, flashed an official-looking courier's card, and had gone swiftly up in the lift. There were hardly any people in the building at that time of the morning. The receptionist had left not long afterwards and hadn't mentioned it to his replacement. Uniformed officers had conducted enquiries, but nobody had noticed anything of significance. CCTV images were not very clear and confirmed what the receptionist had said about the woman. The dashcam footage retrieved so far showed the assailant riding off at high speed, just like a ghost in the night: there one moment, gone the next.

'And the body, Rohan? Did it have the same signatures we found on the victim in Istanbul? Eyes, ears, tongue?'

'Yes. But there was a board round his neck with a rhyme scrawled on it.' I stared at the three ivory-coloured domes of the Sacré-Coeur behind Nicole's head.

'Well, what did it say?'

'Oh, sorry Nicole. It said:

He who betrays The Boss
Will always pay the cost,
Just like God's banker,
The two-faced...'

You didn't need to be Shakespeare to work out the final word.

'Well,' she said after a while, 'one thing's certain.'

'Yes?'

'I don't think "The Boss" refers to Bruce Springsteen.'

We laughed.

'So, Parekh betrayed his boss,' I said, formal again. 'He told me he was an accountant by trade and wasn't making enough money. He branched out into restaurants and jewellery. He was probably involved in moving lots of money around for "The Boss" and knew all the secrets. He thought "The Boss" would protect him when he escaped from us.'

'He thought wrong,' said Nicole. 'Perhaps you were getting too close. The Boss obviously knew this. He was using the drone over his house. Could have had a long-range microphone on it to listen in on conversations.'

'What about the reference to God's banker, Nicole? What's all that about? Any ideas?'

'The poet knows his history, Rohan. So, you've never heard of Roberto Calvi?'

'No, should I have?'

'Go and get yourself a glass of wine,' she replied, 'and I'll tell you about him. I'll fill mine as well.'

A few moments later, we were both sitting comfortably, and I took a long sip from a cool glass of Sauvignon Blanc. Nicole was drinking Pinot Grigio. She took a sip, put her glass down and pulled on a thin gold chain hanging around her neck.

She explained that Roberto Calvi was an Italian banker who was Chairman of Banco Ambrosiano from 1975 until his death in 1982 at the age of sixty-two. The bank had apparently exported several billion lire, all illegally, and he was fined almost twenty million US dollars for transferring twenty-seven million dollars out of the country. The Vatican was allegedly involved in illegal transactions of money and it was feared that Calvi would expose this. The Vatican had always denied involvement but paid more than two hundred million dollars to Banco Ambrosiano's creditors.

'Why would they do this if they were innocent?' continued Nicole. 'Now you can work out why Calvi was known as God's banker.'

'What happened to him?' I asked.

'He escaped from his Rome apartment on 10 June 1982, and his body was found hanging under Blackfriars Bridge in London on 18 June, just over a week later. Some people think he committed suicide, but why escape to London to do it? Why not do it in Rome, like his secretary, who jumped off a tall building?'

'So, he was murdered?'

'Seems to be the accepted theory, but nobody's proved it conclusively. People still argue about it — the fact that he couldn't have climbed up the scaffolding under the bridge to hang himself, the fact that bricks were found in his clothing, and so on.'

'Mr Parekh was found dead in similar circumstances,' I said, 'although there were no bricks in his clothing. And he knew the financial secrets of someone else. Someone powerful.'

'Yes, I think so. And we need to dig round some more in the Panama Papers. Lots of useful information there.'

'When I last spoke to Parekh,' I said, 'he mentioned that the man, "The Boss", used various names, including Jim. He was also known by the initials G.M.'

She didn't reply, apparently deep in thought.

I looked at her, wondering whether to say anything. And then I did. 'I'm worried, Nicole. I'm worried that The Scorpion might be my long-lost sister.'

She stared at me.

I explained why I thought this. 'I can't believe she rode past me at such great speed. And the birthmark on the back of her neck! I can't believe it's her. A killer. After all this time. And in the same city.'

Nicole looked at me, her face full of concern. She said she would give me a hug if we were in the same room.

'I think your partner might object,' I said, trying to make light of it. 'But thank you. It means a lot to me.'

'Look at it this way, Rohan. The chances of it being Maya are remote. The birthmark may have been a patch of dark skin. Or the shadow formed by the edge of the helmet. You were separated in another time and in another place. Anyway, The Scorpion is not a nice woman. She's dangerous. So if you do come across her, please be careful.'

I felt conflicted. I didn't want it to be her, but I also wanted to see her.

'Plenty of young women went to Syria and Iraq to fight for ISIS,' Nicole went on. 'A few became famous, like The White Widow, because of the atrocities they're supposed to have committed. Who's to say what horrors they saw? What horrors they perpetrated? The chances, however, of The Scorpion being your sister, so far away from where she disappeared … they are slim, no?'

'I want so much to believe you, Nicole. I so hope you're right. But part of me also wants to see her.'

'What? So she can kill you?'

I didn't reply.

'It was a warning, Rohan. *Whoever* fired that shot at an already dead man was warning you not to get involved. I'm sorry.' Nicole paused, then continued. 'On another note, this may be relevant or it may not be. I'm not sure. You know the French police, Interpol and other international forces have been tracking a number of people involved in large-scale illegal trade — antiquities, drugs, armaments, and so on. We're tracking four in the UK at the moment.'

'How?'

'By monitoring their cyber activities, especially on the dark web. Also by using spyware in their phones.'

'What? Surely they wouldn't click on any unidentified or dodgy links.'

'No, of course not. Sophisticated spyware has been developed in Israel, which allows you to infect the user's phone just by ringing it. No need to click anything. Our government has bought it. It can take complete control of a person's phone, including email, encrypted message apps and photos. It can also listen in on conversations. You name it. And the user doesn't know it.'

I was staggered. My knowledge of cyber security was not that great and I said so.

'Anyway,' Nicole continued, 'we've come across one man very recently. A few days ago, in fact. He's of great interest. He calls from London and mentions having been in Cyprus, Central Africa, Syria and Iraq regularly. And, believe it or not, in areas not far from your city, along the A1 motorway. He uses many aliases, but we know his Christian name is James. He speaks regularly with a woman called Kel. They seem very close. Could be lovers, I don't know. She uses a pay-as-you-go mobile phone and changes it often. We cannot identify her. She's very careful about what she says, but has made references to cyber security, many other security matters, and to some of the major crimes police forces in the UK are currently investigating. She may have hacked into the Police National Computer. Or maybe she has access to it. Does her name mean anything to you?'

I said no, it didn't. She could have been a mole anywhere in the country — from a serving police officer to a member of the support staff with privileged access to the PNC. I also told Nicole that it was almost impossible to hack into the PNC.

'Nothing is impossible, Rohan. It was a long shot. Sorry, shouldn't have said that. Not after what happened to you on the bridge.'

'Not to worry, Nicole. Don't give it a second thought.'

She said it was getting late and her partner would soon be home. 'But one last question,' she added. 'What about your bird? Your parrot? Any luck finding him?'

My eyes welled up as I said I had given up hope. The chances of finding him alive were non-existent.

She said she felt for me, then went on, 'You know what we have to do, Rohan.'

I shook my head.

'We need to look some more into the Panama Papers. See if there is information there — however small — that could help us. That's our starting point. *Au revoir*,' she said, blowing me some air kisses and waving.

Then she was gone.

CHAPTER 37

The clink of steel on steel greeted me as I walked into the post-mortem examination room. It was several days later, and I was there early on a sunlit morning. Dr Malik, like me dressed in surgical gown, mask, cap and theatre shoes, placed a pair of shiny dissecting scissors onto the surgical tray. He looked up, waved me forward and continued to place an assortment of sterilised instruments required for the autopsy: scalpels, knives, bone-cutters, a chisel, a mallet and a hinged back saw. I tried hard not to think about how these would be used as I stared at Anand Parekh's lifeless body lying on the long steel table in front of me. A couple of hosepipes rested in their crooks above the table, a draining hole in each corner.

'Welcome, Inspector Sharma, to my domain. One customer is almost ready to be served.'

I had wondered whether to ask Grace if she wanted to attend as part of her training, but I decided she had seen enough death in the short period of time we had worked together.

Dr Malik asked his assistant, who was standing near one of the stainless-steel sinks, to make notes about the state of the body. He also had a microphone hanging from his neck to make an audio recording of his observations.

He picked up a camera with a powerful lens and flashgun and started photographing various parts of the body from different angles. The cold of the room made me shiver, even though it was relatively mild outside. I nodded to him and rubbed my arms.

'Well, *he's* not going to complain of the cold, or if the service is no good.'

I ignored the comment.

The skin on the naked brown body, covered by a sheet from the waist down, was shrivelled. The body hair did not stand on end. Anand Parekh's face looked straight up at the ceiling. I tried not to look at his horrific injuries and instead thought of him in life, when he'd said he wanted to go to the toilet.

Dr Malik suddenly stopped and asked his assistant for a magnifying glass. He then stared at the area around the breastbone for a long time.

'Inspector, come and have a look,' he said, handing me the magnifying glass. 'Just there.' He pointed.

I leaned forward and peered at the tiny hole to the left of the breastbone. Before I could say anything, Dr Malik gently pushed a silver probe into it and pulled it out slowly.

'Just as I figured,' he said. 'I initially thought he may've died through severe blood loss. But that might not be the cause of death — or not the primary cause. I'll know for sure when I open him up.'

I remained silent, the humming of the air conditioner and the dripping of water from one of the taps the only sounds.

The pathologist continued, 'I think this hole was made by a long, thin implement like a sharpened knitting needle or a thin screwdriver whose end had been filed into a point. I use something similar here. Would've gone straight to the heart. There will be a lot of blood behind the ribs if his heart was punctured. Could be the cause of death.'

I asked him to continue with the post-mortem and to give me his findings when he could. I was in no mood for electric saws, bone-cutters and scalpels.

I travelled back to HQ, reviewed all the known evidence with the team in the incident room, and had a briefing session with Grace. She informed me no new leads had come to light from the door-to-door enquiries, from CCTV or dashcam footage, or from any appeals on the media, both social and traditional. I asked her to continue with this line of work. We just had to get a breakthrough. After completing the necessary paperwork, I popped into Jamie Shriver's room to see if there had been any progress in trawling through the Panama Papers. He said he and his team would continue working on them, and then I headed home.

As I drove along the Golden Mile, crowds of people thronged the pavements and the edge of the road. Loud Indian music blasted from cars and shops, and the cafes and takeaways were getting busy. I stopped and picked up a container of freshly squeezed passion fruit juice, which had been blended and mixed with ground pepper and a touch of sea salt. At home I prepared some chicken tikka paste, marinaded the pieces of meat for about an hour and then cooked them slowly in the oven.

I could not help thinking of the key question that had been tormenting me. If Parekh's killer was Maya, I would be shattered. How could she have done this? What untold suffering had she inflicted on others? What suffering had she experienced in her own life to drive her to do this?

I could not share my thoughts with anyone — not my mother or father, not my children, and not with Grace. It made me realise how alone I was. The one person I could talk to, ironically, was my ex-wife, Faye. She would be sympathetic and would understand. But I decided not to contact her, not yet. I wasn't ready.

I paced up and down my front room. The noise of car engines, loud throaty motorbikes and buzzing scooters passed by my window. There was the occasional laughter of youngsters walking past and the distinct sound of Gujarati spoken by two women from India, not East Africa, as the inflection and vocabulary were slightly different between the two different parts of the world.

I sat down, put on my wireless headphones and chose to play some Western classical music that would lift my soul. The sound of the choir in the last movement of Beethoven's Ninth Symphony resonated loudly in my head. I waved an imaginary conductor's baton as the immortal 'Ode to Joy' was sung with depth and optimism. This was followed by *Carmina Burana*. My arms waved furiously in front of me to the beat of the bass drums and the wall of sound from the hundreds of singers in the chorus.

My phone vibrated in my breast pocket. I paused the music.

I didn't recognise the number but accepted the call. 'Hello?'

'Hello, Rohan. How're you?' asked the female voice.

I hesitated.

'It's Jenny, Jenny Tyburn.'

I suddenly remembered the curator of the local museum who'd examined and dated the sculpture Hasina had thrust into my hand an eternity ago. 'Sorry, Jenny, I didn't have your number in my contacts, so your name didn't come up on the screen. We haven't spoken in a while.'

'Why isn't my number in your contacts list? Not important enough?' She laughed, then told me she'd been on an archaeological dig in the Atlas Mountains in Morocco for a few weeks, but she was glad to get back to the cooler weather in the UK. We chatted a bit longer; I told her a few things about the case that were in the public domain, and she said she was really keen to hear more. 'Perhaps we ought to get together one evening for a drink or a meal, or both.'

'It would be lovely to do that,' I said, remembering the pub lunch we'd had by the canal, her flirting in the sun, her legs touching mine under the table.

'What about the statue?' she asked. 'Found any more?'

'No.'

'I suppose I can't submit the paper I've written about the statue to any academic journals yet? Or talk about it?'

'No, I'm sorry, you can't. Not yet.'

'Fair enough. Okay, please call me when you can. Oh, by the way…'

'Yes?'

'Make sure you save this number in your contacts list.' She laughed and was gone.

It was getting dark and I decided to clear up and go to bed. It was still early, but the rest would do me good. As I washed up the few items of crockery, I was distracted by a sound at the back bedroom window. *Tap, tap. Tap, tap.* I would not be able to see anyone from the ground floor because of the labyrinth of brick alleyways at the back of the terraced houses.

I darted upstairs, peering out of the back window. I saw some movement in the back alley and opened the window silently. There was the soft sound of footsteps running away.

'Oi, bugger off!' I shouted.

People in the neighbourhood knew who I was and teenagers could be messing around, trying to annoy me. I heard the bedroom window next door being pulled shut. I knew a teenage girl lived there, so perhaps her admirer had targeted the wrong house to get her attention.

As I closed my window, I looked down and saw the metal bracket from which Fernando's cage had hung on the wall a lifetime ago.

I tried not to think about him, but it was difficult.

CHAPTER 38

It was well past midnight when I leapt over the iron railings and trudged across the grass of the deserted park. I sat down on the bench in the long, wooden shed facing the bowling green. Mr Khosla had rung earlier in the day and asked me to meet him here. He had come across some information that he claimed would help me catch his son's killers. I noticed the use of the plural — killers — and wondered what he knew. I did not blame him for continuing to be wary of meeting me openly.

I sat hunched on the wooden slats, grateful for my thermal coat and cashmere scarf on the cool September night. In the distance the leaves of the large, mature trees rustled, occasionally lit by the ghostly headlights of cars driving along nearby roads. An owl hooted and the stream babbled behind me, the tall reeds rustling in the breeze.

Hushed footsteps approached in the darkness and a heavy body planted itself on the bench, a few feet away from me. Mr Khosla grunted, sniffled and suppressed a cough. He reached into his pocket, pulled out a handkerchief and wiped his nose. We didn't say anything for a long time. We just listened to the sounds of nature and the passing traffic.

'Getting colder,' he said. 'Got dew on the grass… My left foot's wet.'

I did not say anything.

'Think there's a hole. A hole in my sole,' he continued.

I didn't know if he meant 'sole' or 'soul'.

In the distance, the two glassy eyes of a cat stopped, looked at us and then continued their slow, stealthy movement.

'I miss him,' Mr Khosla said eventually.

'I'm sure you do,' I answered. 'I've no idea what it feels like to lose a child, though I have come close to it.'

He lit a cigarette, taking care to cup his hands around the lighter so the flame wouldn't be visible to anyone. He inhaled deeply and held the smoke in his lungs, before slowly breathing it out again. 'I needed that,' he said.

I was sure his lungs did not, but I let him take his time.

'I know another club owner,' he said at last. 'He and I go back twenty years and more. He has a similar place to mine, but on the other side of the city. He knew Bobby was my son. Anyway, he rang me earlier today. He'd heard about Parekh's demise through his unsavoury sources. Your constabulary leaks like a sieve. He remembered Parekh coming to his club a couple of years ago, maybe a bit longer. He couldn't remember the exact date but thought it was in June or July because it was a warm, sunny day. He came in with a middle-aged white guy.' He blew smoke out through his mouth and nostrils. 'The two went upstairs to drink and watch porn on the big screen on the wall. It was live webcam stuff where you ask the girls — or men — to do whatever you want them to do. They stayed in the upstairs room, drinking, smoking cigarettes — not weed — and asked for food to be brought to them. Then they asked for three women. The party went on for several hours. They left a lot of mess up there, so said my friend.'

'A middle-aged white man is not a lot to go on,' I said.

'No, agreed. But he had a distinctive scar on his top lip. And he had a dark moustache to cover it up.'

'Doesn't make him a criminal.'

'No, but he had more cash than the king. He was flashing it about.'

I decided not to say anything about the king not carrying cash, as he took another long drag from his cigarette.

'He seemed to be good friends with Parekh,' Mr Khosla continued. 'But he was also mean. He punched one of the women because she wouldn't do something.'

'Not a lot to go on. Nasty bastard, that's all. Presumably there's no name? No CCTV image of him?'

'No to both. No CCTV image because it was too long ago. It got deleted. But there's something better. It ties him to some of the things you're investigating. Believe it or not, he appeared in a television programme. Not a starring role. More of an extra, so to speak.'

'Go on.'

'My friend was watching daytime television while waiting to open his club — stocking the bar, not looking at anything in particular. And then a documentary came on. My friend recognised him. The programme's still available.' Mr Khosla smirked and cleared some phlegm from his wheezy throat. 'Nasty bastard, indeed,' he went on. 'The film of him is a bit old. But it's definitely him, the Grand Master, according to my friend.'

After our meeting ended, I rushed home, made a strong cup of tea, switched on the television and put on one of the catch-up channels. I wondered if I would finally catch a glimpse of the man whom others had referred to as the Grand Master.

The documentary film started with a narrator's overview of how antiquities from the Middle East, including Egypt and Libya, had arrived, sometimes illegally, into Britain and other wealthy countries. It focused on some famous discoveries of the past, including Tutankhamun in the 1920s and mentioned how some items from the dig in the Upper Nile had disappeared, with a few discovered later in Britain. Other missing items from the Aztec, Mayan and Inca civilisations were also discussed. The programme's focus was on the sale of antiquities where legal ownership had been proved, but where questions of morality, and the rights and wrongs of selling such items, still remained. Many of the major auction houses in prominent capital cities around the world were involved in such sales.

'One such controversy,' commented the narrator, 'was the sale of the Sekhemka statue by Northampton Museums some time ago. The limestone statue is seventy centimetres — or thirty inches — tall and dates from the fifth dynasty, making it older than Stonehenge. Sekhemka was a scribe in Ancient Egypt and a photograph of the statue, seen here, shows him sitting on a dais in a traditional pose. On his lap is an open papyrus scroll listing various offerings. His wife, Sitmerit, is sitting by his feet.'

The narrator then explained that the statue was brought back to the UK in about 1850 and presented to the museum by the Marquess of Northampton. It remained on display in the museum for more than a century, but then the local council decided to sell it to raise funds for other projects. Despite widespread opposition from local and national organisations, including the Egyptian Embassy in the UK, the statue came up for sale in London.

'A group of Egyptian protestors are seen here outside the auction house,' continued the narrator, 'and a protestor briefly halted the sale inside by shouting loudly during the bidding.'

Footage obtained illicitly from inside the sale room showed a crowd of people sitting opposite the auctioneer, some bidding in person, while others placed bids on the telephone. As the mobile phone footage panned around, I noticed a man sitting on one of the aisle chairs, taking an intense interest in the proceedings, a catalogue on his lap. I paused the image. He looked to be in his mid-forties and had closely cropped, dark hair, piercing blue eyes, and a muscular body. Just above his top lip, behind a wispy moustache, was a distinct scar running towards his nose. He didn't bid and didn't seem to be with anyone else. I unfroze the image and the scene moved on.

'The statue had a guide price of about five million pounds,' continued the narrator, 'but it was sold to an anonymous overseas buyer for more than three times that amount. The drop of the hammer was met with applause by some. However, despite attempts to stop the statue from being exported, including intervention by the British government, its present whereabouts are unknown. The Egyptian Embassy called its sale "shameful and unethical."'

I fast-forwarded the images to make sure I did not miss anything, inserted a memory stick into the USB socket, started the programme again, copied it, turned off the television set and went upstairs to bed.

Finally, a breakthrough.

Despite the late hour, sleep did not come easily. My mind raced, my left knee throbbed with arthritic pain, and I watched daylight slowly take over my bedroom. At one point, I thought I heard a tapping sound on the back window, but I ignored it as I was not sure if it was part of a dream. The two dodos still danced on the ceiling, seemingly back from extinction. I tossed and turned in bed for an hour, the noise of the traffic outside getting more insistent until, eventually, I decided to get up.

I sensed it was going to be an important day.

CHAPTER 39

As I walked into the incident room very early the following morning, my calf muscles ached, my eyelids were heavy, and my head throbbed due to lack of sleep. The whiteboard on the wall was covered in scribbles — names, dates, locations, and links to various strands of the case. Some joined up with each other, some did not. Some had question marks after names, and some had exclamation marks. I stared at the board, then added some more strands to it.

I made some strong tea in the communal kitchen and walked down the corridor with the mug, the sound of hushed chatter behind me as other early risers arrived. I was about to enter the incident room when Jamie Shriver called out to me, briefcase in hand.

'Good morning, Sir. I was about to ring you from my office. Can we have a chat when you have a spare moment, please? I need to update you on developments.'

'Good morning to you, Jamie. You're one of the people I wanted to catch up with today. A chat would be great. Please come through when you're ready.'

Back in the incident room, I got out my laptop, inserted the memory stick and connected it to one of several USB ports in the middle of the conference table, which were linked to the digital smartboard on the wall.

As I did this, Grace walked in. After the usual pleasantries, I asked her to see Ben Carter on some outstanding issues, including whether we had identified a suspect for the Caucasian sperm found inside Hasina, and to follow-up on Anand Parekh's autopsy report from Dr Malik. I said I was following up on a tentative lead with Jamie, and would brief her if it led to anything substantial. She smiled and walked over to her desk as Jamie came in.

I fast-forwarded the video footage on the screen, froze it when I reached the man sitting in the London auction room, and asked Jamie to blow up the image of the face, to make it as clear as possible, and then to print out several hard copies.

He raised an eyebrow and I briefly explained the significance of the man but did not go into too much detail.

Jamie took the memory stick, left the room and returned a few minutes later. 'It's being done now, Sir. D'you think it's our G.M.?'

I didn't say anything and shrugged.

'My team's been working really hard on tracking down leads in cyberspace,' he explained. 'We've come across transactions between APEX Enterprises and G.M. Hundreds of thousands of pounds were transferred into G.M.'s account over a relatively short period of time. The funds come in from different accounts, including an offshore account in Singapore.'

'That's the one used by Felicity Hardcastle, isn't it? The Fairy Queen?'

Jamie nodded. 'There were many transactions between APEX Enterprises and G.M., after monies had been received by APEX from accounts set up by people in Syria, Egypt and Afghanistan. They could be payments for stolen antiquities, drugs, you name it.'

'So,' I said, 'we have a concrete link between APEX and G.M.'

'Yup. But we still don't know who G.M. is. The only thing we have is the name G.M. Enterprises.'

'God, couldn't they think of another word apart from "Enterprises"?'

'G.M. Enterprises provide a false address not only in the Panama Papers but in their more up-to-date dealings. But we're trying to track them down by identifying their IP address or addresses. They keep changing all the time. We're hoping for a lead eventually from one of the internet service providers. It's difficult to trace because the electronic signals cross many countries and many providers.'

'Good work, Jamie. Thanks. Please keep me posted.'

I was rubbing my temples when there was a knock on the door and one of Jamie's team came in and handed me a large brown envelope.

I looked inside, smiled, and thanked her for her incredible efficiency.

I scrolled down the screen on my phone and rang the auction house in London. I explained who I was and said I would like to see someone senior who could help the police with their enquiries in identifying a possible buyer who may have engaged in criminal activities. This got a prompt response and I was told the sales director would be free later in the day. I asked whether she preferred Zoom or Skype or Cisco.

'Oh, we don't do that, Inspector. It will have to be in person. And please bring all relevant paperwork confirming your identity. Otherwise, our security guards won't let you in.'

I looked up the train timetable, drove to the station, and was on the London-bound train promptly. I arrived at a bustling St Pancras Station, had a light lunch and another cup of strong tea, took a taxi to the auction house and was there by early afternoon.

'Yes, he does look familiar, Inspector. But he hasn't been here for a while. Not that I'm aware of, anyway.' Penelope Goodall, the sales director, looked intently at the photograph and handed it back to me across the table. She tucked her immaculately groomed shoulder-length blonde hair behind her right ear, the diamond stud in the lobe glittering under the bright ceiling spotlights.

'It's the scar above the lip. I remember that,' she continued, as she lifted the rim of the bone china cup to her lips. 'He bid for some items before, not always successfully, but he stood out because he paid in cash. Sometimes large amounts.'

'Doesn't it worry you, Mrs Goodall? Somebody paying large amounts in cash?'

'Not really, Inspector. Money's money. Although, with more recent legislation about money-laundering, we have to be careful about what we accept and how much. Generally, though, we know our customers. They are upstanding, wealthy citizens from all over the world.'

'What about a name and address for this man?'

'I think he lived in Cyprus. He gave us bank details and an address there. I assumed he was in our Forces over there. He has a military bearing — the way he talks, the way he walks. You can usually tell. You see, my husband was a senior officer in the Marines, so I know the type.'

Her sky-blue eyes stared at me. I wasn't sure if she found my questions tedious, but she answered them as best as she could. The sleeve of her navy Armani jacket fell as she took another sip of coffee, the thin, square watch glinting under the lights.

'Sorry, I can't remember his name, Inspector, but maybe my personal assistant will.' She picked up a telephone handset from its cradle on the teak desk, pushed a button and asked him to come in. As she did so, the understated scent of jasmine, freesia and rose floated into my nostrils. 'Rupert,' she said, 'what's the name of this client? Do you remember?' She smiled at me.

'Oh, yes. I remember him,' said Rupert, staring at the photograph. 'He was interested in Middle Eastern antiques. He also collected vintage chess sets. Especially those made from ivory —'

'Pre-1948,' interrupted Penelope Goodall. 'You can sell that legally.'

'— pieces inlaid with precious and semi-precious stones, especially the eyes on the king, queen, and the two knights. He was fascinated by them. I once overheard him say he loved the game and played it to a very high standard.'

'His name, please,' I said.

Rupert pushed his elegant fingers through the dark curls on his head. His cream shirt and thin blue tie complemented his boss's hair and attire well.

'Sorry, Inspector, but it's connected, you see; because of his obsession with the game, he said he'd acquired the name Grand Master in the army.'

My heart lurched.

'Anyway, on the odd occasion he bought anything, he signed himself Jim Masterson. And that was the name on the account in Cyprus.'

'Any chance of getting me details from his file? You do keep them, don't you?'

'Not sure we do anymore, Inspector. Not had any dealings with him for quite some time. But I'll go check.'

I tried not to sound too excited, or too desperate.

CHAPTER 40

On the early evening train journey back to Leicester, I upgraded my ticket to first class to secure a seat and, hopefully, get some privacy. I looked across the table at the woman opposite me, sitting with her son, who looked about ten. They had obviously been to London for the day, and she was now struggling with the cryptic crossword in *The Times*. The boy was playing an electronic game on his tablet. The *ping-ping-ping* was irritating, but it also reminded me of my son, Karan, and the fact I had not seen my children for a while. I gazed out the window at the giant Swiss rolls of harvested hay in the empty fields, trying to ignore the guilt. A tattered scarecrow fluttered its dark rags in the breeze; a large bird of prey hovered and swooped down like the angel of death. I saw some cattle grazing, then a blur of trees.

I sent a text message to Nicole stating I had made some progress in the possible identification of G.M. Although the auction house had given me a name — Jim Masterson — there was a good chance it was fake and the address in Cyprus had been abandoned long ago.

To my surprise, Nicole messaged back immediately, saying they were still tracking Jim and Kel in the UK.

Could Jim be G.M., d'you think? I asked.

Her reply was cautious: *Could be. Not sure. Also got help from US drones monitoring phone conversations. When they're not spying over Ukraine, Iraq, Iran and Afghanistan, that is.*

I explained I had rung the Ministry of Defence to see if somebody in HR could help identify the man, but I'd been informed I had to make a proper appointment once I had been cleared, for security. It was late in the day, so I didn't push it.

We agreed we would speak again soon when there were any new developments. I remembered I had not contacted Grace. I moved to the empty space between carriages. She told me there was no match on the Caucasian DNA, and the post-mortem on Anand Parekh had confirmed the cause of death to be the deep puncture wound to the heart. I explained I was on a train as I had made an unexpected trip to London and was trying to track down a retired army officer called Jim.

We cut the connection, I went back to my seat and smiled at the woman and her son sitting opposite. The train travelled swiftly at more than a hundred miles an hour, and the swaying movement of the carriage and dipping, late afternoon sun made me close my heavy eyelids. I woke with a start as the brakes squealed and the train slowed as we approached my station. The young boy smiled and I wasn't sure if I had been snoring.

'You got a text message, Mister. A little while ago,' he said, pointing to my mobile on the table.

I thanked him and read the message, then read it again. My heart thumped.

The woman opposite said, 'Are you okay? You're white as a sheet. Sorry, I hope you don't think that's racist.'

I forced a smile, said it was fine, and hurried onto the station platform. I sat down on one of the benches as people jostled past me, bumping into my knees, the thud of a heavy briefcase against my elbow making me wince. I looked up at the middle-aged man in a pinstripe suit as he rushed along, making no apology.

I sent a text message to the person I needed to speak to. I received a fairly prompt reply to say she was going out for an evening meal, but could she ring me after nine? I said that would be fine.

I tried to push the feelings of jealousy down. After all, her life had nothing to do with me.

I had another restless evening. After pacing up and down in my front room, I went for a walk along the Golden Mile, staring mindlessly at the brightly coloured sarees in shop windows, the squares of orange, cream and yellow sweetmeats in silver trays covered in rice paper, and the vegetarian restaurants with their mouth-watering aromas.

I hurried back as darkness smothered the remnants of daylight. I turned on the television and stared at it mindlessly, waiting to be called.

A few minutes after nine, Faye called, prompt as ever. After I'd thanked her for finding the time, she said, 'Sounded urgent. You wanted to speak to me?'

I explained I had received a text message from an anonymous number that had unsettled me. I read it to her and asked what she made of it.

She was silent for a long time, then said, 'Please read it to me again. Slowly this time.'

'Hi bhaia, it's your sis Maya here. Know this is a surprise. We grew up in Kenya but got parted. A kind family raised me in Somalia and then we went to Syria. I found out we were bro and sis recently. Saw you at the bridge. We must meet when we can. How's mum and dad? Will be in touch again.'

'And it ends with two kisses,' I said.

'*Bhaia* means brother, right?' she asked.

'Yes.'

'How did she get hold of your number?'

'Very easy to do. It's on my calling card, which I give to anyone who can provide information. Like Mr Khosla, for instance. Hundreds at HQ must also have it.'

'What d'you think, Rohan? The facts fit, right?' asked Faye.

I had contacted my ex-wife because she was the one person who knew what I had gone through with Maya's disappearance. She'd comforted me when we were living together, calmed my spirit, and made me feel less guilty about her abduction, knowing how it tore me apart.

'Yes, they do, as far as I can tell. Obviously, I don't know about the Somalia and Syria bit. But the sniper at Bow Bridge was a woman and she shot the noose hanging Anand Parekh. She could've killed me if she wanted. But for whatever reason, she didn't.'

'Could be a hoax, of course.'

'Well, that's the thing, Faye. She attached three photographs to the message. One when she was young with a Black couple in Somalia — the ones who raised her, or so it seems. The father's holding her in his arms, looking at the camera. The mother's smiling. The girl, who's about four, looks just like me. Smile, dimples, thick, dark hair. Same colour skin. The second photograph,' I continued, 'is of a girl aged twelve or so. She's standing in front of a tent, hard snow on the ground, nose running, hair straggly and unwashed. It must be northern Syria or Iraq, because you don't have snow in Somalia. There's a black flag fluttering from a tent in the distance — looks like the ISIS flag. And the final photograph shows a young woman in her late twenties or early thirties. It looks like a selfie. She's standing in front of the Blue Mosque in Istanbul. So, she must have escaped from the warzone.'

'Could the images have been doctored? Airbrushed?' Faye asked.

'Difficult to tell. Especially on a mobile. But I've already asked Jamie in the IT unit to work on it. But she looks just like me, Faye. How can you doctor that?'

'I'm so sorry, Rohan. You want it to be Maya, don't you?'

'I just don't know what to think,' I said after a pause. 'You were the only person I could talk to. I couldn't ring my parents. This would freak them out, to put it mildly.'

'You need somebody in your life, Rohan. Somebody you can talk to. You need a new woman in your life.'

'Please don't, Faye,' I said, realising that her words echoed what my mother had said recently.

'I don't know what else to say, Rohan. Give me a ring if you need to. If there're any developments.'

'There'll always be developments.'

'Haven't you forgotten something, Rohan?'

I thought, and then said, 'Thanks, Faye.'

There was another long silence.

'You're so engrossed in everything,' she said, 'you haven't even asked how your children are.'

She was right. I should have enquired about them first. They were supposed to be the most important people in my life. Had I become that callous? That self-centred?

I tried to back-pedal and asked if I could speak to them. Faye said Karan was already in bed and Yasmin was doing her homework.

The knife twisted. It served me right.

After hanging up, I poured myself a Glenmorangie whiskey, sat down and sipped it. I didn't often drink spirits, but tonight I felt the need for one. My mind was restless, my body weary, my soul not at peace. I refrained from pouring another one and went to bed.

I tossed and turned, staring at the two dodos on the ceiling. I cast the duvet onto the floor, started shivering, leaned down and picked it up. I listened to the steady stream of traffic on the road outside, the gentle patter of raindrops on the tiled roof, and hushed voices under the window as people walked past. I started drifting in and out of consciousness. The insistent pattering noise on the back bedroom window grew louder and louder. I got up, really annoyed. Why the hell didn't Romeo — and Juliet from next door — work out which window was which? I rushed to the window, opened it, and peered out through sleepy eyes, ready to shout a mouthful.

But the back alleys were quiet. There was nothing and nobody to be seen. I craned to look at the window next door. It was closed tight. The stars shone brightly on a black velvet sky; a silver crescent moon winked on the horizon.

Fuck, I thought, and went to slam my window shut. Just then, I caught a movement below and looked down.

I could not believe what I was looking at.

CHAPTER 41

'Fernando?'

Big, round eyes looked up at me. Rainwater dripped from his scrawny body, the feathers a dirty grey and white.

'Fernando come home,' he said.

I grabbed him from the metal bracket that had once held his cage, pulled him inside, and said, 'Oh, God, Fernando, is that really you?' I cuddled him close, desperately hoping this was not a dream. 'Oh, Fernando, Fernando, where the hell have you been? You've lost so much weight.' Tears welled up in my eyes as I held onto him.

'Fernando come home,' he repeated.

I took him downstairs, quickly cut up some fresh fruit, found some cashew nuts and fed him. He ate ravenously, bits of pear stuck to his beak, and drank copious amounts of water.

'Oh, Fernando, Fernando. I've missed you so much. You'll never know.'

'Fernando a bad boy,' he said.

'Yes, you were. Flying off like that. Thought you were a goner. In more ways than one.'

He blinked, sorrow in his eyes, as if he could understand everything I was saying. I was overjoyed. He picked up a piece of apple in his claw and put it to his beak, staring at me as he ate.

'Oh, Fernando! What the hell happened to you over the last few weeks? You've lost weight. But you must have managed to eat something, right? Berries? Scraps left by picnic goers? At least there was plenty of water at the reservoir. I'm really glad the ospreys didn't get you.'

He ignored me, picked up a raisin with his claw and munched it, followed by a cashew nut. He then dipped his beak in the water tray.

'Fernando come home.'

'Yes, Fernando. You've come home. Where you belong.'

I just looked and looked at him and stroked him endlessly. The smile on my face resembled the crescent moon dangling in the sky.

I had lost track of the time as hazy daylight filtered through the gaps in the curtains. I did not care.

I got up late the next morning, checked my phone, checked Fernando's return was not a dream, fed him and chatted to him while having breakfast, my chest bursting with happiness and relief. At least something in my life seemed to have worked out. I was just waiting for some bastard to come along and ruin it. Well, there were plenty of opportunities for that. *Now, now, let's be positive*, I thought. The balance between sadness and happiness had just shifted.

As I refreshed Fernando's water tray, my phone rang.

'Hello, Sir,' said Grace. 'Hope you're okay. Not known you to be late.'

I assured her I was fine and explained about Fernando's return. She was really happy for me and wanted to know the full story.

'By the way,' she continued, 'Jamie was here earlier. He said it was difficult to tell if the photos on your mobile were genuine or not. The one of the young Asian girl with a Black couple that was taken somewhere foreign — he said it looked genuine because of the lighting and the way the shadows fell. But he couldn't be certain. What's all that about, Sir?'

'I'm sorry, Grace. I haven't had a chance to brief you on all developments because of what's happened over the last day or two.'

I explained the importance, or otherwise, of the photographs on my mobile, of the possibility that the young girl — and grown woman — was the sniper near the bridge, but I didn't say more because it was simply conjecture. I said I had gone to London yesterday to try and identify a man at an auction who could be an important suspect in the case, but had drawn a blank. I suggested she and I get together once I'd heard from the Ministry of Defence and had spoken to one of their HR officers. I saw no point in both of us going to London at this stage. In any case, Superintendent Breedon would have jumped up and down at the expense involved.

'Nothing from Afghanistan or from the Afghan Embassy in London, is there? Have they taken us up on our offer of sending the victim's DNA samples?'

'No, Sir. I've been ringing them on and off, and I've sent endless emails to Kabul. No luck, sadly. Not surprising, I suppose, given all that's going on in that sad country.'

'Suppose not. Thanks, Grace. Please keep on trying.'

We hung up. She was not the bubbly Grace I had got to know. Something seemed to be bothering her and I wasn't sure what. I wondered if it had something to do with the post-traumatic therapy she had been having. Maybe I would ask her when I saw her next.

I rang our own HR department and arranged for them to send my identification, and other security documents, to the MoD and to make an appointment with whoever I needed to see. Once they had identified the name of the HR officer, I wanted them to send a photograph of our suspect — Jim — to the responsible individual. I scanned and sent a copy of the photograph to HQ.

I knew bureaucracy, especially in the Civil Service, was long and slow, so I wasn't expecting a quick response. As the day passed, I sent a message to Nicole asking for a virtual meeting when she had the time, so that we could compare notes. It was the middle of the day and, again, I wasn't expecting an instant response.

I sent text messages to my children, asking if I could collect them after school because I had a happy surprise for them. I sent Faye a message to clear it with her first, again not expecting a quick response because she would be teaching at her school.

As the late morning turned into early afternoon, I fancied a stroll along the Golden Mile but did not want to leave Fernando. He was dozing on his perch and I had left his cage door open, feeling guilty about locking him up again. But he made no attempt to fly out. He looked serene at times, eyelids drooping, nodding off and waking up with a start. He kept staring at the chopped fruit and nuts at the bottom of his cage.

I listened to some uplifting music, including the Second Waltz by Dmitri Shostakovich, some Mohammed Rafi songs from classic Bollywood films, some Billy Joel and some Neil Young. Then it was time to collect my kids.

Yasmin and Karan were overjoyed to see Fernando as they walked into my front room. Fernando squawked on recognising them, stretched out his grey and white wings, flapped them furiously, and jumped up and down on his perch.

'Oh, baby, how're you?' said Yasmin, after the initial surprise. 'We thought you'd gone forever.'

Fernando blew a wolf whistle.

'Oh, Fernando!' cried Karan. 'I'm so happy to see you.'

Both of them took turns to hug him, wide smiles on their faces.

'How did you find him, Dad?' asked Yasmin.

'I didn't. He found me. Knocked on the back bedroom window.'

'But how, Dad?' asked Karan.

'Well, he pecked the window with his beak,' I replied.

'Oh, Dad,' said Yasmin, grinning, and prodded my midriff with her elbow.

'I really don't know how he survived,' I said, 'or how he found his way back home. He's lost some weight but seems to be okay. I'll get him checked out at the vet's soon. Maybe someone kept him for a while and then he escaped. Maybe he fended for himself — could've fed on berries and leftover picnic food.'

'Glad the ospreys didn't get him,' said Yasmin, the dimples in her cheeks pronounced. I pushed aside any similarities to the young girl standing in the frozen and broken landscape in Syria.

'But Dad, how d'you think he got back here? Back home?' asked Karan, eyes shining.

'No idea. Some animals and birds are really intelligent, like house martins. They're birds that fly all the way from South Africa to this country every year. Thousands of miles. And they build their nests in the same house every year. Nobody understands how they find it again.'

Yasmin said, 'I remember seeing a Disney film ages ago. It was a really old film about two dogs and a cat who walked hundreds of miles in America or Canada — I forget which — to find their owner's house. They thought they'd been abandoned with a friend. And they made it.'

'Animals are wonderful creatures,' I said. 'And African grey parrots are highly intelligent. Fernando will have remembered this house, and the iron bracket holding his cage. I'm not sure, but he might have tried to get my attention before. I often heard noises on the back window. Didn't think in a million years it'd be him.'

'Oh, Dad. We're so glad he's back. We're one big family again,' said Karan, eyes wide and smiling.

CHAPTER 42

Several days later, I sat in the main reception area in the Ministry of Defence building in Whitehall, London, having been cleared by the security team. It was early afternoon. The area was teeming with people in uniform — army, navy, air force — and in smart civilian clothes, hurrying from one side of the massive ground floor to the other. Silent, efficient escalators carried people to the floor above and brought down others, while further away along the gleaming marble floor, the lifts were busy. I knew the building had ten floors or so above ground and three floors below, the latter for top-secret work.

As I sat on the soft leather settee, I thought of how life had changed for me in a relatively short space of time. When I was five years old, not long after Maya had been abducted, my mother and I had gone to the cinema in the Rift Valley town of Nakuru, much bigger than Naivasha. The Indian hero and heroine in the Bollywood film had been in Trafalgar Square, the leading lady in a colourful saree, pigeons fluttering uneasily on her head and outstretched arm, dipping their beaks in her small container of wheat. The leading man in an Indian air force uniform had been smiling next to her, trying to shoo the pigeons away. The camera had panned from them to the mighty Nelson's Column, and I remembered wondering whether I would ever visit this magical place of old Georgian architecture and the circular BT tower, with its rotunda restaurant, standing majestically in the background. Now, nothing remained of the leading man or the leading lady or of the pigeons, apart from memories on a roll of fading celluloid.

As I watched people hurrying past, the irony struck me that the boy from a remote part of the African landscape was now sitting in one of the most powerful places on earth, while a middle-aged African woman asked me to move my legs as she polished the marble floor with a buffing machine.

'Captain Thomas will see you now, Sir,' said the young attendant as he walked towards me, smiling. 'This way, please.'

Captain Thomas was the officer who had responded initially to my enquiries, and she had agreed to meet me once she had conducted a thorough investigation of my request. She said she was part of the Adjutant General's Corps and dealt with the full range of personnel matters relating to serving and former members of the army.

As I was led into one of the upstairs offices, through dark and heavy wooden doors twice my height, Captain Thomas, undoubtedly South Asian in origin, stood up from behind the long conference desk and walked towards me with a wide smile, her hand outstretched. She was wearing a pale cream blouse and well-fitting combat trousers. A lanyard displayed her name and role. We exchanged pleasantries and she offered me a cup of coffee, which I gratefully accepted. I placed my briefcase on the long, mahogany table and gazed at the giant painting of a standing Field Marshall Montgomery in uniform and beret, a baton in his hand.

'I'm sorry it's taken longer than normal, Inspector,' Captain Thomas said. Her aubergine-coloured hair was tied tightly at the back in a bun, and her big brown eyes shone as she indicated for me to sit in a plush chair with armrests. Traffic moved silently on the busy road below us. 'We didn't have much to go on. The brigadier I'm working with thought it'd be good for me to be involved in this case, since it's a serious police matter involving death, after all. I'm on secondment here from my normal regiment.'

'I'm grateful to you, Captain, for seeing me, and for any information you can share about the individual. And before you say anything, I'll try not to besmirch the army's reputation in our investigations.'

'Not a word I hear often. "Besmirch".' She smiled and then continued, 'Well, I interrogated our personnel database with the information you provided. It threw up the files of thousands of individuals. There was no way to go through each one individually. Would've taken a team of officers several months. And the photograph you provided wasn't useful because the personnel records don't have photographs of individuals.'

I had a sinking feeling that this trip was a waste of time and our investigation was going to stall. It was short-lived.

'But I wouldn't let that defeat me,' said Captain Thomas. She smiled. A small nose stud glinted. 'All personnel with security clearance have to have an ID card, of course. I asked our ID team based in Portsmouth to scan the photograph and see whether they could come up with a match, using the latest facial recognition software. I also circulated the photograph to other members of the Adjutant General's Corps, to those who've served a long time in case anyone recognised the man.' She paused.

'And?' I asked, impatiently.

'Both the ID team and one of the HR officers confirmed the same name. The officer — or should I say former officer — is called Graham Maxwell. This is the photograph we have on file for him.'

She pulled out a ten-by-eight photograph from a manila folder and passed it to me. There was no mistaking the man.

He had dark hair and piercing blue eyes and was muscular, but there was no scar or moustache on his top lip.

'He was a major in the Parachute Regiment. He retired a few years ago — sadly, on a full pension. Nasty piece of work, by all accounts. It didn't become apparent to his superiors until much later. He saw action in Iraq and Afghanistan and was disciplined a couple of times. He worked with warlords, became greedy, got involved in the opium trade and helped the warlords in Afghan take the opium out of the country. It was smuggled into Iran and Turkmenistan, to be processed into heroin.

'He was also rumoured to be involved in human trafficking, especially young women. His superiors hushed it all up — they didn't want the publicity. It would have been bad for the army, as well as their careers. But Major Maxwell had built up a good network of mules, informants and others by the time his regiment left. It was noted in his file that he'd become good friends with members of the Special Boat Service. A few of them were involved in some dodgy dealings too.'

The connection with Peter Fraser, the dead diver we'd found in Charnwood Forest, made sense. He had been a member of the Special Boat Service.

As Captain Thomas sipped her coffee, I said, 'What about his pension? Where's it paid?'

'To a bank account in Cyprus. But I can't get any more information out of them because of client confidentiality. And since he hasn't done anything wrong that we're aware of — or can pin on him — we can't insist. But they did tell us the account's been dormant for a long time. No withdrawals or transfers.'

'Any next of kin? Parents? Siblings?'

'No siblings. He was an only child. Some senior recruiting officers in the army prefer it that way. There's no emotional baggage and they can be trained and sent on special missions — life or death situations, so to speak. His father died when he was young, but he did have a mother when he joined. This is her last known address. She must be quite old by now, if she's still alive.'

Captain Thomas had already written the address down on a piece of paper and handed it to me.

'What about the scar above the lip? Any ideas?' I asked.

'He had difficulty controlling his temper sometimes. I'm surprised he was promoted to the rank he was. Maybe he was good at fooling his superiors and passing all the required assessments for promotion. There's a note in his file. He was involved in a serious brawl with one of the other officers after a night of heavy drinking, in Aldershot of all places. A flick knife appeared from nowhere. He was cut above the lip in the fighting. There were no witnesses, so they couldn't be disciplined.'

'Any other relevant information, Captain?'

'He was an expert marksman. Scored highly. He was seconded to the SAS for a while, but they kicked him out. They don't explain why. But given what I've told you about his temperament, I suspect he's not the type they wanted. And, under "hobbies" on his form, it states Maxwell was an excellent chess player. He played to a very high standard. Is that relevant, Inspector?'

'Could be,' I replied. 'Tell me, he wasn't known as Jim at any time, was he? For whatever reason?'

'No, I don't think so,' she said, flicking through the papers on her desk before scrolling down her laptop. After a while, she said, 'But what have we here? His middle name's James.

Maybe he called himself Jim sometimes, to lay a confusing trail.'

I looked up at her beaming face and asked, 'Address?'

'No current address for him. Sorry. But his mother's address is in your neck of the woods. Nottinghamshire. She may still be there.'

'Near enough.'

After thanking Captain Thomas for all the help she had given me and promising to write to her brigadier to express my gratitude, I left the Ministry of Defence buildings and walked towards Charing Cross Station, from where I would take the tube to St Pancras Station and then back to Leicester. It was the height of the rush hour and I was dreading the journey back, packed like sardines and smelling every scent of the human body. As I walked along The Strand, staring at Nelson's Column in Trafalgar Square, my mobile rang.

'Hello, Sir,' said the male voice, who said he was calling from one of the local police stations in Leicester. 'Got somebody called Jalil here. He said you know him. He wants to speak to you urgently.'

'Jalil?'

'He says he's a waiter at The Omar Khayyam. Or was.'

'Yes, I know him. Not seen him in a long time.' I remembered asking after Jalil when I had eaten at the restaurant with Grace. 'What's he want?'

'Says the Afghan woman — the murder victim — was his sister.'

CHAPTER 43

Autumn light shone through the windows of the interview room at the local police station in the east of the city. Grace and I sat across the desk from Jalil Barakzai, the waiter from The Omar Khayyam. He was a slim man in his early twenties, and his big brown eyes darted from me to Grace and then back to me. He looked very different to the erect, biddable waiter he had once been, always immaculately dressed in a silk collarless shirt, dark waistcoat, baggy silk trousers that tapered at the ankles, and thin, embroidered leather shoes with turned-up toes. He was now in a tattered T-shirt and salmon-coloured fleece. I was not sure if the musty smell was from the old carpet, or from his clothes.

I expressed my condolences to Jalil.

'Hasina and I, we both travelled from Afghanistan in the back of a lorry — very hard journey across many countries. We were hidden in different lorries, always afraid we'd be found and sent back, or worse. We came through Iran, Iraq, Turkey and then Greece, Hungary, Germany. Don't know all the countries the lorries go through.'

He stopped and had a sip of black coffee. There were beads of sweat on his forehead, running out from beneath his thick, dark curls. I looked out of the low window at the cracked paving stones. The fading yellow leaves of a dying dandelion fluttered in the breeze, reminding me of one I saw near the abandoned garages where I spoke to Bobby, the drug dealer.

'Our older brother had borrowed lots of money from moneylenders for our journey,' Jalil continued. 'It would be difficult to pay back — many thousands of dollars. He said he'd find a way.'

'What happened when you got here? To this country?' asked Grace.

'Hasina, well, she and other women were taken off first and put in a different lorry at big lorry park near Peterborough. I was brought here to Leicester. We had a hidden phone to keep in touch, but they found hers. Don't know what happened to her. Then one day her friend Amina saw me going into restaurant for work. She couldn't believe it. We all come from the same village. She said she escaped and was trying to get to London. She did not say much — she was scared — but she said Hasina was with the same group. All locked up. Made to do dirty things with dirty men.'

Jalil stopped, tears welling up in his eyes. His long eyelashes flickered. Grace offered him a tissue, which he did not accept.

'And now, now she's dead… Allah in his mercy wanted her back. To keep her safe.' He sobbed, putting his head in his hands.

After a while, he said, 'I worked in different factories, different restaurants, different carwashes. All my money was taken away. They said it was to pay for our trip to the UK. No papers — couldn't go to the police or anyone else. Mr Rahimi, the owner of the restaurant, he treated us well. But he doesn't know where we live, or how. We just did work. He was given all the right papers.

'I know Hasina tried to escape before, both she and Amina. Both were caught, Amina told me. They're not nice people. And when my sister tried to escape again, she was not seen again.'

'And what about Amina? Are you still in touch with her?' I asked.

'No, not heard from her for a long time. One of the other waiters said she escaped to London and is hiding there.'

He took another sip of coffee, his hands trembling as he put down the mug on the desk. There were nicotine stains on his long fingernails. Grace looked at him with concern.

'And then I escaped, like it says on this T-shirt.' He pulled open the front of his fleece and I saw the familiar phrase, *Just Do It*. 'Because I know they will kill me too. My older brother, Ghulam, he sent me a text message sometimes, telling me he will pay back the money. He said he would try to come to the UK. But his messages, they stopped. Don't know what happened to him.'

He looked out of the window. A sparrow rummaged in the hedge, while a robin looked on. A magpie looked longingly at both.

'They know Hasina is my sister,' he continued. 'They knew I would go to the police. But I hid in Birmingham, away from them.'

That would explain why he'd suddenly left his job at the restaurant.

'I'm so sorry, Jalil, about Hasina. And I hope you find your brother, Ghulam,' I said.

'Somebody told me he was killed in Syria. By *Bichchoo*. The Scorpion. But I don't know if it's true.'

My stomach tightened into a knot.

A teardrop ran down his cheek. He took the tissue Grace offered.

'Look, Jalil,' I said, 'we'll keep you safe and try to get paperwork and other things sorted for you. So please don't worry. Then you can have Hasina back. But we also need to confirm your DNA with hers. And we'll decide what's best to do after that.'

He looked confused, not quite sure what I was saying to him. I asked Grace to accompany him back to HQ on the other side of the city. It would take a while for the paperwork to be filled in and for other actions to be undertaken, including finding him a safehouse. I also asked Ben to arrange for a mouth swab to be taken and for DNA samples to be analysed.

As Jalil and Grace left, I was wondering whether to have a cup of tea in the canteen when my mobile rang.

It was a member of the admin section back at HQ. 'Sir, it's about the address you asked us to follow up yesterday — the one in Nottinghamshire that you got from the MoD. Sadly, the lady who lived there moved on. The current occupants bought the house from somebody else. They didn't know her.'

'Oh, shit!' I said, and then, 'Sorry.'

'Not all's lost, Sir. That's why it's taken me a while to get back to you. I rang a few local estate agents. I eventually found one who handled the sale of the house a few years ago. Apparently, the lady in question moved to Lincolnshire. I didn't have an address, but I looked it up on the electoral register. She's still there! Not far from Stamford.'

'Well done. That's excellent! Please send across the details.'

I ended the call. The location of the house in Lincolnshire, not far from east Leicestershire, placed it near the calls Nicole and her team had pinpointed recently, from the man named James. It also confirmed what Jamie Shriver and Nicole Laurent had told me about various electronic signals being picked up by particular masts in the area. Since I was in the east of the city, I thought I may as well pay a visit to the house.

CHAPTER 44

It was late evening; Nicole had been working on a number of cases with Interpol and the French police, and she apologised for not video-calling sooner. I brought her up to date with Fernando and she was happy for me. Then she called out his name and blew a whistle. He went wild, squawking, wings beating furiously.

'Nicole's a bad girl! Nicole's a bad girl!' he shrieked.

Fortunately, the inspector laughed.

Through the kitchen window behind Nicole's head, Montmartre looked full of life. The white stone of the central dome of the Sacré-Coeur was lit up, gleaming bright under the dark Parisian skyline. Electric lights in hundreds of apartments were switched on and, in the distance, the ghostly glow of car headlights danced and disappeared among the trees of the nearby park.

'I'm over the moon to have found him safe and well. I now leave him with neighbours when I'm away working, so he's not lonely.'

I sat in my front room with my laptop, trying not to think of the contrast between the two settings. The television in front of me was switched on, the volume down low. I sipped a glass of tonic water and placed it on the table beside me. I updated Nicole on my visit to the Ministry of Defence, Captain Thomas's identification of Major Maxwell as the Grand Master, and my visit to the house of the suspect's mother.

'I parked in an isolated spot and watched the comings and goings for a couple of hours. During that time, nobody went in or came out of the house. I drove up and down, pretending to be lost, and looked at the house, but nothing.'

'Maybe she went shopping,' suggested Nicole.

'Perhaps. I have a couple of officers watching the place. I cleared it with the appropriate authorities, including the Lincolnshire Police.'

'And what about the Scorpion? Have you heard from her?'

A shard of glass pierced my heart when she asked this question. 'She sent me a text message recently saying she was my sister. Attached were three photographs of herself at different ages, in different parts of the world.' I described the photographs to Nicole and forwarded them to her.

'Or she may not be your sister,' Nicole said, after looking at them. 'I still think we're on the right road,' she added, trying to change the subject. 'Or do you British say "right track"?'

'Could be either,' I said, and smiled. Her English was considerably better than my almost non-existent French.

'The geographical connection is important,' she continued. 'Leicestershire and Lincolnshire. And Interpol have evidence of a link between two people in those two areas — a woman named Kel and a man named Jim. Well, this man Jim is heavily involved in selling arms to groups all over the world. He's also involved in selling other contraband.'

'Well, Jim must be the Grand Master. And Kel…' I stared at the television screen.

'And Kel?' Nicole repeated.

'Oh, fuck! Nicole, I'm really sorry. Gotta go. I'll call you back.' I cut the connection.

The voice on one of the movie channels continued, '*To mark the forthcoming anniversary of Grace Kelly's birthday, we have a special weekend of her films.*' On the screen were short clips of her various films, together with cinema trailers from the 1950s, when the originals were screened.

'*She was a highly versatile actress whose wide repertoire of acting roles reflected her abilities. Many critics have focused on her privileged background and her subsequent marriage to Prince Rainier of Monaco, but they do not give her enough credit for her true acting talents. The films, clips of which you can see on your screen right now, include* High Noon, *the Academy Award-winning Western with Gary Cooper;* Mogambo, *the African adventure with Clark Gable;* Rear Window, *the murder thriller with James Stewart; and* High Society, *the musical with Bing Crosby and Louis Armstrong.*'

Oh, God.

When Grace and I had eaten at The Omar Khayyam, she had said how much she liked old films and had mentioned a number that all starred Grace Kelly. *High Noon. Mogambo. Rear Window. High Society.*

Grace Kelly.

Grace.

Kel.

Could Kel be a nickname? A play on the name of the famous actress?

I suddenly recalled something that had been bothering me. Grace had asked whether the flyers I had stuck around Rutland Water seeking Fernando's whereabouts had yielded any success. I knew I had not said anything about the flyers to her, or to anybody else I worked with. Only my children and Faye knew about them. So how did Grace get hold of this information?

Then there was the information both Jamie Shriver and Nicole had given to me: they'd said there were pings on mobile phone masts in the north-east of the county, not far from where Grace lived, and certainly on masts on her way home from the city.

I fired up my laptop, connected with Nicole again, and asked her a question, the answer to which would confirm my suspicions.

'Do you have a voice recording of the conversations between Kel and Jim?' I asked.

'*Oui*,' she replied. 'There is one from today. But I have not yet listened to it. No time. Need to connect to our central database. Give me a moment, please.'

She connected a USB cable to her computer and typed in a few passwords.

'Ready?' she asked.

I nodded, muting the television.

Through my laptop speakers, I heard the unmistakable voice.

'*Where're you, James?*' Grace asked.

'*In Amsterdam at the moment. Tying up loose ends. Should be back at East Midlands Airport in the next couple of hours. What's going on at your end?*'

'*Oh, not a lot. Been interviewing an illegal from Afghanistan today…*'

'*Your boss, has he found his bird yet?*' the man asked.

'*Why are you so bothered about his parrot? And, yes, as a matter of fact he has…*'

I asked Nicole to switch the recording off.

She leant towards the camera, eyes wide. 'She knows you, Rohan. The comment about your bird. Who is she?'

I nodded sadly. 'My sergeant. I'm sorry, Nicole, I have to go. I need to decide what to do. This is a bit of a shock.'

'I understand. Maybe we'll speak later. Let me know.'

I thanked her, and we said goodbye.

I paced up and down, took a sip of water and stared at Fernando. 'What would you do, Fernando? Eh?'

'Watch the birdie, Rohan, watch the birdie.'

'Thanks! You're a great help!'

After a while, I picked up my mobile, dialled a number and let it ring. It went straight to voicemail.

It was quite late. I wondered whether to ring again. Then I took another sip of tonic water and redialled.

'This had better be good, Rohan,' came the reply.

'It isn't.'

'Isn't what?' demanded Superintendent Breedon.

'Isn't good, Sir.'

A female voice in the background said, 'Darling, switch it off. Come back to bed.'

'I'm really sorry, Sir. But you need to know this.'

As I brought him up to date on developments, I could hear the cogs turning in his head. Damage limitation. Preserve the reputation of the force. Preserve *his* reputation. Not necessarily in that order.

Then he told me what to do.

CHAPTER 45

It was almost five o'clock in the morning. Grace Nicholson sat in the cold, drab interview room at police HQ. I looked at her from the other side of the two-way mirror, the interview room wired with microphones so I could hear the conversations.

'You've got to be joking,' said Grace to DI Fiona Whittingdale, who sat opposite the interview desk. In the corner, another officer was present and the interview was being formally recorded.

'Can you please get hold of DI Sharma, my superior? He'll clear this up. There's been a terrible misunderstanding, Ma'am.'

'All in good time, DS Nicholson. All in good time.'

Grace wrapped her coat tightly around her body and crossed her legs. Her hair was unkempt. She looked across the desk, wincing at the two fluorescent lights.

'We possess information that you're helping this individual called James. He's well known for his criminal activities, both here and abroad,' said DI Whittingdale, her blonde hair tied in a bun, glasses resting on her head.

Grace shook her head. She looked down.

DI Whittingdale's gaze lingered on Grace's face. I walked in and sat down on a chair at an old, beaten-up metal table in the corner.

'Oh, Sir, thank God you're here. I don't know what's going on. But I haven't done anything wrong. And neither has James.'

DI Whittingdale turned and smiled at me. Grace Nicholson twisted the tissue she held in her hands, pulling it apart bit by bit. Her fingers trembled when she put the remnants on the battered, metal desk.

'Why am I here, Sir? What's going on?' she pleaded.

'I'm sorry, Grace. DI Whittingdale's in charge. As you can imagine, it would look odd if I arrested my own DS.'

'But why? Why won't anyone tell me what's going on?' She looked down and stifled a sob.

I stood up, opened the door and asked one of the duty officers to bring some coffee into the room.

There was silence.

I stared at the top of the dented, grey metal table where I sat. Someone with a penknife or a steel nail had scratched the words, *Fuck the pigs*, to which somebody had replied, *No thanks*. Below that was a newer statement: *But I'll do the lezzies. Remind them of wot their missing.*

The coffee arrived several moments later. Grace sipped hers slowly.

'What's your relationship to James?' asked DI Whittingdale, as she put down her mug. 'You sound like longstanding lovers on the recordings we've got.'

'What? What recordings?' asked Grace.

The DI didn't reply.

'Look, I don't know what you've got. But James has looked after me for many years — cared for me and, yes, loved me. When there was nobody there. We haven't seen much of each other lately. But since he left the army, he's been around a bit more. He's seen more of me and his mother.'

'He's much older than you, isn't he? At least a dozen or fifteen years. Like older men, do you?' asked DI Whittingdale.

'What's that got to do with anything?' replied Grace.

'Like them with a bit more experience, do you? Know what they're doing — more than some of the younger ones?'

Grace stared at DI Whittingdale, whose glasses were back on the bridge of her nose. Then she looked at me. 'James,' she sighed, 'is my *brother*. My stepbrother. And, yes, he's a bit older than me. He's always looked out for me. He stopped me being bullied at school; he cared for me. And, to stop your sick mind some more, no, we were not, and *never* have been lovers!'

'What?' I said.

'Yes, my stepbrother!' replied Grace, raising her voice. 'I told you in the restaurant, when we first met. He's much older than me. He was an officer in the army but left a while ago. He buys and sells things. I'm not exactly sure what. He has clients all over the world. He's not involved in murder, or any nasty things.'

'But the house in Lincolnshire — that's his, isn't it?' I asked.

'Yes,' replied Grace. 'His mother, my stepmother, lives there at the moment. They have a different surname to me. My father divorced her. Told you that before, too. James bought the place for her. He visits her every now and again when he's in the country. I tried ringing her tonight but got no reply. James told me afterwards she'd gone to a friend's house for a meal and forgot to take her phone.'

'Is this James?' asked DI Whittingdale, standing up and thrusting forward a photograph of a middle-aged man with a noticeable scar above his lip. It was Graham Maxwell, who also went by the name 'Jim'.

'No idea who this man is,' said Grace. 'Never seen him before in my life.'

DI Whittingdale clenched a fist and stared at me. 'And the address, Grace. The address of the house. What is it?' she asked.

Grace gave her the name of the street and the house number but wasn't sure of the postcode. She took out her mobile phone and showed them a photograph of James.

DI Whittingdale indicated that we should meet outside. She closed the door behind her and whispered, 'Well?'

'That's not the address we've been staking out. Not the house I went to. Shit! We got the wrong person and the wrong fucking address!'

'Not me! You! What do we do now?' asked DI Whittingdale, the dark bags under her eyes more pronounced.

'Her brother's involved in some dodgy dealing,' I eventually said. 'Interpol wouldn't have picked up on him otherwise. The French wouldn't have got it so badly wrong. Illegal arms trading was mentioned by Inspector Laurent. Probably other things as well.'

'But it doesn't mean DS Nicholson's involved too,' said Fiona Whittingdale.

'No,' I replied. 'But she held on to information which would have helped my investigation.'

'Maybe naivety?' said Fiona Whittingdale.

'I so hope you're right, Fiona. Let's keep her under investigation. Release her under bail. I'll ask the super to suspend her pending blah, blah, blah.'

While DI Whittingdale returned to the room, I asked the duty officer outside to remove the offending desk as soon as they were done.

'Will do, Sir. Sorry, had to use it from the custody suite. The usual one in the interview room was badly damaged by a suspect recently.'

CHAPTER 46

I felt the warm arm nudge the side of my back.

'C'mon, Rohan, time to wake up.'

'Oh, I don't want to. Can't we stay here a bit longer?'

'Wakey, wakey, time to go to work.'

'Oh, Faye…'

I drifted out of the dream. It was something Faye used to say to me years ago. Then she'd cuddle up behind me, naked, hold me tight and not let go. Eventually, when I had to break free, she would giggle and say, 'Oh … spoilsport.'

I blinked and rubbed my eyes as daylight poured in through the gaps in the curtains. The clamour of voices outside was getting louder and then fading into the distance. People were hurrying past, some shouting in Gujarati, some in broken English with the unmistakable Leicester accent.

The bedside clock told me it was almost midday and I'd had about four hours' sleep. I had returned from HQ at about seven-thirty in the morning, had fed Fernando and then crashed into bed. It took me a while to go to sleep, as my neighbour had woken up to go to work and was listening to *Sunrise Radio*, which consisted of a mixture of interviews with prominent local businesspeople, Bollywood gossip, the latest fusion music and some classical Hindi songs.

I had tossed and turned, thinking about Grace's betrayal and the phone recordings of her divulging confidential information. I wanted to think it was naivete on her part, that she did not mean any harm, but what she had been doing was unforgiveable. Who knew what else she had leaked, or what else she had been doing? Still, Superintendent Breedon had agreed, while travelling to the office in his car, to suspend her pending a full investigation and informed me that HR would deal with it.

I had also rung the two officers staking out the house where Graham Maxwell's mother lived. They informed me that all was quiet and nobody had been in or out. The evening lights had come on, and they suspected they were on a timer. I asked them to keep me informed.

I went downstairs, cleaned out Fernando's cage, topped up his water tray, fed him some more and then made myself some Indian tea. I needed a dose of powdered cinnamon, cardamom and cloves with the tea leaves and the milk, all boiled in a saucepan. It would wake me up.

'You're probably confused, aren't you, Fernando? Normally, you'd be with the neighbours while I went to work.'

He looked up, his dark beak covered in flecks of peach and pear. His weight had improved considerably. 'Thank you, Rohan. Thank you,' he said. I wasn't sure if he was thanking me for the food, or for keeping him company.

'You're welcome,' I replied, taking another sip of tea, which was having the desired effect. I pulled the dressing gown cord tighter and watched the midday news. Then my mobile vibrated.

'Hi, Jenny, how you doing?' I asked Jenny Tyburn, the curator from the local museum.

'Lovely to speak to you, Rohan. Not heard from you for a while. Was wondering if the investigation was almost complete, and if you fancied meeting up for a cup of coffee or a meal.'

'Would love to, Jenny. But, as the Americans say, can we have a rain check on that, please? Just a bit too busy at the moment.'

'Oh, that's a shame. Been looking forward to it. So, I still need to sit on my article?'

'Afraid so. For the moment.'

She sounded disappointed. We agreed to meet before too long and certainly when the investigation was over.

'For a meal. It's on me,' were her final words.

As soon as I'd ended the call, the screen lit up and Ben Carter's name appeared on it.

'Hello, Sir. Just thought I'd give you the forensic results on the tests done recently.'

What he told me threw me completely.

It was mid-afternoon. I got out of the pool car, which I'd parked in a cul-de-sac on a sprawling council estate on the edge of the city. The heavy, dark grey cumulonimbus clouds rested low over my head and stretched into the distance. Broken glass crunched under my leather shoes as I walked towards the blocks of two-storey maisonettes, each one joined to the other in a long line. The blocks reminded me of prisons in Siberia, or those in western China. The uneven pavements, overflowing waste bins and discarded fast food containers blew in the strengthening breeze. The cracked and broken roof tiles, some lying on the ground, had long ceased to protect the people inside, now housing many with broken lives and broken dreams.

In the distance, groups of parents, some women with toddlers in pushchairs, waited for their children outside the school gates, some laughing, some smoking, some arguing. The sound of children's excited voices and their laughter soon filtered through the air. I tried not to think about the used syringe I'd just avoided, nor the bright red bra and used condom lying on the side of the road. I nodded at one of the undercover officers, who was innocuously dressed and walking past.

I entered the block of flats and climbed the side stairs to the upper floor, my briefcase bumping my thigh. The plaster on the wall was missing in places, and the pockmarked breeze block showed through. A fading swastika and other right-wing graffiti were spray-painted on the walls. I knocked on the brown door on the top floor and waited, while I was checked through the peephole in the middle. The turn of the mortice lock and then the Yale lock and then the removal of the door chain was followed by the door opening tentatively.

'It's all right, Jalil. Can I come in, please?'

'Oh, Mr Rohan, I'm pleased to see you. Please, please come in.'

We went through the hallway and into the sparse lounge. The curtains were tattered, the room cold. I sat down on an old settee with uneven, uncomfortable springs. Jalil sat on a wooden chair opposite me, next to a vinyl-covered table. He offered me some Afghan tea, the black leaves boiled with cinnamon, cardamom, cloves and sugar. I thanked him and sipped it. His eyes were furtive, looking up and down and from side to side. A heavy smell of nicotine was in the air.

'Is this place okay for you, Jalil?'

'Not good, Mr Rohan. But better than being on the streets. I know two policemen keep an eye on this flat all the time. I also get food and drink delivered. But I want to have a normal life.'

He was dressed in some new clothes — pale blue faded jeans, a dark sweatshirt and a pair of Nike trainers. A cream-coloured fleece was draped on the chair behind him.

'But people, they're good to me. Got better clothes, can eat better.'

'I'm glad to hear that, Jalil. You know we're trying to keep you safe, until we catch some of the people involved.'

He nodded.

'And that's why I'm here. I'm not sure if this is good news or not. But the DNA sample you gave — you know, the mouth swab — doesn't match that of the female body. That's the poor woman who was murdered and found in the river.'

'So not Hasina?' he asked, wide-eyed.

'No, it's not your sister, Hasina.'

'Thanks be to Allah.'

'But, Jalil, it doesn't mean she's safe. She could still have come to harm.'

His head, full of dark curls, bounced up and down. 'But she could be alive,' he said, relief etched on his young face.

I did not want to crush his optimism. 'Yes, Jalil, she could still be alive,' I said, though I knew the chances of that were slim.

He smiled and looked down at the ground. 'But where could she be, Mr Rohan?'

'I have no idea. But please don't go looking for her and place yourself in danger. Let us do the looking. Do you promise?'

He nodded. 'What about the poor dead woman you have? Who is she?'

'I'm not sure, Jalil. But I'm hoping you can help me.'

I took another sip of tea. He tapped his fingers on the dark blue vinyl covering the table, next to the overflowing ashtray. He took my cup and placed it beside him while I switched on my laptop. I scrolled down and showed him the same photographs of the writing between the toes of the dead woman that Grace and I had shown to the university academic, Dr Khorram. I'd learned a lot from him about Pashto but didn't say anything to Jalil about our meeting.

'This writing, Jalil. Can you read it?' I asked and explained where it had been found.

He stared at the screen, shivered, and asked me to scroll through all the images.

'It says *Loy Bagh*, which is our village in Afghanistan — mine, Hasina's and Amina's.' His gaze lingered on my face at the mention of Amina's name. 'The other writing is not finished. It says *"ina"*, which could be part of a name.'

He paused, tears welling up. 'Oh, Allah the Merciful, please not Amina,' he said. 'We all grew up together as children. She and Hasina are good friends. Both there and here.'

'Do you know if she has any relations in this country? Brothers? Sisters? Cousins? Even those who entered illegally? I promise we won't do anything to them. We won't have them deported. But we need to find out who this poor woman is. We tried contacting the authorities in Afghanistan, but nobody's replying. Given all the other difficulties they're facing, something like this isn't a priority for them.'

He looked at me as I spoke but seemed to be in world of his own. 'Can I smoke, Mr Rohan?'

'Your flat, Jalil. Not mine. Please do whatever you want.'

The trail of the bluish-brown smoke meandered above my head, a slight whiff of it making me wretch. I hid my discomfort. I did not push him, but walked to the window and looked at the depressing skyline. Raindrops puttered on the windowpane and ran down into the decaying timber frame.

Finally, when he was about to stub out the cigarette end, he said, 'Amina has a brother in London. But he came here under a lorry, from Calais. He works in restaurants, sometimes does carwashes, and in summer he goes to pick fruit in Kent. I don't know where he is. But I have a phone number for him, only to be used in an emergency.'

'Jalil, please. This is important. We need him to do a DNA test, like you did, to find out if it's Amina. We'll even meet him, bring him here. Or we can do a test where he is. But we need to find him.'

'Okay, Mr Rohan, I'll contact him.'

'But please, Jalil, let me or one of my team speak to him, to explain the situation. You're not trained in these things.'

'I will see what I can do.'

I shook his hand.

'And thank you for everything, Mr Rohan,' he said, as I closed the front door behind me.

Later in the evening I had a video call with Nicole and explained what had happened over the last twenty-four hours. She was apologetic but also said the information about James McNamara, Grace's stepbrother, was largely reliable. He used his biological father's name and had been involved in the sale of illegal armaments using forged end-user certificates. These certificates allowed arms to be legitimately sold to countries and no questions would be asked. There was also evidence of his involvement, with others, in the drugs trade and in protection rackets in different parts of the world. She said she would ask her superiors to issue an international arrest warrant for him.

CHAPTER 47

The cold rays of the autumn sun pierced the large, reinforced window behind Superintendent Breedon. It was early morning and I had been summoned to his office. His feet stretched out under the large desk, and I could see the tips of his finely polished black shoes when I sat in the chair opposite him.

After I'd briefed him on current developments, he rested his elbows on the desk and steepled his long fingers. The nails had been clipped and the cuffs of his dak uniform were starched. The bright sun made me squint as I looked at him. I did not mention the one thing that was tearing me apart. Was the woman who'd sent me the text messages and who claimed to be the shooter at Bow Bridge really my sister? God, I so wanted it to be her. She knew so much about me, though she could have picked that up from the media, especially after the publicity I'd received for the Shiva the Destroyer case. But the photographs she'd sent me looked real. Part of me wanted to tell my superior, but part of me didn't. After all, the woman had committed no crime. She claimed to have fired the rifle at the bridge, but there was no evidence to say it was her.

As I wrestled with my conscience, I heard the words, 'Are you listening to me, Rohan?' Superintendent Breedon was speaking to me the way a teacher would speak to a child.

I looked across the desk and said, 'Yes, of course, Sir. Just got a fair bit going on at the moment.'

He cleared his throat, letting his gaze linger on me. His thin lips stretched tight. 'I understand why you took the actions you did, Rohan,' he said, eventually, 'but some of the local politicians are treating it as yet another gaffe by us — raiding the home of one of our colleagues, breaking the door down. I told them we acted on what we regarded as reliable information from Interpol and the French police.'

I was not sure what to make of the royal 'we' and 'us' and treated it with suspicion.

'Be that as it may,' he continued, the sun's rays bouncing off the gleaming epaulettes on his shoulders, 'DS Nicholson acted highly improperly. In addition to the phone calls to her stepbrother — who's involved in the illegal sale of arms to foreign powers and God knows what terrorist groups — the team for professional standards investigating her conduct has found other incriminating evidence.' His brows furrowed. 'They found she had been interrogating the PNC for any information on her brother — obviously to keep him posted. She typed in her password on the computer and used the search engine numerous times. The searches were nothing to do with any cases you and she were working on. There's no going back for her.'

I wondered how she knew about the flyers I'd put out for Fernando. Her brother must have had contacts within the rangers at Rutland Water, or somebody in the police must have heard about them. There was no way for me to know.

'No, I guess not, Sir,' I replied to Superintendent Breedon. 'Oh, by the way, can you make sure we've got all the paperwork ready from the magistrates? It's for search warrants and the like. We need them quickly.'

I explained which type of warrant was necessary and why.

He looked at me, nodded, and then said, 'As you know, for some things we can use anti-terror legislation to justify our actions. But I'll bear in mind your request. Okay, that'll be all.'

As I walked down the corridor, my mobile vibrated.

'Oh, hello Mr Rohan,' said Jalil when I answered. 'I contacted Omar, Amina's brother. He wants to know if she's okay or not. He hasn't heard from her for a long time. He says he will meet you for a DNA test, but not in London. Doesn't want anybody to know where he lives. He hasn't got any papers. He says he will meet you at Hemel Hempstead station.' He then gave me a day and time.

'Thank you, Jalil. That's really good. Please thank Omar for me. But I can't meet him myself. It will have to be two members of the forensics team. They know what to do. Will you go down with them? I'll arrange for your train ticket.'

He hesitated.

'Please, Jalil. This is really important.'

After a much longer pause, he agreed. I said I would contact the head of forensics and would then let him know the names and numbers of the two support staff who would go down with him. I asked if he was comfortable with that arrangement and he agreed.

As I ended the call, a disturbing text message arrived:

Hello, bhaia. Been so long. Want to meet you, mum and dad. We should be one big happy family. Been apart too long. Is Fernando okay? Will be in touch again. Can't wait to see you all. Your loving sister Maya xxx

The icy grip tightened around my heart. I so wanted to see her and talk to her. But how on earth would Mum and Dad react? And was it really her?

As I walked back to the incident room, a female colleague passed by in the opposite direction.

'Are you all right, Sir? You look pale.'

'Oh ... do I? Yes, I'm fine, Debbie. Thanks for asking. Just working hard, that's all.'

She smiled and carried on walking.

I wondered what the balance was now between happiness and sadness.

As the day progressed, I tried not to think of Maya, or of Grace. But it was difficult. Faye and the children also came into my thoughts, and I pushed them to one side of my brain. I evaluated the mountain of evidence on the case — the paperwork, the computer files, the medical reports and the witness statements, making sure I had not missed anything. I wondered whether I ought to ask for Grace to be replaced.

The phone rang.

'Sir,' said the male officer who was staking out the house on the outskirts of Stamford, 'it's been quiet here for a long time. The house was empty. But an ambulance has just pulled up, and an old woman on crutches was helped in by the paramedics. It's quiet again now.'

'Any carers with her?'

'No, Sir.'

'Okay, thanks for letting me know, Steve. Keep an eye on things. See if she uses the phone. There's no mobile registered to that address, but the landline's still working. The house is bugged, isn't it?'

He confirmed it was.

'Landline's bugged too. Keep listening. I'll join you as soon as I can.'

'Okay, Sir.'

CHAPTER 48

I squinted and stared at the ceiling as the tinkling chimes of my mobile phone sounded on the bedside table. The breeze whispered through the gap in the window, and the fraying curtains sighed in response. The pale yellow sunlight danced on the uneven ceiling.

I looked at the clock and saw it was past eight in the morning. *Shit!* I thought, grabbing my phone. The call was from Steve, the officer from the armed response unit who was staking out Jim's mother's house with a colleague.

'Sir,' he said, 'she just received a call.' He played me the recording:

'Jimmy, where've you been? I was in hospital. You didn't even ring to find out how I was.'

'I'm really sorry, Mum, I didn't know. I've been abroad.'

'You're always abroad. Don't care about your poor mum anymore. I got nobody else.'

'I'm really sorry, Mum. But I got to work. What was wrong with you?'

'You want to know now I'm back home. You couldn't care less before.'

'Oh, please Mum.'

'Well, I fell down the stairs. Couldn't get up for hours. Not till Mrs Wright from next door looked through the letterbox and saw me. She said she was worried about me because I hadn't come out for my daily walk. She let herself in with the spare key, then rang the ambulance.'

'Oh, Mum, I'm really sorry. But you're okay now, aren't you?'

'No thanks to you. They kept me in hospital for two days and did all sorts of tests and X-rays. Wouldn't discharge me until I was mobile, they said, because I live on my own. Wish your father was still alive…'

'*Look, Mum, I'm home for a while now. I'll come up to see you soon. Maybe even later today, as I've got things to do up there.*'

'*That's right. You're not coming to see me, but because you got things to do.*'

'*Please, Mum. I'll be there later. Probably in the evening. Promise.*'

The line went dead.

Both Anita Thomas at the Ministry of Defence and Rupert at the auction house in London had confirmed that Maxwell used the name 'James' or 'Jim'. James was his middle name, and his mother must have preferred 'Jimmy' to 'Graham'. I thanked Steve and told him to maintain his position and ring me about any developments. I would be there later.

'All's quite ordinary, normal chit-chat between mother and son,' said Steve.

It was about nine-thirty at night and we were sitting in the unmarked, powerful BMW estate that was parked in a secluded spot. I sat in front with the driver, while Steve sat in the back. The detached house with the old lady stood in a quiet cul-de-sac in the distance, a large tree in the small front garden. A silvery-white crescent moon lingered low over the cool horizon, a final smile on another day. Through the gathering clouds, stars competed for their twinkling light to be visible. Parked on the drive was a dark Range Rover, with Maxwell's driver wearing a baseball cap, the face difficult to make out. We listened intently through our headpieces. The conversation between Graham Maxwell and his mother inside the house was banal. He asked about her health, and she said it was good to see him and that he looked well. She also asked whether he had eaten. Mothers were the same the world over. Eventually, after he had finished his cup of tea, he said he would be back soon and kissed her. They said goodbye.

He came out of the front door and got into the Range Rover. The car reversed, drove past the side road we were parked on, and made its way towards the main road. As it passed, his driver removed the baseball cap and a mane of long, dark hair swung and rested between their shoulder blades.

'Looks like an Asian woman,' said Steve. 'Definitely not white.'

My heart almost missed a beat. God, was that Maya in the car? Could it really be her, after all these years? So close, yet so far. I tried to keep calm. I needed to be professional about this, and not let personal matters interfere.

The Range Rover kept to the speed limit and travelled west towards Oakham and then north to Melton Mowbray. We followed at a discreet distance, not sure of the route the car was taking. It was definitely not the most direct route to Leicester, if that was where it was heading. There were no bugs in the Range Rover, so we could not hear anything.

It was quiet along the dak country road, an occasional car coming in the opposite direction. The storm clouds rumbled and moved at speed across the horizon, light from the silvery moon and the handful of stars barely visible. Steve's semi-automatic rifle poked through the gap between the two front seats, the infrared sight fixed on the barrel.

The smooth whirring of the four-litre engine broke the silence, the light from the dashboard and connected computers dimmed to a minimum. We skirted the main road around Melton Mowbray and then headed south, towards Leicester.

'Strange route, Sir, if I may say so. Could easily have followed a more direct route to the city, if that's where they're heading. But why?'

'Hmmm … and they're keeping to the speed limit, almost as if they know they're being followed — like a driver who's had too much to drink and clocks a police car behind them.'

As we approached the outskirts of Leicester, Steve said, 'Perhaps they're going to join the M1. It's not far from here, and it would take them north or south. That would make more sense.' The car's brake lights came on and it made a sharp turn on the slip road towards the city centre.

'There goes your answer, Steve. Not the motorway.' After a few moments I said, 'Just got a bad feeling about this.'

I radioed HQ and asked for another armed response unit to join us. I gave them our current position.

We travelled down the main arterial route into the city, along the Golden Mile, which was quiet and mostly locked up for the night, apart from a few stragglers wandering along the pavements. I turned to my right and could almost see my house as we drove past the side streets of Victorian terraces. I hoped Fernando was okay and not feeling too lonely.

A few minutes later, as the other armed response unit with four more officers positioned itself behind us, Steve said, 'I get the feeling we're being given the run around —'

A black Audi estate drove at speed from one of the side roads and smashed into my side. Our car swerved to the right and missed an oncoming one by inches. We stopped. I grabbed my left arm. The pain was excruciating. The Audi raced past us and stopped. A dark woman with a rifle leaned out of the roof of the car. A burst of semi-automatic fire hit our radiator grille. We ducked. Shots ripped open the gap between the windscreen and roof. Three shots zipped through the glass and into the car. The driver put his foot down, head down but squinting over the dashboard. Officers from the second car behind us opened fire. Bullets were breaking the tarmac and zinging on the metal as sparks flew. They chased the Audi as it sped away to the right.

I screamed at our driver to follow the Range Rover, shouting to Steve behind me not to open fire. It would be too dangerous for bystanders. I turned round and saw him slumped to the side. There was a gaping wound in his neck with blood spurting out. I looked at the driver, who was ashen-faced. 'Think I've been hit in the shoulder, Sir,' he said. The Range Rover raced along one of the main roads in the city centre, shops on either side, the railway station a mile away. There was a squeal of brakes and the smell of burning rubber. He turned a sharp left, onto a road of office blocks. High in the sky, I saw a helicopter with flashing lights. It was descending. What the hell was it doing so low?

The Range Rover swerved again to the left, mounted the pavement and crashed into the glass front of the office block — Bishop's Tower, the tallest building in the city. The pale, brightly lit rectangular façade stretched seventeen floors into the night sky, each floor riddled with square windows. The two occupants flung open the doors, jumped out, and raced towards the lifts. I told the driver to radio for help, grabbed his pistol, and ran out as our car lurched to a stop. I clutched my arm in agony, running as fast as I could. I jumped towards the lift doors as they closed.

I looked to the left, found the service lift towards the back and dived in. It had to be the top floor they were heading for. But why? Why bring us here?

All of a sudden, the whole building shook. An enormous explosion sounded from somewhere below — maybe halfway up. The lift was moving from side to side, the winding gear struggling. But it was still moving, with the creaking sound of tired cables about to snap.

There was a second explosion, this time a lot closer. The smell of petrol fumes, of oil, of cordite and nitrate explosives rushed in.

I stopped the lift. It felt too dangerous. I got off at the sixteenth floor and ran up the service stairs. I could hear the *chop chop chop* of the helicopter above. I hadn't called in the police helicopter, so it wasn't ours. Maxwell must have radioed his pilot at East Midlands Airport earlier to pick them up here. Had it landed on the roof? I flung open the doors as a hail of bullets zinged into the metal. I dived through and rolled along the apron, firing clumsily with the pistol in my hand. My left arm was burning.

The helicopter was getting ready to lift off. Graham Maxwell ran towards it. No mistaking the muscular physique, the haircut, the army training. He dived in. It started taking off. There was another burst of machine gun fire. The *pfft pfft pfft* of bullets tore the apron at my feet and slammed into the metal doors behind me. I shot back. The woman jumped up into the half open door. I grabbed her legs as the chopper blades increased their revolutions. The downward draught got stronger and stronger. I jerked. I pulled. She let go, falling to the side. I was on my stomach, the cold, grey pavement eighty-four metres below. The helicopter took off. She hung onto the railing, legs dangling over the side. As her hands slipped, I grabbed her wrist. I almost screamed in agony as the pain flashed from my hand up to my shoulder. Looking down, I stared at her terrified face, the sweat on her forehead. Her dimples. The unmistakable Sharma mouth. Her hair blown about by the rotor blades.

'Maya, please hang on. Maya, please. Don't let go.'

'Rohan. Don't let go. Please.'

'No, I won't. I promise.'

The helicopter swung to the right, moving upwards into the night sky. Shots rang out from below. A line of bullets hit the cockpit glass. The helicopter swung again as the pilot pulled it away. There was a further volley of gunfire. The cockpit was smashed. The engine sputtered. The craft went round and round, banking right and left. It tried to fly towards the park nearby. Below me, two of the floors were on fire. Glass shattered. Flames spurted several metres into the air.

I held on to Maya's wrist, my hands sweating. The sharp pain in my shoulder was unbearable. I leaned over.

'Maya, give me your other hand.'

'I can't... I... can't.' I noticed the blood running down her arm. God, had I shot her?

'Please!' I shouted.

As I said this, her wrist slipped from my grasp. I tried to grab her other hand and caught two fingers. She looked at me, wide-eyed. Her body grew heavier. Her fingers slid out of my hand.

Her mouth formed into a scream. Her arms flailed. She tumbled backwards, hurtling to the pavement below.

I looked up, numb.

There was an explosion, a glowing ball of fire in the distance. Below me, I could see the armed officer leaning out of the BMW, his rifle in his hand. He gave me a thumbs-up.

On the far horizon, the thin silvery-white crescent moon smiled on another night. A steady drizzle hit my face.

CHAPTER 49

A week later, I looked out of the window at the dirty, grey sky. Daylight was fading fast and it was getting colder. The traffic whizzed by and brown teenage faces in school uniform walked past, speaking English in a Leicester accent. There were middle-aged women in colourful sarees and gold jewellery, speaking and laughing in Gujarati. High up in the sky, a flock of swallows sliced the air with their pointed wings, racing south, back to Africa for the winter. My heart ached. I wanted to fly with them — back to Naivasha, to a happier life, a happy family, where nothing could go wrong. But it was now a dead world, with dead, shattered dreams.

I walked into the kitchen and made myself a cup of masala tea, the full works. I brought it to the boil, strained it into a mug and let it cool for a while.

I made the tea with some difficulty, as my left arm was in a sling. It had been X-rayed and nothing had been broken. Parts of my body were still heavily bruised. I sat down and watched some mindless game show on television. The regional news broadcast came on afterwards. I didn't pay much attention, but my ears pricked up when I heard the following from the newsreader:

'...and finally, the well-known principal of a successful academy in Leicester, David Griffiths, is leaving for personal reasons. Mr Griffiths, who has been absent recently due to ill health, said he would now like to enjoy a less stressful life by working at a private school in Dubai. Mr Griffiths is highly respected by his students, staff and the wider community. The Chair of the Board of Trustees stated that he would be sorely missed.'

We had not charged David Griffiths with anything because he hadn't committed a crime, but the trustees had obviously been informed of our investigations into his personal life when we had released him on police bail.

The phone rang. It was Yasmin. After a few pleasantries, she said, 'So, is your boss going to give you a medal? Or a pay rise, Dad?' Both my children rang every day to make sure I was recovering well. This was the first time Yasmin had said anything about my work.

'You got to be joking, darling. He told me off for using the pistol, since I'm not a trained firearms officer.'

'But he knows you did some training with guns in the Met, doesn't he? When you were a rookie, when you and mum had just got married.'

'Yes, darling. He knows. He eventually said he understood why I did it. Heat of the moment and all that. But please remember a good officer died too. They're carrying out an external investigation because of it.'

'I'm glad you're all right, Dad. But I'm sorry for the poor officer and his family... Both Karan and I, we're really looking forward to going to the cinema with you. It will be great.'

'I'm looking forward to it, too, darling.'

'Anyway, got to go, Dad. Mum's just arrived at the school gates. She's giving me a lift home.'

'Take care. Love you lots.'

'Love you too, Dad. Bye.'

At four o'clock I logged onto the secure online connection, waiting while the pixels danced and waved on the screen.

'*Bonjour*, Rohan,' said Nicole. This time she was sitting at an office desk, her back to a large window, the Eiffel Tower behind her, the shimmering river Seine in a corner not far away. The Parisian skyline was dotted with long cirrus clouds, and was turning an orangey-red colour. A flock of pigeons flew across.

'*Bonjour*, Nicole. Hope you're well.'

She smiled, said that all was well with her, and that she hoped I was recovering quickly. She saw the sling holding up my arm and offered her sympathy. 'So, my friend,' she went on, 'I hope it's all right to ask a few questions, to make sure I understand what's going on.'

'Shoot,' I replied, then quickly added, 'You know what I mean.'

'The girl victim. The headless body. Was that Amina?' she asked.

'Sad to say, the DNA matched the brother. He was distraught when we told him. I offered to get some support for him, including meeting the cost of the funeral. But because he's in the country illegally, he wouldn't accept anything from the authorities, and certainly not the police. He said he'd get members of his own community to help him.'

'Then what about Hasina? The girl you met outside your door — the one you thought had been killed? Where's she?'

'No idea. May be dead somewhere. We haven't found a body.'

'And what about the most important question of all? Was The Scorpion your sister?'

I picked up my mug of tea and sipped some through the cool, milky film which had formed on top. 'No.'

Nicole looked at me quizzically.

'Her DNA didn't match mine,' I continued. 'I have no idea who she was. But she looked a lot like my sister, or how she would have looked at that age. I think Graham Maxwell, the Grand Master, must've seen her in one of the refugee camps in Syria. He probably saw the family resemblance, and he knew me and my reputation well after all the publicity I got for catching the serial killer. All the important information about my life is readily available online.'

'What about the photographs? The ones of her growing up in Somalia and Syria?'

'The IT team analysed them in detail when we found her mobile. The one in Somalia with the Black couple is false. The pixels don't match properly. The photo of the small girl has been superimposed and doctored. The shadows of the couple and the girl don't match either. The one of the girl taken in northern Syria or Iraq is false, too, for the same reasons. They think the last one — of the woman standing near the Blue Mosque in Istanbul — is probably genuine. That was taken recently, and its origins and time can be digitally traced. The birthmark on the back of the neck, believe it or not, was done using plastic surgery.'

'Well, they certainly went to a lot of trouble to fool you. To fool us.'

'Yes, I've thinking about it long and hard. She could easily have killed me by shooting me.'

'Oh, don't say that.'

'Well, it's true, isn't it? But the Grand Master liked playing games — he thought he was highly intelligent. And maybe he was. Since he had such a lucrative operation in and around Leicester, he put a plan in place to deal with any problems, in case we ever threatened his empire. He knew his cover was blown to a certain extent by the leaking of the Panama Papers. He tried to cover up some of the information contained within them, but he knew I'd probably come for him at some stage. It would obviously be me because of the background of many of his associates. Also, Amina and Hasina escaping was something he didn't count on. And he didn't give enough thought to Bobby the dealer and his father. He blamed Anand Parekh for a lot of this, I'm sure. Given his connections in the city, he must have had informants within the police. But I have no idea who they are. He set a trap for me, wanting me to fall into it. He must have known we would find his mother eventually. And he used her as bait.'

'And the young woman,' said Nicole.

'Yes, and the young woman. As I said, she looked a lot like my sister. My sister's photograph appeared in the newspapers. My mum and dad gave it to one of the reporters when she wanted to do a profile on me. The Grand Master must have noticed the woman in the refugee camp and brought her out. He then groomed her, taught her to kill and paid her well. He knew she would be useful to him. She played mind games with me about my sister, and almost succeeded. The Grand Master also brought out the other woman we caught — the one in the Audi that rammed us. She was Syrian too. She's not saying any more — she only says she didn't know The Scorpion. Once he'd got rid of me, Graham Maxwell would have expanded his drugs, sex, antiquities and arms empire again. He wanted to go out with a bang, show the world who's boss.'

'Speaking of bangs, why were there two explosions? Where were they?' Nicole asked.

'One on the eight floor and one on the fourteenth. They were caused by large quantities of Semtex smuggled in by two workmen in overalls. They carried large holdalls and used the service lifts. Different receptionists on duty on the front desk believed the false identity cards they flashed and the fake signatures they used. We've got them on CCTV. Once, a woman followed them in. She was The Scorpion — they were obviously working as a team. They probably wanted the building to implode, like the Twin Towers in New York. But

Bishop's Tower, though severely damaged, withstood the blasts. It won't be long before we get the two responsible.'

'What about the bullet in her shoulder? What did forensics say about that?' she asked.

'The bullet fragments didn't come from my pistol. It was a rifle shot. I haven't told the officer who was with me yet. Not sure I will.'

'And what about your sergeant, Grace Nicholson? What has happened to her?'

'Don't know if you have experienced anything like it, Nicole, but I was devastated by her betrayal. She was just starting out in the police and was highly efficient. I really liked her. She would've been a fantastic detective inspector, but she took a wrong turn. In her interviews with DI Whittington and HR, it became apparent she was the victim of coercive control by her older stepbrother. Maybe he did more to her, but we're not sure. She won't admit to anything. But that's often the case with such victims.'

Nicole nodded, smiled and waved to somebody behind the camera.

I carried on. 'Needless to say, the force is trying to cover it all up to protect its reputation. She was told to resign. There will be no further action against her as long as she doesn't say anything to anybody. She jumped at the offer. Can't say I blame her, given all the circumstances. Her stepbrother, James McNamara, was arrested and charged. He'll spend a long time in prison.'

'Did you speak to her before she left?'

'Yes, I did, even though I wasn't supposed to. I rang her and explained how sorry I was about how things had ended. I told her I'd really enjoyed working with her and that I appreciated she was trying to deal with a situation she couldn't always control. I offered to help her in any way I could in the future. She thanked me for everything and said she might well be in touch.' I could sense Nicole was not paying attention anymore.

'I hope we work together again,' she said. 'And I hope we meet one day. My partner is here to give me a lift home.' She looked up and said, 'Come say *bonjour* to Rohan.'

An attractive redhead, slightly older than Nicole, smiled at me.

'Hello,' I said.

She waved to me and said, 'Bonjour Ro-*haan*.'

I waved back.

Nicole came back on screen. 'That is Angeline.'

'Well, she's lovely,' I said.

Nicole smiled and replied, '*Au revoir*, Rohan.' She blew me an air kiss.

I returned it and said I hoped to meet her and her partner sometime.

Later that evening, I sipped a glass of chilled Pouilly-Fuissé after I had just finished eating some takeaway tandoori chicken, shish kebabs and fish pakora. My arm hurt and I had not fancied cooking.

I let Fernando, who was sitting on my left shoulder, take a sip.

'Not too much, Fernando. Don't want you getting drunk.'

He bit my earlobe.

'*Oi*, stop it!'

He jumped onto my head and I let him stay there.

'Just you and me again. Just you and me.'

I put the glass down and sent a text message to Jenny Tyburn: *Okay to publish article. Am happy to cash in rain check for meal.*

She would be ecstatic and would make a name for herself. That's what she had once said to me.

I sent the message and waited for a response. Nothing. I checked it had been received and opened. It had been. I rang. No reply.

'Ah well, Fernando. Outlived our usefulness, I think.'

'Bad girl,' replied Fernando.

'Yes, bad girl.'

His claws dug into my scalp and I placed him on the edge of the settee.

I could not drive and wasn't sure where I would have gone to if I could. I rang my mother and father, making sure all was well with them. I was glad I had not said anything to them about the woman who claimed to be Maya. It would have broken their hearts to think she was back and then gone again, this time forever.

I let Fernando take another sip of wine from the dregs at the bottom of the glass. He lifted his head and looked at me with his big, round grey eyes.

'Why don't we watch a film to cheer us up? How about *When Harry Met Sally*? Is old but I love it.'

Fernando hiccupped.

As we watched the film, Fernando's head began drooping and then became erect again. The phone rang. It was not a number I recognised.

'Hi Rohan, it's Anita. Anita Thomas. How're you?'

'Fine, Captain Thomas. What a pleasant surprise to hear from you.'

'Well, I'm with the brigadier at one of our barracks in Yorkshire. He's going to stay here for various meetings. No need for me, he said. I was wondering if you wanted to meet up for a meal tomorrow evening. I'm on my way down.'

'I'd love to.'

The famous scene of Meg Ryan pretending to have an orgasm in the café came on.

'Who are you with, Rohan? Is it an inconvenient time? Especially for your friend?'

'No, no, Anita.' I explained what was happening.

She laughed.

I pointed the phone to the screen and we both heard the older woman customer say, 'I'll have what she's having.'

Anita Thomas laughed again. 'Now, that's an opening if ever there was one,' she said.

I blushed.

EPILOGUE

The physiotherapist said it was all right for me to drive a few days after my meal with Anita Thomas. It had been a delightful evening. She was excellent company, and I offered to book her a hotel room for the night, but she declined and said she had many things to catch up on and had to get going. We agreed to meet again.

After we had separated, I was listening to Leonard Cohen singing about the transient nature of life when my mobile pinged. It was a WhatsApp message, and not from a number I recognised.

I read the message: *Went to Ireland on a lorry first. Then to Brittany, to escape to Morocco from Spain. Jalil has joined me. All good. Am sad about Ghulam and Amina. Thank you for your help.*

Attached to the message was a photograph of Hasina with her arm around Jalil. They were both smiling and giving a thumbs-up. They held a card with today's date on it to show it was genuine. In the background was one of the royal palaces in Marrakesh.

There was a kind God after all. The balance between sadness and happiness had swung again.

I messaged her back: *What about the ankle bracelet I saw on your leg when you came to my house? I thought you were the one in the river.*

She replied straight away: *Oh, poor, poor, Amina. She lent it to me. I returned it to her before she was killed. My best friend.* The message ended with an emoji of a tearful face.

I explained how sorry I was about Amina and Ghulam, and I wished them both well.

Jenny Tyburn had returned the statue to me some time ago. I would ensure any reward for its recovery, or proceeds from its sale, would go to Hasina. The money would change her life, and she was the rightful owner.

A NOTE TO THE READER

Dear Reader,

Thank you taking the time to read the second DI Rohan Sharma thriller, *Shattered Dreams* and I sincerely hope you enjoyed reading it. I grew up in Leicester and I still visit friends and family regularly from my current home not too far away. I am proud to call it my home city and, like many other communities there, my father moved to Leicester from Kenya. My mother and the rest of my siblings followed him several years later. I hasten to add that the prologue is a work of fiction and bears no relation to the life of my late father. As many of you will know, Leicester is a vibrant and thriving city, and an important part of its history and changing nature is reflected in the area of the Golden Mile to the north. This is an exciting world, and I wanted DI Rohan Sharma to be located there because it is his spiritual and cultural home, despite having lived in other parts of the world and in other cities.

As regular readers in the genre will know, there are not many protagonists who are from Rohan Sharma's background. I wanted to write about an ordinary detective of South Asian origin who is trying to make a positive difference within his home city. But he also faces particular challenges because of his background, which he tries to overcome. I have not been a police officer, but Rohan Sharma's professional life is comparable to that experienced by others of a similar background. I also wanted to develop a complex character who straddles a multi-dimensional world, and this is evident in many aspects of his life.

I undertake an enormous amount of research for each book, for example on history, geography, forensics and, in the case of the first book, *The Dance of Death*, the geological make-up of Leicestershire. I try to ensure that procedures for homicide investigations are accurate, but I have taken a few liberties with this novel in the belief that police procedures should respond to an evolving situation and not be set in stone.

Finally, if you enjoyed reading *Shattered Dreams* could you please spare a few moments and post a positive review on **Amazon** and **Goodreads**. You can **follow my author page on Facebook** for updates on my books.

Many thanks.

C V Chauhan

Sapere Books is an exciting new publisher of brilliant fiction and popular history.

To find out more about our latest releases and our monthly bargain books visit our website:
saperebooks.com